"Listen to me, Beth!"

Cole's gaze shifted here and there for any signs of the raiding party. "I'm going to try to get us out of this alive, but I'm going to need your help. Should we meet up with the Indians, I don't want you trying to outrun them."

Beth's panic exploded in her ears. "I'll not give up without making a run for it!"

She leaned forward, ready to plant her heels in her horse's ribs, but Cole grabbed the bit. Beth could do nothing as long as Cole held on. She whipped unmercifully at him with the ends of the reins.

"Dammit, Beth, stop fighting me!"

Beth continued to struggle. "I'll never listen to you again...you yellow-bellied—" All other accusations were left unsaid. Her mouth was suddenly dry, and she became very still.

Five mounted hostiles in full plumage were riding toward them. They, as well as their horses, were splashed with all the colors of the spectrum.

Cole stated coldly, "You wanted to see scalpings and you wanted to see Indians. Well, here they are...."

Dear Reader,

DeLoras Scott's first book, *Bittersweet*, was published by Harlequin Historicals in 1987, and she continues to be one of our most popular authors. This month she is back with *The Devil's Kiss*, a romantic comedy about two misfits who discover love, despite Indians, outlaws and themselves. Don't miss this wonderful story.

The Trail to Temptation is the second book for Rae Muir, a featured author in our 1996 March Madness promotion. It's a Western about a star-crossed couple who fight their attraction on a trail drive from Texas to Montana. Award-winning author Margaret Moore's *The Wastrel*, the magical story of a disowned heiress and a devil-may-care bachelor, introduces her new series of Victorian romance novels featuring a trio of "most unsuitable" heroes that she has aptly named MOST UNSUITABLE....

And March 1996 author Tori Phillips returns this month with an unforgettable story, *Silent Knight*, the tale of a would-be monk and a French noblewoman who fall in love on a delightful journey across medieval England.

Whatever your taste in reading, we hope Harlequin Historicals will keep you coming back for more. Please keep a lookout for all four titles, available wherever books are sold.

Sincerely,

Tracy Farrell
Senior Editor

Please address questions and book requests to:
Harlequin Reader Service
U.S.: 3010 Walden Ave., P.O. Box 1325, Buffalo, NY 14269
Canadian: P.O. Box 609, Fort Erie, Ont. L2A 5X3

DELORAS SCOTT

THE DEVIL'S KISS

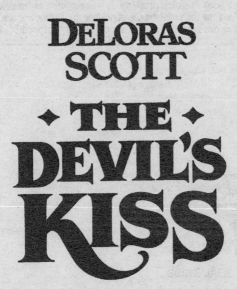

Harlequin Books

TORONTO • NEW YORK • LONDON
AMSTERDAM • PARIS • SYDNEY • HAMBURG
STOCKHOLM • ATHENS • TOKYO • MILAN
MADRID • WARSAW • BUDAPEST • AUCKLAND

ISBN 0-373-28946-4

THE DEVIL'S KISS

Books by DeLoras Scott

Harlequin Historicals

Bittersweet #12
Fire and Ice #40
The Miss and the Maverick #52
Rogue's Honor #123
*Springtown #151
Garters and Spurs #179
Spitfire #204
*Timeless #225
Addie's Lament #277
The Devil's Kiss #346

Harlequin Books

Harlequin Historical Christmas Stories 1991
"Fortune's Gift"

*Springtown Series

DELORAS SCOTT

was raised in Sutter's Mill, California—an area steeped in history. At one time it was gold country, and the legacy of wagon trains, cowboys and miners has remained. It's no wonder she enjoys writing about a chapter of history referred to as the Old West.

Author's Note

When my parents moved to Sacramento, California, in the fifties, there were still thousands of acres with nothing but rocks left from the mining days. A hundred years ago the miners dredged everything. Especially the soil needed for plants to grow. This bit of knowledge, Sutter's Fort and a land steeped in history drew my fascination. Now, having lived and traveled extensively across these United States, my interest hasn't diminished. Of course, everything comes full circle and I am again living in Sacramento, and enjoying that wealth of history.

The idea for *The Devil's Kiss* came from old pictures I happened across in a library. A lady of obvious quality was seated on a horse—sidesaddle—a rifle lying across her lap. The picture next to it showed a burly sharpshooter standing beside a towering pile of buffalo pelts. My imagination churned and came up with *The Devil's Kiss*.

I love to hear from readers. Please write.

DeLoras Scott
P.O. Box 278042
Sacramento, CA 95827-8042

Prologue

Texas

Cole Wagner watched the freckle-faced young man enter the saloon and sidle up to the bar. It was doubtful the pup had yet reached his seventeenth birthday. Cole's gaze dropped to the .35 resting in the kid's holster—hand level for a quick draw. There was a cockiness about him that Cole easily recognized. He had seen it many times before.

"Are you goin' to call the bet or not?"

Cole glanced down at the cards he was holding. A jack high. He called the wager and drew three cards. Tonight he'd barely been able to stay even in the game, but things were starting to look up. He'd just been dealt two jacks to go with the one he held.

On the other side of the room the kid downed his drink, then turned. Eyes narrowed, he slowly, methodically scanned each man in the saloon.

Cole dropped what was left of his cigar into the spittoon beside his foot. "Tell you what," he said to the other four players. "Its been a long night, and I have to hightail it to Missouri on the next train. So, I'm going to make this my last hand." He shoved his stash to the center of the table. "Anyone care to match it?"

The banker shook his head and tossed his cards in. The barber thought a moment before calling. The other two also called, making it the biggest pot of the evening. The three jacks were good and Cole started raking in his winnings.

"Cole Wagner!"

The call was loud and the saloon was small. Everyone heard the name. Cole shoved his winnings into his coat pockets.

"Has old age made you a yeller belly?"

The other players at the table suddenly realized whom they had been sitting with. They made a dash to get away, knocking over several chairs in their haste. It had always amazed Cole how quiet a saloon could become when a gunfight was about to take place.

"Well? You jest gonna sit there? Maybe you ain't as good as I heard tell?"

The chair scraped the wooden floor as Cole shoved it back and slowly stood. There were *some* things he just couldn't abide. Being called yellow was one, and being called an old man was another. He started walking toward the bar, his body a taut spring waiting to uncoil. He smelled the rank odor of unwashed bodies, Rosebud whiskey and stale smoke. Even a whisper seemed amplified a hundred times. "You'd be wise to reconsider, pup."

"I didn't ride no hundred miles for nothin', old man."

"You're not even dry behind the ears. It's too bad you're not going to live long enough to find out that thirty-two isn't old." When Cole came to a halt, there was less than twenty feet between him and the cur. With a resigned sigh he tucked the front of his black longtail coat behind his guns. His hands dropped to his sides... ready...waiting. "It's your move, boy."

Beads of sweat began popping out on the kid's forehead. As usual, the mutt wasn't as brave as he was making out to be. Then Cole felt the steel barrel of a shotgun jammed between his shoulders. It had all been a setup. The kid's partner must have been waiting until he could get behind him.

"I wouldn't make a move for that gun, Wagner," the man behind Cole warned. "It makes no difference if I turn you in dead or alive. All I want is the bounty."

"Damn you, Perkins!" the kid yelled. "What took you so long? Hell, I thought I was fixin' to get killed!" He grabbed the neck of the whiskey bottle and with a shaking hand lifted it to his lips and guzzled the contents.

Cole felt his .45 being lifted from his holster. As the bounty hunter came into view, Cole chuckled. The one with the rough voice was a skinny weasel, had a glass eye and was considerably older than his friend.

"Dammit, Jake, get over here and tie him up!" Perkins yelled.

The kid slammed the bottle down on the bar. As he hurried forward, he wiped his mouth with the sleeve of his dirty shirt.

"Is he really Cole Wagner?" one of the patrons called.

"The one and only," Jake boasted now that he knew the outlaw couldn't harm him. "Or maybe we should call him Sir Outlaw. Look at him. He was talkin' real big a minute ago, now he ain't nothin'. I'll bet I could've outdrawn him." He took the rope Perkins handed him. "He ain't gonna be seein' the outside of prison for a hell of a long time. If he don't get hung, he'll probably die there."

"You'd best hope so," Cole warned, "'cause if I get out, you're a dead man."

"Shut up, Jake," Perkins ordered. "If you gotta act so almighty, do it after we get our money."

The saloon became a hubbub of voices as the two men marched their prisoner outside. Perkins was being especially cautious. Jake, on the other hand, kept giving the outlaw unnecessary shoves. As Cole swung up on his horse's back and settled himself in the saddle, young Jake stepped forward, ready to taunt the prisoner again.

With Jake between him and Wagner, Perkins couldn't prevent what happened next.

The outlaw swung his foot upward, the toe of his boot catching Jake beneath the chin. The boy staggered backward, falling into his partner, knocking him down. By the time Perkins had scrambled to his feet, Wagner had his horse galloping down the road. Perkins fired several times, but the wanted man had already disappeared into the night.

Chapter One

Independence, Missouri, 1874

Bethany Alexander folded her hands in her lap trying to look pleasant, when in reality the chairs in her small hotel suite were most uncomfortable. "I was pleased to see you had the carriages waiting for our arrival."

The portly man seated across from her smiled.

"Have my other instructions been carried out?"

"I have done everything you requested in your letters," John Smyth assured the wealthy and very beautiful redhead. "However, I did have a problem with your telegram."

"Oh?"

"The telegrapher must have misinterpreted your message. It said something about buying an outlaw."

"What was confusing?"

He cleared his throat. "How do you expect me to do that?"

"I'm the one paying for your services, not the other way around. I've decided a bank robber or someone of such a nature would be perfect."

"Apparently you have not considered the impossibility of such a purchase, or the danger in hiring a man of that caliber."

"Oh, but I have, Mr. Smyth." Beth leaned forward, excitement shining in her eyes. "I am looking for a man who can show me the real West, and who better to do that than a real outlaw?" She leaned back in her chair. "I'm disappointed that since my trip from Boston began, I have yet to see a man wearing a weapon on his hip."

"I can assure you the people hereabouts are just as civilized as they are in Boston. And, contrary to the picture you apparently have in mind, wanted men do not go about sporting hardware on their hips, nor do they make themselves available. They would be hauled off to jail."

Why would a woman of obvious quality even consider such a thing? Smyth wondered. It certainly couldn't be for the money. Well, it wasn't any of his concern. When she left Independence, he'd be finished with her.

"If you are unable to get what I want," Beth said calmly, "I will locate someone better qualified to handle the matter."

John frowned. "There is a jail, but I wouldn't recommend—"

Beth stood. "Good. I knew you would come up with something. We'll leave immediately. I want to get everything settled as quickly as possible so I can be on my way."

John pulled his handkerchief from his pocket and mopped his forehead. It had been a tedious day. "Instead, why don't *I* look into the matter and report back? I'm certain you would rather rest after your long journey."

"May I remind you that I stepped off the paddle wheel two days ago? Besides, I can rest after I die." Beth anointed him with a radiant smile. "Well, are we going?"

"Y-yes, of course, but I doubt we'll be immediately successful in our quest," John hedged. "However, given proper time, I'm certain I can find the type of man you are looking for."

"Well, we won't know until we try. Shall we be on our way?"

The gentleman stood. He had tried to dissuade Mrs. Alexander from going to the jail. Now he could only hope Wagner had had enough time to get there from Texas. As they walked down the hotel stairs he thought about how shocked the lovely Mrs. Alexander would be should she discover she was about to be used by the government to track down a band of outlaws. When they entered his coach Smyth swallowed a chuckle. And wouldn't the widow *really* blow off steam if she knew he wasn't the real John Smyth? He was simply there to set up everything.

When the carriage pulled to a halt, Beth was surprised to see the size of the jail. She hadn't expected the Tower of London, but neither had she expected such a small brick building. Could prisoners actually breathe in such a place?

The deputy inside was snoring so loudly he didn't hear the visitors enter—until Smyth shoved the man's feet off the scarred desk.

Deputy Carson jumped to his feet. Startled at seeing the well-dressed lady, he sputtered, "Ah...ma'am, I think you've come to the wrong place. This here's a jail."

"Obviously," Beth stated tartly.

"Mrs. Alexander is looking to buy an outlaw," John announced.

The statement caused the deputy to choke on his tobacco juice. After a coughing fit and several gasps, he finally managed to catch his breath. "Whoever heard of
such a thing? 'Sides, all I got is a couple of men sleeping
off a drunk." *Easterners sure can come up with some of
the damnedest things,* he thought.

"Mrs. Alexander is willing to pay you handsomely for
the *right* outlaw." John winked at the deputy trying to
indicate that money could be made from this deal.

"Of course, he must be good at what he does. And a
gentleman," Beth added.

Carson was beginning to get Smyth's message. "It just
so happens I *do* have such a man." He certainly wasn't
above making money off a drunk.

"And he must know how to shoot and talk to Indians," John added. The only problem with this entire setup
was not letting the deputy in on the deal. But orders had
been to let no one else know what was really going on.
Even he didn't know all the facts.

"Oh, he does," Carson assured Beth. "Yes, sirree.
Why, he's even robbed a bank or three," he threw in for
good measure. He glanced at John to be sure he was saying the right things. Just how much money was this
woman willing to pay?

John nodded his encouragement.

"There's a reward for him," Carson added as an after-
thought.

"How big of a reward?" Beth asked.

"A . . . five hundred?"

Beth clapped her hands. "Wonderful. I'll buy him."
She looked at John. "See how easy that was?"

Carson couldn't believe his good fortune. He should
probably feel guilty about taking advantage of the lady,

but he didn't. "Plus what he owes for tearing up the Gun Runner Saloon last night."

"Who shall I pay?" Beth inquired.

"Me. You can pay me." Carson said.

"I want to take a look at the man first," John insisted.

The deputy opened the door leading to the two cells. John stepped into the narrow walkway.

"And how much do I owe the saloon?" Beth asked the deputy.

As soon as John saw the big man lying on the bare straw mattress, he released his breath. He should have known Wagner would be there as arranged. This had to be an important assignment for President Grant to send his best man. He was also the most cold-blooded son of a bitch John had ever worked with—but that was neither here nor there. The man always seemed to get the job done.

"What is your name?" John asked, loud enough for the others to hear.

"Who the hell wants to know?"

"I do. I might have a job for you."

"Just call me Sir Outlaw." The big man laughed at his own joke.

"I have a lady who is willing to pay a good wage for a man who can show her the West. Would you be interested in such a proposition?"

"Hell, yes. Beats staying in this confounded place. I'd make a good guide."

John walked back out just in time to block Beth from entering. He closed the door behind him.

"Perhaps I should take a look. I don't want to spend money unnecessarily."

"He needs to be cleaned up before being presented to a lady."

"Well, what do you think?" Beth asked.

"He seems to be just the man you're looking for."

The deputy tried not to stare as the lady reached into her reticule for the money, but he was having an awfully hard time believing his good luck. "The prisoner's name is Cole Wagner, ma'am," he stated. He couldn't believe the amount of coin that was being placed in his hands.

"Thank you," Beth said sweetly. "I will send two men to take him away. Even so, it might be wise to have him manacled."

Inside the cell, Cole Wagner scratched his bearded chin, grinned, then returned to his smelly mattress. So far everything had gone as planned. But for now, he needed all the rest he could get. His trip from Texas had been long.

The rhythm of rain splattering on the tin roof soon had him sleeping as soundly as a newborn babe.

That afternoon Deputy Carson and his handcuffed prisoner stood just inside the doorway of the jail, staring at two brawny men who were climbing out of a coach. Cole could tell by their hesitant smiles that they weren't too sure how they were supposed to handle him.

Since the good deputy had already repeated his conversation with the woman, Cole saw no reason to delay his departure. He nodded at the men, ducked his face from the rain, then ran to the coach. In truth, he needed to get away from the jail as quickly as possible. At any time the deputy could have recognized his picture, if the Wanted posters had already been distributed. Too many explanations would have had to have been made, and under the circumstances he couldn't afford that to happen. But that was exactly why Smyth had selected this particular jail. The deputy was new and gave no inkling of ambition. It was doubtful he even looked at the Wanted posters.

Cole quickly discovered that this particular style of carriage wasn't made to carry three big men. The vehicle seemed to sink a foot when the other two joined him inside. One sat facing him, the other sat beside him. Cole felt like a squashed gnat. He studied his companions. They had to be brothers. They both had light brown hair, blue eyes, and were devoid of any quality that would make them easy to identify.

Because the men seemed nervous, Cole decided to make their acquaintance. "Since we're apparently going to be working together, it's only right that I introduce myself. The name's Cole Wagner." He gave them a wide, friendly smile.

"I'm Wilber Jones," the older of the two replied, "and this is my brother, Decker."

Cole raised his hands. "I'd shake but, as you can see, that would be a bit difficult."

They both laughed, already starting to feel relaxed around the stranger.

Decker cleared his throat. "You don't look like a man who would rob a bank."

The statement slid off Cole's shoulders as easily as satin. Over the years he'd had a lot of practice at coming up with answers people wanted to hear. "Looks can be deceiving. Don't tell anyone, but I'm quite harmless, if that's what is bothering you. That bank thing happened a while back. I was trying to feed some of my family whose farm had been ravaged by grasshoppers."

The Jones brothers fell silent.

Cole had just drifted off to sleep when the conveyance came to a halt in front of the hotel. A few minutes later he was escorted through the back entrance, up the stairs and was finally brought to a halt in front of a large door.

When the door opened he found himself facing a petite beauty. Servants didn't wear such expensive gowns. He suspected he was facing his soon-to-be employer.

"Please come in, Mr. Wagner." He stepped forward and she closed the door behind him, leaving the others to stand in the hallway. "I am Mrs. Bethany Alexander."

A slow grin spread across Cole's lips. This situation had possibilities. Besides the lady's pleasing physical qualities, he liked her apparent lack of fear at being alone with an outlaw. He snatched off his top hat, then sauntered farther into the room.

A quick glance at the expensive surroundings told Cole a great deal about the lady he was going to be working for. She was wealthy and accustomed to the very best. The price he had planned to charge for his services escalated.

Cole held up his manacled hands. "Do you plan to leave these on me?"

"For now."

"I'm curious. Aren't you worried that I might attack you?"

"Why should I be? Decker and Wilber are on the other side of the door. Besides, we're not alone."

Out of the corner of his eye Cole caught sight of a man sitting in a chair, partially hidden by the room's shadows.

"Please join us."

Cole followed her to the other side of the room.

"You've already met the Jones brothers. This is Howard Bench. He will be second in command during our trip."

Howard stood and nodded.

Cole figured him to be approximately ten years the woman's senior. He had a touch of gray at his temples and his clothes were fashionable and expensive. But the gentleman wasn't just a soft greenhorn. He had the look of a hunter in his eyes, a look Cole easily recognized. Cole knew immediately that Howard knew how to take care of himself and would probably be dangerous if crossed. Because he and the lady had different names, he wondered if they were lovers. "What trip are you talking about?"

"We'll discuss that in a moment." Now that Beth had a good look at the man, she began to slowly shake her head from side to side. His beard, height and build were the only images that made him look even half dangerous. Undoubtedly his black eye and facial abrasions were due to tearing up the saloon she'd paid for.

"You don't look like an outlaw," Beth commented, more to herself than to Cole. She shouldn't have relied on Mr. Smyth's opinion.

"What is an outlaw supposed to look like?" Cole asked.

"Well...I...I certainly wouldn't expect one to be dressed in a plaid tweed suit and wear a top hat, even though the suit is quite worn and outdated." Beth sat on a cushioned chair, leaving him standing. "Even your hair and beard are well trimmed," she said with obvious disappointment.

"I take it outlaws dress differently and do not trim their hair."

"They would hardly have time for such things when they're constantly running from the law. I had also expected someone younger. How old are you, Mr. Wagner?"

Where had the woman come up with these ridiculous ideas, Cole wondered. "Why do you ask?"

"Beth, don't you think you're being rather hard on Mr. Wagner?" Howard asked. "Mr. Smyth told you that men do not dress as such in town."

"Had the deputy not said he was a bank robber, I would never have suspected him of a single wrongdoing." She looked at his black eye. "Other than partaking in a brawl." She shook her head again. "There is whiskey behind you on the end table, if you care to have a drink."

The invitation surprised Cole. Mrs. Alexander was a complexity. She did not strike him as a woman who offered whiskey in her parlor. Was she testing him? "Thank you, but I think not. This is Sunday and it's against the Lord's teaching."

From the looks on their faces, it was evident that the lady and gentleman were dumbfounded. Cole knew he'd made the wrong choice. He should have accepted the damn drink. He certainly could have used one.

"That obviously wasn't a hindrance last night. All outlaws drink whiskey, smoke, gamble, curse, practice debauchery and are quick draws. But maybe you weren't a good outlaw. You don't even wear a gun and holster. It's no wonder you got caught!"

"I had a gun. As luck would have it, the sheriff had walked into the bank right behind me," he lied. "I didn't have a chance."

Howard rubbed the back of his neck. "See, Beth? You're being completely unreasonable."

Cole was somewhat pleased that her face softened a bit. He shifted to his other foot. "Do you mind if I sit?"

"Yes, I do."

"Beth!" Howard protested.

"He has been in jail, Howard. He's probably covered with lice."

Cole rolled his eyes. Damn! If only he knew what this was all about and what was expected of him. All he knew was that he was to go to work for the lady as a guide, just as the deputy had told him. "Where did you learn all about outlaws, Mrs. Alexander?"

"From dime westerns. That is the reason for this trip."

Cole had to turn away to keep from breaking out laughing. "Never have I met anyone quite like you, Mrs. Alexander," he finally managed to say soberly.

"Nor I you."

"Tell me. If all outlaws looked the same, don't you think it would be easy for the law to spot them?"

Howard chuckled. "Touché! I've tried telling her the same thing."

Beth knew they were right. She shouldn't have let her disappointment at not finding what she had expected override common sense. And why should she continue to badger Cole Wagner? Hopefully he had the qualifications she needed. After all, he was the only man she had for the position as guide. He would have to do until she found someone better. She really didn't need a desperado if he could show her what she needed to see.

Howard walked over and poured himself a full glass of whiskey.

So far, Cole had learned that Beth was not only the one who seemed to be calling all the shots, she was also quite blunt. He needed more information. "If it's not too much trouble, ma'am, I'd like to know what you expect of me. Are you seeking revenge on someone, am I to kill a lover, or maybe you just fancy having a wanted man for yourself?"

The whiskey spewed from Howard's mouth as he broke out in a thunderous roar of laughter.

"Your questions weren't called for, Mr. Wagner," Beth snapped.

"Then why do you want an outlaw?"

Beth marched to the door and opened it. "Decker, Wilber," she beckoned.

The men appeared immediately.

"Take him to his room. I have already made arrangements for his clothes to be cleaned and for him to bathe. Later, Mr. Wagner, we will dine and discuss what I want of you."

"Because it seems to be so important to you, Mrs. Alexander, I am thirty-two," Cole said just before walking out the door.

As soon as the door had been closed behind the men, Bethany glared at Howard. He was using his handkerchief to wipe the front of his vest where he'd spewed whiskey. He was still chuckling. "Howard!"

"Come, come, Beth. Even you have to see how comical this entire situation is. And you did ask for what you got."

Beth's face relaxed and a smile toyed with the corners of her full lips. He was as close to a father as she had ever known. "You are impossible."

Howard nodded. "I hope this time you haven't taken on more than you can handle, Priss." He set the glass of whiskey on the mantel.

"What do you think? Can he show me everything I want to see?"

"I have a strong hunch you've met your match with our Mr. Wagner. But to answer your question, I have no idea what the man can or cannot do. Maybe we'll know more after supper." Oddly, it flashed through Howard's mind that he had been watching over Beth for nearly ten years and it was time for someone else to take over the task.

Beth decided to change the subject. "Esther is still in bed, but I thought you'd like to know that color has returned to her cheeks."

"I never expected it not to." Howard finished his drink. "Don't blame yourself for her sickness. You had no way of knowing the Missouri River would be so choppy."

"You're right, of course, but I hated seeing her so miserable."

"I'll see you at supper, Priss." Howard left, feeling uneasy. Over the years he'd known a lot of men. Some good, some dangerous. Which was Cole Wagner? He still wished he had been able to talk Beth out of this foolish trip.

With Howard gone, Beth suddenly felt alone. It was a familiar feeling. She'd known it for so many years it had almost become a friend. Howard had said she needed to find a *good* man to marry. One she couldn't order about. Esther had said the feeling was caused from never really knowing her parents. Her uncle had taken on the responsibility of raising her when her parents had died somewhere in Europe, but Uncle Oliver bore her no true affection. She smiled faintly. Howard and Esther were her family. Frank had joined them a little later. He was just a boy then.

Beth glanced at the wag clock, then quickly stood. She had to meet Mr. Smyth downstairs in fifteen minutes. She wanted to be sure all final arrangements had been completed—something she could have let Howard take care of, but she needed to be busy instead of just sitting around feeling sorry for herself. She also wanted to tell Mr. Smyth how disappointed she was in the outlaw he'd selected. Other than his size, Cole Wagner seemed more like a domestic cat than a lion. And it wasn't right that he should be on the handsome side. He was supposed to appear villainous.

Chapter Two

Not until Cole was ready to sit at the supper table did Howard remove the handcuffs. Cole rubbed his wrists, noticing the red abrasions. The deputy had locked them too tight.

From the moment Cole had entered the room, his eyes had not left the beauty already seated across from him. The bodice of her green grown dipped low enough to allow him an ample view of full, creamy breasts, waiting to be released from their confinement. Her hair hung in soft, copper ringlets and the green bows at each side of her face matched her gown. It had been a good three years since he'd formally dined with a lady of such absolute loveliness.

"Please be seated, Cole," Howard said. "I'm sure you could use a meal under your belt."

The moment Cole was settled, a parade of servants appeared. Bowls of vegetables and platters of beef and fowl were held out for his selection. At least his hostess's attitude had improved from earlier.

"Excellent meal, Mrs. Alexander," Cole complimented when he had finished his dessert.

"Thank you. Please call me Beth. Everyone else does."

"What do you do with what's left over?"

"As you will soon discover," Howard answered, "Beth has a lot of people in her employ."

Beth dabbed her lips with her linen napkin before placing it beside her plate. "I think it's time for us to get down to business."

Cole leaned back in his chair and smiled. "Excuse me for not mentioning sooner that you are a vision of loveliness tonight."

The compliment took Beth completely by surprise. "I... Thank you. Ah..." Beth regained her composure. "Until I started this trip, I had never traveled in my own country. I've never seen a man robbed or shot, or a gun drawn. I haven't seen savage Indians. This is where you come in. I want you to show me all this. I want to see stagecoaches and trains held up. In other words, I want to see the real frontier. Naturally I'll be making sketches and taking notes the entire time. I intend to write novels." Beth looked him straight in the eye. "I am writing about outlaws."

Cole was dismayed. She was serious! There wasn't even a hint of humor in her expression—or Howard's. Now, how the hell was he supposed to react to this? Damn! Someone had better supply him with some answers—and soon. What was her part in this assignment? "Do you realize what you're asking?"

Beth stood. "Of course I do," she replied indignantly. "I've done a considerable amount of reading on the matter."

"Are you going to let her do this?" Cole asked Howard as they followed Beth into the small parlor.

"You will learn that the lady has a mind of her own."

"Why would you ask such a ques—" Beth broke off and laughed with delight. "Howard, I do believe he thinks we are lovers."

"I gave it some thought," Cole admitted.

"Why, I'll wager you were even convinced that I'm a kept woman."

Cole kept his comments to himself. He was still trying to digest all the woman planned to accomplish during her travels.

"Actually, Howard, I can see where he could have reached that conclusion."

Nothing was going right, and Cole would very much have liked to join Howard in a drink of that whiskey the debonair gentleman was pouring himself. He was having to second-guess everything, and his guesses were not getting the results he'd expected. Figuring out Beth Alexander wasn't going to be easy.

"You are wrong on both accounts," Beth assured Cole. "Howard and I are good friends. He watches after me."

Cole watched her sit on the divan with the grace of a queen.

Beth looked directly at the tall man. "Now, I believe the time has come for you to tell me if you can provide what I want. Are you familiar with the area from here to Dodge City, my final destination?"

"Oh, I can provide what you want, and yes, I do know the territory. The question is whether or not I want to provide your entertainment. Are the men you've hired to go on the trek aware of what you are planning? I would think they would have concern for their lives, even if you don't."

Beth's eyes flashed with indignation. "Let's settle all the questions you might have so we will not have to broach this subject again. I want to write dime westerns. You are asking yourself why, when they are about men, and I don't need the money. Because the editor at *Beadle Library* turned down my proposal. He said it was obvious I didn't know what I was writing about. He was right. However, I can be a very determined woman. I *will* write those novels and prove my worth to the world, but as the editor said, first I must become acquainted with the real West.

"As for our trip, there will be nothing to concern yourself about except getting me to my destinations and providing what I want. Those who work for me have specific jobs and are quite capable of taking care of themselves. I am also capable of taking care of myself. There is little that I haven't seen or done, including hunting tigers in India and playing matador in Spain."

Beth paused, then added, "And I have seen death. When I was hunting, one of the maharaja's beaters was mangled by the tiger."

This time Cole didn't ask if he could be seated. The high-backed chair looked the most comfortable.

"As for my people," Beth continued, "I interviewed and hired each one individually. I made sure they would be loyal, willing to follow my orders without question and, most important, willing to take personal risks. They are a daring group, even the women. Does that take care of everything?"

"How long do you think it's going to take to accomplish what you have planned?"

"I hadn't thought about it. Are you in some sort of a hurry?"

"Not really. Just curious."

"I have even purchased a house. It is presently being readied. I thought we could use it as a central base."

"Let me see if I understand this correctly. You're planning to ride out, watch a stage being held up, then return to town? Then after a good rest, do we ride out again and watch Indians scalping settlers? What do you need me for?''

''To be my guide!''

''Anyone can do that. Go find an ex-lawman to do your running back and forth.'' He knew he was taking a big gamble. He could only hope that she was as determined a woman as she'd stated and didn't like things or people slipping out of her hands.

Beth raised her lace handkerchief to her nose and inhaled the scent of jasmine perfume. ''I'm well aware that we may have to bivouac for two or three days on some occasions.''

One thing was certain. No matter what Beth was involved in, she definitely needed watching after. ''*If* I took this job, we would leave and not return until everything has been accomplished. Seeing someone murdered or scalped by an Indian is a lot different than being mauled by a big cat.''

''I'm quite brave, and you needn't try to frighten me. You might also like to know that I'm not easily dissuaded from what I set out to do.''

Cole leaned forward, resting his elbows on his knees. ''If that is so, how come you kept me handcuffed until this evening?''

''I have an investment in you and I want to make sure you don't run off, at least not until I feel I no longer need you.''

''And what is to keep me from leaving right now with you as my hostage?''

''Howard, and the men waiting outside.'' Beth pulled a small revolver from her pocket and pointed it directly at the outlaw. ''I hope you're not foolish enough to think that because I'm a woman I don't know how to use it.'' She gave him a warm smile. ''Mr. Wagner, I will not be a handicap. My horsemanship and marksmanship are every bit as good as some men's and exceedingly better than others. I have nerves of steel and do not faint in a crisis."

"I'm afraid you've got the wrong man, Mrs. Alexander," Cole bluffed. "That deputy lied to you. No man can provide you with what you're looking for. You seem to be a sensible woman, so think about this. Of all the thousands of miles of track, who can make a knowledgeable guess as to where outlaws plan to stop a train, for instance? Not only where, but when. You'd do better to just rob the damn thing yourself." Cole stood. "Also, Indians do not scalp people for ladies' entertainment. Shoot me if you like, but I'm leaving. We both know I'm not the man you're looking for." He headed toward the door, gambling she would stop him.

"A hundred dollars for every time you provide what I want!"

His ploy had worked!

"Two hundred. It's not as if I have to actually rob a train. We could pretend."

Cole reached the door but didn't turn the knob. He was listening to her offer, and at the same time wondering what she would come up with next.

"Five hundred," Beth offered.

"A thousand." He turned and faced her.

"Very well, a thousand. Do we have a deal?"

"Only if we keep going. I can show you everything on the way. I have no desire to keep retracing my tracks."

"Done." Beth's smile showed her satisfaction.

"When will everything be ready to go?" Cole asked.

"Other than some last-minute supplies, we can leave any time you say."

"Fine, but I'll want to check everything personally. If all is in order, we'll leave at four in the morning, two days from today." He couldn't picture her willing to get up so early, but he didn't receive the reaction he'd expected. "In the meantime, I need money to get what I'll need, like a horse and gear." He rubbed his wrists. "Have you decided what you want to see first?"

"I think I would like to rob a train."

Cole chuckled. The woman did have guts. "Then a train you shall rob. Let's just hope you don't get caught by some marshal."

"Have you ever been to Dodge City?"

"Yes."

"I have saved newspaper articles about it being..." She picked up the cuttings she had gathered. "'A perfect paradise for gamblers, cutthroats and girls.'" She flipped to the next one. "'Fast men and fast women.'" Another, "'The wickedest little city in America.'" The next clipping. "'Seventeen saloons furnish inspiration, and many people become inspired—not to say drunk. Every facility is afforded for the exercise of conviviality, and no restriction is placed on licentiousness.'" She laid the papers on the seat beside her. "Would you say the critiques are correct in their depiction?"

"I'd say so," Cole replied.

"Good. I would like to know the route you would take to get there."

"Probably drop down to Wichita and over. Anything else?"

"I'll let you know if there is."

"Good night, Howard." He nodded at Mrs. Alexander. "Good night." He left, certain that this beauty had to be quite insane. Or else there was more behind her starched demeanor than he realized, such as a wild taste for adventure. He headed down the hall to where he'd bathed earlier, the Jones brothers trailing right behind him.

Later that night Cole's door was unlocked from outside, and a man dressed in black stepped in.

"Well?" he asked.

"Send a wire that so far everything has worked out as planned," Cole replied. "We'll be leaving in two days."

The man handed Cole a large envelope and left, locking the door behind him.

Cole made himself comfortable on the bed and read the familiar handwriting.

I know you've expressed a desire to quit my little organization, but I really need you on this one, Cole. The assignment certainly won't bore you.

Grain destined for our forts is being augmented by chaff and something else. We're lucky if we get half the grain originally purchased, and soldiers and their families have already been poisoned. The man who handles most of the grain is named Samuel King. He and some congressmen are in cahoots in this swindle, but the mastermind is Quin Turner. We have no description other than he is English and a tactical genius. His gang have wreaked havoc for over five years, killing and robbing, and of course stealing grain from the farmers. No one has been able to locate his headquarters. If we can get our hands on him, we'll not only destroy a band of thieves, we will also have proof of the men in Washington involved in the swindle.

I arranged for one of Turner's gang to escape from the Kansas State Prison so he can lead you to the others. His name is Tex Martin. He was followed to

Independence, where he signed on with Mrs. Alexander. Now the bad part. Our spy was killed and the only description I have of Tex is that he has brown hair and no distinguishing features. As usual, you're on your own to figure everything out and catch the scoundrel Quin Turner.

Also, knowing your reputation with women, I am ordering you to keep your britches up and your hands off Bethany Alexander. As bad luck would have it, the widow's uncle is a senator. Not one under suspicion. The woman is a bit of an eccentric. The one good note is that the senator is seldom aware of her escapades and won't interfere.

You and I both know you're the best I have, and your disguise as an outlaw should work in your favor.

President Ulysses Grant.

Mrs. Alexander was a bit eccentric? That was putting it mildly. Cole lit a match to the paper, then dropped it in the fireplace. So much for his thoughts of bedding the beauty. As determined as Beth had been to see robbers, murders and Indians, he'd come to believe she was involved in his assignment. As it appeared now, she was nothing more than an innocent party. How ironic that she had been thrown into a situation very similar to what she was looking for, which in turn put more responsibility on his shoulders. He needed her help if he was to get to Turner.

The Turner gang. He'd heard rumors about them. Word was that all outlaws were welcomed, but, under penalty of death, each member had to take an oath to never reveal the location of the hideout or the names of the other members. For years lawmen and the government had tried to put an end to the band's ravaging and slaughter. Now he was expected to take care of the matter with nothing more to go on than a man named Tex who no one could identify, and that was supposed to lead him to the hideout that no one could find.

Which one of the lady's men had he disguised himself as? Could there possibly be a brother no one had known about?

After finishing this assignment, he was going to retire and purchase land in California.

Chapter Three

Cole twisted in the saddle, his dark eyes scanning the parade stretched out behind him. Satisfied that everything was moving well, he turned back around, his gaze automatically scanning the horizon for any signs of trouble. Even after being on the trail a week, sight of the caravan still left him speechless. For some reason that absolutely escaped him, a damn household was being transported from one spot to another. The only thing lacking was the wooden structure.

There were five new canvas-covered wagons, each being pulled by six yoked oxen. These were for the furniture and apparently every convenience known to mankind. Besides these, there were three additional farm wagons filled with supplies. The wagon wheels kicked up enough dust to be seen for miles around and would make a tempting parcel for any outlaw bands or Indians lurking about. Cole could only hope that marauders would mistake the dust for a small, well-armed wagon train and would prefer to give it a wide berth.

And then there was the menagerie of servants—eight men and four women in all. The rest of the flock consisted of five steers, one milk cow, horses, oxen, one pig and four sheep.

Though Mrs. Alexander's entourage seemed never-ending, Cole had to admit it was well planned. The women handled the mending, cooking, serving and other womanly duties. The men drove the wagons, did the loading and unloading, set up tents and collected firewood, as well as doing anything else they were needed for. Besides their work on other chores, the Jones brothers were experts on wagon building and repairs, George Higgins was a blacksmith, Frank Doolan cared for the stock and Tucker Washington was a doctor. Evan White and Jeff Dobbs filled in where needed. Howard Bench kept Beth's fancy carriage moving in front of the line to avoid the dust. It had become increasingly evident that her comfort was of the utmost importance. At least, as far as she was concerned.

Preferring to just observe for the time being, Cole hadn't developed a close friendship with the men. However, he had learned that none of them would admit to ever having traveled through Kansas before. Tex Martin was keeping a low profile. Had Cole not been assigned to join this caravan, Beth could have found herself in a heap of trouble. She could have been stranded in some remote spot, having been attacked, with all her valuables gone. Indians would have taken care of the rest.

More than once Cole had seen Beth busily writing in a journal at night. Without a doubt, she was keeping a record of everything that transpired during the day. He wondered if her determination to be a writer was nothing more than a phase that would soon fade.

If Beth or Bethany—depending on who was talking about her—wasn't riding in her carriage, she was on one of the three magnificent riding horses she'd brought along. Besides the two geldings, there was a black mare that was faster than any horse he'd ever seen. Beth had told the truth about her horsemanship. She handled the frisky animals as if she'd been born on one. The sidesaddle she used made the act all the more difficult. However, the lady had a bad habit of taking off in one direction or another, which led to his second complaint.

So far, they hadn't even managed eight miles a day. The copper-haired dictator seemed to find an unending array of reasons for delays, none of which he deemed necessary.

Cole's keen eyes scanned the tall grass and trees stretched out before him. It was still early spring, and the rains had been plentiful enough to leave behind a green sea of grass. The sky was blue and songbirds were in spectacular voice. He shifted his weight. It felt good to be in the saddle again.

Originally Cole had planned to leave Missouri and head straight into Kansas. He didn't care to find some sheriff waiting around the bend and he'd hoped to avoid trains simply because he didn't want some Pinkerton man hounding him. However, if her highness wanted to rob a train, Kansas wasn't the right place. It would be better to stay in Missouri and head north, well away from everything. And he knew just the right spot.

"Cole! Cole Wagner!"

Cole groaned. What the hell did her majesty want this time? He turned his mount around and started back toward the caravan—which had already come to a stop. The lady was climbing out of her carriage when he brought his buckskin horse to a halt in front of her. He stared down at the woman, forced to admit that even beneath the heavy clothing the boss's figure was something to behold—and untouchable, he reminded himself. The next few months were undoubtedly going to be a living hell—in more ways than one.

"I have to go behind the bush. Please try to remember that women are unable to relieve themselves as easily as men. Therefore more stops are going to have to be made along the way."

Cole grinned at her lack of embarrassment. Other women would have turned ten different shades at having to admit to such. On the other hand, Beth could hardly be compared to other women. "Do you realize—"

"Surely this discussion can wait until after I've tended to my duty."

Cole watched her hurry off toward a long line of tall shrubs, some thirty yards away. With that hat, veil and blue velvet riding dress, it was no wonder she continually fanned herself.

As the other women fell in behind Beth's coach, Cole swung to the ground with the grace of a man used to being in the saddle. So far, they had yet to travel long enough for him to even grow saddle weary.

After five minutes, Cole pulled his hat down to shade his eyes from the afternoon sun. Another five minutes found him flicking the ends of his horse's reins across his gloved palm. What the hell were the women doing? He glanced around at the men, who were patiently waiting.

Which is Tex Martin? Cole wondered. Certainly not the doctor, Washington Tucker. He and his wife were black. He had already decided that his only recourse was to cull the men out, one at a time.

Cole had started with Howard, Beth's second in charge. Cole had spent more time visiting with him than anyone else in the caravan. Though it was doubtful Howard was the man Cole was looking for, Tex could have dyed his hair—and there were no age restrictions to go by.

Cole squatted, his thoughts still on Howard. The older man had even gone so far as to say that though he would protect Beth with his life, she was an absolutely unpredictable cavalier. He'd blamed it on money and having been on her own too long. But while Howard was so willingly informative, Cole knew the gentleman was also making *his* mind about whether the outlaw was trustworthy.

Cole checked his pocket watch. Another twenty minutes had passed, and his patience was nonexistent. He stood and looked toward the bush. "It's time to head on!" he yelled.

Esther, Beth's personal maid and companion, ran into view, her breathing already heavy from her exertion. "Mrs. Alexander has decided we will camp here for the day."

"What?" Cole bellowed. "We can still get in four more hours of travel!"

The woman's ample chest swelled with indignation. "*Mrs. Alexander* is bathing in the stream. It has been a week since she's been allowed such pleasure, and she's not about to forgo it!" Esther disappeared again into the foliage.

Magda, the cook, Lizzy, Tucker's wife, and Molly Dee, another helper, were starting campfires for cooking. Some of the men were already unloading Madam Alexander's furniture, while the others were setting up camp. Cole looked up at the sky, trying to keep a lid on his temper.

"Come, come, my friend," Howard said as he walked from the carriage to where Cole stood. "You must learn to relax. Over the past ten years I have been on many trips with madam, and they are always the same. One eventually grows used to it."

Cole's temper had won the battle. "Maybe you, but not me." He dropped the reins to the ground and started forward. He'd had enough of this foolishness.

After he had forced his way between the thick shrubbery, it quickly became apparent that neither Esther nor Mrs. Alexander had heard him approaching. Instead of harsh words, he was greeted with a titillating view of the "countess's" slender bare back as she bent over on her knees, allowing Esther to rinse the soap from her hair. On any other occasion it would have been a pleasing sight, but Cole wasn't feeling hospitable.

"What the hell is all this about? We're supposed to be on a journey, not a social!"

"How dare you invade my toilette!" Beth stormed.

Cole received a considerable sense of pleasure at seeing the lady grovel for her blouse, then snatch it up to cover her breasts. "How dare *you* leave me standing while you pamper yourself? I wasn't aware I'd be expected to wait over a half hour to finish what I had started to say! So I'll spill it out now. If you plan to accomplish anything on this so-called journey, we sure as hell can't be stopping every few minutes because of your whims. At the pace we're going, it'll take a month just to reach the area where you can rob your train! Believe me, that isn't going to be easy with an entire caravan behind you!" He started to walk away, then turned back. "What do you think happens on wagon trains? They don't stop, madam, except to water the stock."

Still clutching her blouse in front of her, Beth climbed to her feet, her wet mane falling into her face. "Who do you think you are?" she asked while trying to shove her hair from her eyes. With the beard covering his face, it was impossible to see his expression. "I do not take orders from anyone, no matter who he may be!"

"It was you who caused this confrontation, not me."

"Furthermore, I cannot tolerate a man who ignores gentlemanly manners," Beth hissed.

"Then, lady, you had no business hiring an outlaw! But just to clear the air, my manners are unquestionable when there is a lady about, not some spoiled, thoughtless female who wants to lord it over everyone."

A deep, guttural sound rolled from Beth's throat. "Don't you dare speak to me like that!"

"You pull another stunt like this, and I'm gone," Cole warned.

"Fine. Go. Leave. I don't need the likes of you." With unwavering eyes Beth watched him turn on his heel and head back toward the wagons. As soon as he was out of sight, she shook her blouse and held it out for Esther. The water from her body and dripping hair had soaked it.

Esther hurried forward with a dry cloth. "He should never have talked to you like that. It's good you got rid of him. He's too brash."

Beth bent over at the waist and began toweling her hair. "He can rant and carry on all he wants," she said between clenched teeth, "but I know he isn't going anywhere. He's not about to leave without the money we agreed on, and I'm not about to give it to him until he shows me something I want to see!" Her hands paused. "Maybe it was a good thing we had this confrontation. He apparently needed to be reminded that I give the orders. Once he accepts that, he'll settle down. I can't really let him go. We need him to get to a town, then I'll replace him." She straightened. After her hair had been combed, she would let the afternoon sun finish drying it. "I think I'll wear my hair in a braid from now on. It will prevent tangles. And while I'm thinking about it—"

"We don't even know if the man owns a pistol," Esther persisted. "So far all he's done is prove he can stay on top of a horse."

"Mmm. I have been thinking the same thing. When Decker and Wilber went to get him at the jail, Wagner told them he was quite harmless and the only reason he'd robbed a bank was to get money. His family needed food. A worthy cause, but certainly not the type of man I had hoped to hire."

"His family? Is he married?"

Beth thought a minute. "I don't know. I was told he was a wanted man, so I assumed he wouldn't have a wife. Oh! The nerve of the man to speak to me like that!" Beth suddenly became very still. "Did I hear a horse gallop away?"

"I think so. You don't suppose . . ."

Beth snatched her wet blouse from the grass and shoved her arms into the sleeves.

"You can't go like that," Esther said. "Wait until I at least get your corset." But Beth was already on the run. Esther didn't hurry after her. She knew that nothing distracted Bethany when she was in such a mood.

As soon as Beth cleared the bushes, she came to a halt. Her fingers were still working at the buttons on her blouse as she scanned the area around the wagons. Neither Cole nor his bedroll was anywhere in sight. "Howard!" she called as she raced forward.

Howard appeared from behind one of the supply wagons. There was little doubt in Beth's mind that he had been imbibing the liquor she always carried on trips. "Where is Wagner?"

"He rode off. Would you like me to go after him?"

"No, I'll take care of this myself. Get my gun and holster!" She continued on to where the big roan was tethered to a line rope.

By the time Beth had untied the lead, made a loop and placed it around the gelding's muzzle, Howard had returned. He handed her the gun belt which she quickly buckled around her waist. The big .45 was shoved into the holster. He gave her a boost up onto the horse. After a few tugs at her skirt so her legs could hang down evenly, she looked back down at Howard.

"Which way did he go?"

The moment he pointed north, Beth sank her heels into the powerful roan's sides.

As the horse sprang forward, Beth was considering the head start Cole had on her. It couldn't be more than five minutes. If she pushed the gelding hard, she should be able to catch up with him. There had to be other criminals available who were agreeable and of a more gentlemanly nature. They would probably be even more familiar with the West than the man she had foolishly hired. Surely if the caravan continued on in the same direction they had been going, they would come upon the town Cole had mentioned. Or at least they would meet someone who could give them directions. But that wasn't the issue. She had made an agreement with Cole Wagner and she'd be damned if she'd let him run out on her. She was the one to do the dismissing, not the other way around!

Cole leaned against the thick tree trunk, enjoying the shade. There was no doubt in his mind that his nemesis would be coming after him. Mrs. Alexander was not a woman who delegated such matters to others. Cole smiled. He didn't want to make it too difficult for her to find him. Once she realized they were stranded and vulnerable without him, he'd have the leverage he wanted. Stopping every thirty minutes was going to come to a halt.

Cole had sung only a couple of bars of "She'll Be Comin' Around the Mountain" when he heard the cadence of hooves pounding against the earth. The rider was in one hell of a hurry. He jumped to his feet. It took but a minute to move his horse behind the tree and cup his hand over the buckskin's muzzle to prevent him from nickering. He had to be sure the rider wasn't some sheriff. Cole had no desire to be looking down a lawman's gun barrel. He should probably shave off his beard so he'd look less like the poster.

When Bethany Alexander rode by, Cole chuckled softly. Yes, indeed. The big boss was going to handle him all by herself. Her copper mane flying in the wind and her wet shirt clinging to full breasts was enough to set fire to any man's loins.

He raised his fingers to his mouth and released a whistle loud enough to startle every creature for a mile around. Though her ladyship was already out of sight, he was certain she'd heard him.

Cole leaned his shoulder against the tree and waited. Would she be as wild in her lovemaking, or would she continue to act the authoritarian witch he'd had to put up with for over a week? The thought of her instructing him on how to make love brought a smile to his face.

When Beth came back into view she was holding her mount to an easy lope. Cole had already acknowledged that she was a capable horsewoman, but until now he'd had no idea just how good. What else was she an expert at? "Were you looking for me?" he asked when she stopped in front of him. He liked the fire that danced in her brown eyes and the flush in her cheeks from her wild ride.

"We had an agreement," Beth snapped.

"You told me to leave."

"You needed to be reminded who gives the orders. I'm beginning to think I'd be better off without you. So far you haven't accomplished anything you agreed to. Now, mount up and we'll return to camp.''

"Oh, no." The material of her blouse was almost dry and no longer molded itself to her body. "We agreed on several things, but one of them wasn't to give you a leisurely tour of the countryside. Just how do you plan on accomplishing anything if we can't even average two miles an hour? We start out late morning, halt for a lengthy period every half hour or so, and set up camp early afternoon! I have no intention of spending the spring, summer and fall on this…journey. I plan to be on my way to California before winter sets in.''

Beth tossed her leg over the horse's withers and slid to the ground. Not once did her gaze leave the outlaw. Though he hadn't raised his voice, the precise words left no doubt that he was serious. She wanted to be prepared should he try anything.

"And just how do you think we should travel?'' she asked, her voice laced with sarcasm.

"You lied to me, lady.''

Beth rested her hand on the butt of her revolver. "What do you mean by that?''

"You said you wanted to learn about the real West. You're never going to learn the way you're traveling. I'm beginning to think you haven't the salt for it.''

"That's a lie!''

Cole was slowly closing the gap between them. He wanted to get his hand on her gun before she ended up harming both of them. Suddenly she pulled the weapon, pointed the barrel downward and squeezed off two shots. Both bullets hit the ground between his feet.

"That's so you'll know not to come any closer.'' Beth saw his jaw muscle twitch. He hadn't taken kindly to being shot at. "Maybe now you'll think twice about trying to disarm me."

Cole stood his ground.

"Toss your horse's reins over that branch above you."

Cole was tempted to kick her feet out from under her, but instead he did as he was told. It galled him that a woman had actually gotten the draw on him.

"I'll ride your buckskin and you can ride my roan back to camp. Don't try to escape, because I would have no qualms about shooting you." She reached out and handed him her mount's lead rope. "You do know how to ride bareback, don't you?"

"I think I can manage." Cole pulled her horse to him, then taking a handful of mane, easily swung himself up on the steed's back.

Keeping the gun pointed at Cole, Beth mounted his horse. The stirrups were too long, but that was of no consequence. "Before we go, there are a couple of things you should be aware of. If you ever come upon me again when I'm bathing, I shall have you killed. Secondly, I take an agreement very seriously. Should you try to escape I promise you'll regret it. Have I made myself clear?"

"Quite," Cole snapped back at her. Damn if she wasn't making him her prisoner!

"Good. Then let's be on our way."

Cole turned his mount and started back to camp. This was definitely not going the way he'd planned it. The lady hadn't even taken the bait when he'd said she hadn't the salt needed to find out about the West.

As the copper-headed beauty rode behind him, Cole thought about what had just taken place. A grin slowly spread across his face. Things were getting interesting. He'd win out in the end, which made every order, inconvenience, gun pointing and any other undesirable situation worthwhile. He began whistling "The Bonnie Blue Flag."

Not until their return to camp and Beth had given orders to keep an eye on Cole, did she truly feel safe. There had been a certain air about Cole Wagner that left her with the impression that he was biding his time—possibly even toying with her.

As she made her way to the big tent near the stream, she pondered what would have happened had Cole given her any trouble. It had been a miracle that she'd managed to put two bullets between his feet instead of shooting him in the boot. She was accurate with a rifle, but so far she hadn't managed the art of drawing a revolver from the holster and shooting a target. Of course, she could never have killed him for backing out on their agreement, no matter how angry she had been. After all, only minutes before he'd ridden off, she had been thinking about replacing him.

"Did you bring him back?" Esther inquired the moment Beth stepped inside the tent.

"You need not sound so worried. Of course I brought him back." Beth unbuckled her gun belt and tossed it onto a low table. "As soon as I get out of these dirty clothes, I'd like a cup of that tea you're brewing."

Beth unbuttoned her blouse and let it fall onto the huge ornamental rug. The rest of the clothes quickly followed. A heavy sigh of pleasure escaped her lips when she slipped into the ruby red silk caftan Esther handed her. "I'm surprised that all European and American women haven't died from wearing so much clothing."

"So you've said before."

Beth lounged on several of the brightly colored pillows scattered about the floor.

"Did the outlaw give you any trouble?" Esther inquired as she handed Beth her tea.

"No, none whatsoever." Beth sipped the delicious brew. "Mmm. Just what I needed."

"You should have let him go. What kind of man would allow a woman to take him prisoner?" Esther moved to a low chair near Beth. "If you ask me, I think your outlaw is a coward. He's nothing like the magnificent men you have known over the years."

"Call it woman's intuition, but I have a hunch we're misjudging him. However, I still fail to understand why he doesn't wear a gun...especially when we are in the wilds. All my people are armed."

"And rightly so. Here's a thought. Perhaps he doesn't know how to shoot."

Beth drew up her knees and wrapped her arm around them. "Then if he isn't an outlaw in the truest sense, and if he doesn't know how to shoot, why doesn't he show any fear?"

"Nothing has happened to frighten him."

"Don't you find it strange that he's never shown any concern for his well-being? There is a hardness..." She set her teacup on the floor beside her. "It's difficult to explain."

"I also mentioned to Howard the possibility that Cole is out to get your money." It took several tries before Esther managed to pull herself to her feet. "He has to know about the money you're carrying. How else would you be able to pay for everything?"

"Esther, you keep contradicting yourself. You say he is a coward who can't shoot, then you turn right around and say he is planning to steal everything I own! As long as he does what I want, you can stop concerning yourself over the matter."

"You can't keep him a prisoner forever."

Beth grabbed a pillow and shoved it behind her back. "Do you know what 'not having the salt to learn' means?"

"Salt? Mercy, no."

"That's what Cole said to me. It sounded more like accusation. Oh, well, it isn't of any significance. He also complained about the lack of time we spend traveling. Perhaps he and I need to talk. I believe I'll have him dine with me. Yes. That's what I'll do. As soon as you pour me another cup of tea, go tell Magda I want her special chicken tonight, as well as several of her other delicious dishes . . . and a custard."

"Don't you think—"

"Hush. I don't want to hear anything more about it."

When Cole entered the big tent and saw Beth, he had an immediate, unexpected, erection. Lord a-mighty! He was reacting like some young pup who had never had a woman. Yet in all fairness he sure as hell hadn't expected to see his hostess in such a costume. Howard had warned him to be prepared for anything, and he should have listened. She'd never catch him off guard like this again.

In an effort to take his mind off the fetching female, Cole glanced around the interior of the tent. It was like stepping into another world. A large rug covered the floor, and an assortment of brass objects were scattered about. He had no idea what they were used for. The furniture consisted of a lot of colorful pillows and low tables and chairs.

Having regained his composure, he let his gaze shift back to the object of his discomfort. Bethany Alexander was reclined against some of the pillows. Her skirt, made of green-and-blue sparkling material, barely covered her hips, leaving a clear view of a flat stomach and a jewel embedded in her navel. The upper portion of her costume allowed just enough material to cover her breasts. Diaphanous veils of various colors draped from the top of her head and extended over creamy white shoulders and body. Her long, thick mane hung down her back, with short copper curls caressing her smooth cheeks.

"I hope you don't intend to remain there all night. Do come in."

"Do you often dress for supper like that?" he asked. Even he was amazed at how calm he sounded.

Beth laughed. "Only on special occasions. You see, I am just finishing my book on Turkey, and it helps me to write when I can create the right atmosphere. This is what women wear in Turkey. Do you like it?" She didn't bother to inform him that it was a belly dancer's costume.

Cole heard a jingling noise when she moved a bare foot. Only then did he notice the tiny bells circling her small ankles. He cleared his throat. Traveling with this woman certainly brought its surprises. "It's different," he finally replied. At this moment he couldn't think of a thing he wanted more than to grab the beauty, lift her onto the pillows and make unrestrained love for the rest of the evening. "At first I thought you might be out to seduce me."

"And what would you say if I was?"

Convinced she was now safe, she was playing with him. The whole thing verged on the unbelievable. Here he was in a situation that any man might dream of, yet he had to keep his britches up! "I'd have to refuse." He chuckled. "I never let a woman bed me unless we're well acquainted."

"Surely you must find me... tempting?" she asked good-naturedly.

He had to say something that would keep her away from him. More specifically, keep him from her. "Contrary to what you may think, I do have my morals." He rather enjoyed taking a virginal woman's side of the issue.

Beth broke out laughing. She laughed so hard tears began rolling down her cheeks. She had deliberately set out to shock him, only to end up with the man preaching morality!

"Maybe I should come back another time."

"No, no," Beth managed to say. "The...food is... ready." As she tried to regain control of herself, she pointed to the other side of the table, motioning her guest to be seated.

After wiping her eyes and blowing her nose on the handkerchief she retrieved from beneath one of the pillows, Beth realized the outlaw was still standing just inside the tent. "Come, sit down. I don't bite. I take it you haven't been around many women."

Not any quite like you, Cole thought. "I've known a few."

Beth wished he would shave off that confounded beard so she could get a good look at his face.

Cole moved forward. "Where am I supposed to sit?"

"On one of the pillows." Beth suddenly wondered why she had felt the need to taunt this man. She should have been aware of his shyness. Or was it shyness? He hadn't been backward when he complimented her in Independence. He had said she was a vision of loveliness. A shy man didn't come up with words like that. "I've had a special meal prepared just for you."

"I'd prefer it if you'd tell me the purpose of my being here." Cole sat on a pillow, then tried to figure out what he was supposed to do with his long legs.

"You said we needed to talk about our trip. I thought this was a more civilized way of doing it than yelling at each other."

Cole finally crossed his legs Indian-style. "What I've been trying to tell you—"

"Let's wait until after we have eaten. It isn't proper to discuss business during a meal."

As the women began parading in with various bowls of food, the delicious aroma quickly permeated the air, making Cole's mouth water. Having eaten only a couple of biscuits that morning, he was ready for a good meal.

Cole pitched right in. The bowls didn't have a lot in them, but he still managed goodly-sized portions on his plate. None of the dishes looked familiar, but he wasn't picky. He took a big bite of the chunky meat.

Beth raised her finger, but the food had already disappeared into Cole's mouth. She flinched when his eyes became large circles of obsidian.

Cole was convinced the woman had tried to kill him. The hot spices were not only cooking his mouth, his skin was turning red! He glanced around the table for water, even though he knew it would only make the burning worse. There was none. Not even a saltcellar to sprinkle salt in his mouth. His eyes watering, he snatched up the glass filled with heaven knew what and downed the contents. Gawd almighty! It was vinegar! He jumped to his feet and ran out of the tent, already removing his coat and welcoming the feel of fresh air against his hot flesh. Each breath he took was like inhaling fire.

"Are . . . are you all right?"

Cole spun around and glowered at his hostess.

"I started to tell you the food was spicy, but you had already taken a bite." Beth raised her hand to her throat. There was no warmth in those black eyes staring back at her. "I had wanted something different to serve you. I'm used to the food, so I had forgotten how hot Turkish food can seem to others." Seeing his breathing was returning to normal, she relaxed somewhat. She honestly felt bad about what had happened. "If you'll come back in, I'll get you some water and have Magda prepare something more to your liking."

"I'm not hungry." He started to walk away.

"What did you mean when you said I have no salt for the West?"

Cole kept walking. "Guts, lady, guts," he called over his shoulder.

Beth watched him walk away. Impossible man. Why was she singling him out from the others? All she had to do was give him an order or spend five minutes listening to what he had to say. It certainly didn't require asking him to dine with her.

She went back inside the tent. The food was getting cold and she was hungry. Strange, she hadn't noticed how broad Cole's shoulders were until he'd taken off his coat. No guts, indeed! Just wait. She'd show him.

Chapter Four

When the sun touched the western horizon, Cole waved for the caravan to make camp. Seeing they had stopped, he scouted on for another mile, making sure there wasn't any trouble waiting ahead. Satisfied, he turned his buckskin around and headed back to where he'd left the others.

As he relaxed in the saddle, Cole was feeling a bit euphoric over how smoothly the past few days of travel had gone. Each morning camp broke shortly after dawn. They stopped for a quick noon meal, then continued on until a half hour before sunset. There had been no unnecessary delays, nor had he heard a complaint. Though he hadn't spoken to Beth since the supper disaster, he knew she was the only one who could have arranged the changes. But rather than ponder on how long this routine was going to last, he preferred to enjoy it while he could.

As soon as Cole guided his horse around a big, stately oak tree, the caravan came back into view. The wagons were in a horseshoe alignment, food was already cooking on the campfires and tents and cots were being set up. Except for Beth and himself, it was arranged so the men slept on one side of the camp and the women on the other. Beth slept on a comfortable bed in her tent, while he pre-

ferred the ground, some distance from the wagons.
Should there be an attack, the marauders would head for
the main group, leaving him free to defend the others.

A short distance from the wagons Cole dismounted,
then untied the rawhide strips that kept his bedding snug
against the cantle. After laying out his bedroll between a
pair of willow trees, he unbuckled the cinch and pulled the
saddle and blanket from his horse's back. The smell of
food cooking was pleasing to his nose as well as his stomach.

Cole was leading his buckskin to the stream for watering when he heard Doolan approaching from behind. The
young man took his job as horse groom very seriously.

"I'll take it from here, sir," Doolan said.

Cole nodded and handed over the reins. He was starting to like having everything done for him. It would be an
easy life to get used to. He glanced at the tall, lanky
groom. Frank Doolan had to be nearing twenty, but he
was still as clumsy as a floundering stud. He seemed too
young to be Tex Martin, but at this point Cole couldn't
afford to rule anyone out.

Cole decided to follow along. He had discovered the
boy was of a talkative nature. A great source for information. "How long have you worked for Beth?"

"Eleven years," Doolan said proudly.

"You were just a boy when you started."

"Yes, sir. My folks got killed in a fire, and Mrs. Alexander—it was Mrs. Jarvis then—insisted her first husband let me learn to be a groom."

Two husbands? Cole wondered. "I suppose before
much longer you'll be wanting to head off on your own."
If he could get rid of Frank Doolan, that would be one
less man he'd have to be suspicious of.

Doolan thought a minute. "I got everything I could possibly want. I've traveled all over and the mistress takes real good care of her people. But to be honest, sir, I'm going to have to make some changes soon."

"What's wrong?"

"It isn't easy to talk about. Promise you won't laugh or say anything to the others?"

"Whatever you say is safe with me."

"Well, you see…I mean…I've never had a woman," Doolan finally blurted out. "Molly Dee knows, and she teases me something awful."

Molly Dee assisted the cook, Magda, and did any duties handed down by Esther. The pretty brunette was always giving Cole friendly smiles, and if she knew he was watching she would make a point of suggestively swinging her hips when she walked. Molly Dee was definitely a flirt.

"I have an awfully bad yearning, and sometimes I think I'm just going to split my britches. I thought…well, I thought…"

The boy led the buckskin into the water, then let him lower his head to drink. The honking sounds made Cole look to the sky. The Canadian geese were quite a sight flying against the backdrop of the descending sun. They were headed north. The weather was still cool at night, but that would change before long. "I'm surprised your mistress hasn't thought to take care of that matter for you."

"She'd never think of bedding—"

Cole chuckled. "That wasn't what I meant. It's a situation I'd have expected her to rectify, especially since she seems hell-bent on ruling mankind. Surely you've been places where your problem could be taken care of?"

"Yes, but I could never get up the guts to go in a whorehouse by myself."

"You want some advice, Doolan?"

Doolan lowered his head. "N . . . yes, sir."

"My advice is not to worry about it. All things happen in due time. There's nothing wrong with a man being a virgin, Doolan. How come you haven't talked about this to one of the other men?"

Doolan stroked the horse's thick neck. "They treat me like a boy. They never speak of women and such things when I'm around. I tell you, Cole, I believe a man needs to experience life before he goes and commits himself to a woman."

Cole nodded. "You planning on marrying soon?"

"No, I was just expressing how I feel. I guess I'm trying to ask if you'd maybe . . . when this is all over would you go with me to . . . ?"

Cole patted the boy's shoulder. "Just give it time. So, the mistress has been married twice, huh? That's a lot of marriages for a woman so young."

"She's twenty-eight!"

"Oh, really?" Cole grinned. "That old, huh?" he teased.

"Yes, sir."

The horse stopped drinking, and the two men headed toward the meadow.

"She's actually been married three times."

Cole raised a brow. "Is that where she came by all her money?"

"Her husbands were very wealthy."

"She probably killed them off with her food."

"Her first husband, Ernest Jarvis, was in his sixties when they married. His heart gave out."

Cole wondered if it had happened while the man was enjoying his conjugal rights.

"I've heard tell the marriage was arranged by her uncle. The second husband, Cornelious Webber, was in his eighties and as proud as all get-out to have such a beautiful woman by his side. He died in his sleep. The third husband, Mr. Alexander, was a mean bastard. No one grieved when he was robbed and murdered." Doolan raked his fingers through his sandy-colored hair. "I'll say one thing, they all had a flair for living even if some did die young. I probably shouldn't be telling you all this."

"A man has to have someone to talk to. Besides, it's all in the past."

"True."

"Sounds as if Mrs. Alexander has spent most of her life married."

"Several years ago I overheard Esther tell Magda that the mistress was married at sixteen and widowed at seventeen. The three marriages only lasted a little over five years."

They stopped in the meadow. The sun had already disappeared and dusk was quickly turning into night. Cole inhaled deeply. The light fog rolling in made everything smell damp.

"Frank, what do you know about Evan, George and the others? Do you feel they're good at their trade, reliable and that sort of thing? The reason I'm asking is because if we should be attacked by Indians or such, I'd like to know who I can rely on to help in the fight."

"I think you could rely on all of them. They may tease me, but they're good, hardworkin' men." Doolan removed a short rope from his back pocket. He hobbled the buckskin then slipped off the bridle so the horse could graze with the others. Both men heard the clanging sound informing everyone that supper was ready.

Cole was a bit disappointed. Apparently Frank had no information that might help him track down Tex. Doolan couldn't be the outlaw if he had indeed been with Beth for so long. An easy fact to check out.

"How much longer before we reach our first destination?" Doolan asked as they made their way back to the caravan.

"At our present pace, about three days."

"Cole!"

Cole turned and saw Howard Bench coming toward him.

"Beth would like you to eat in her tent tonight."

Cole groaned. He didn't want another night of going without supper. He'd much prefer eating with the others. "When am I supposed to make my command appearance?"

Howard chuckled. "She said right away."

Cole watched Howard and Doolan hurry off to the long table, where the others were already starting their meal. His gaze shifted to the tent off to itself. He'd be damned if he'd bathe, as he had last time. He moved forward. No sense putting off the inevitable. If he hurried, he might get away before all the food had disappeared from the long table.

"May I come in?" Cole called when he reached the canvas opening. This time he was prepared for anything.

"By all means."

Assuring himself that this would be brief, Cole ducked his head and entered the feline's den. Again he was taken aback by the sight before him. Everything had been changed. Now the furniture was dark, big and heavy. Though the tent was the same, it now appeared to be much smaller. To add to the overwhelming picture, Mrs. Alexander had on a heavily beaded black bolero, with a white, ruffled shirt front and a bright red waistband. The black satin pants were molded to long, perfect legs and ended just below her knees. White hose covered the rest of her legs and black slippers completed the costume.

"Well, aren't you going to say anything?"

"Working on another book?"

"No. Who wants to dress the same all the time?"

Cole's gaze traveled back up to the beautiful face. Her hair had been pulled tightly back into a knot on top of her head, exposing an oval face with a proud brow, large, heavily fringed brown eyes, high cheekbones and a wide mouth with full, tempting lips.

"Are you just going to stand and stare at me?"

"Since you've gone to all this trouble, I assumed you wanted a complete assessment." He removed his hat.

"I hope you don't think I did this just for you." Beth took his top hat and placed it on a small, heavily carved side table. "However, since you mention it, are my furnishings more to your liking?"

"Well." He pretended to consider his answer. "I would say it depended on what you wanted to use it for."

"And my clothes?"

Cole chuckled. Mistress Alexander was fishing for a compliment. "Again, it would depend on what you had in mind."

"That's no answer."

Cole's grin broadened. "I know. That way I don't get myself into trouble."

"I'm wearing a matador's suit." Seeing his blank expression, she added, "It's what the men wear in Spain when they fight bulls."

Cole looked at the small table that had been set for two. "Why would any man want to fight a bull?" he asked offhandedly. This was all taking too long. There would be no leftovers if they continued to chat. He wondered what she planned to feed him tonight. "Did Howard make a mistake when he said we would be sharing supper?"

Beth was becoming vexed. What was it about her that he didn't find attractive? "No, he made no mistake. I guess we should eat."

Cole went straight to the table, but to Beth's delight, when he pulled out a chair, he motioned for her to be seated. The man had manners after all. She was suddenly curious as to his background. "I had a special dinner prepared."

Cole managed to hold in his groan. She had said the same thing at the last meal. He looked at the fine china and sterling settings. He was trying damn hard to get along with this woman, but she wasn't making it easy.

"You will be pleased to know that there are no hot spices in the food. Though I'm wearing clothes from Spain, I selected pasta dishes from Italy. I thought they might be more to your liking." She clapped her hands.

Molly Dee immediately appeared carrying a large bowl of something white. It reminded Cole of worms. When Molly Dee set it on the table, Cole wondered if her breast brushing against his shoulder had been an accident. Magda was right behind the cute little brunette, with two smaller bowls.

"Please, serve yourself," Beth said eagerly. She had always loved to entertain. Unfortunately, Cole was the only one she had to practice on. "The sauce goes on top of the pasta. Eating it can be a bit tricky."

Why not? Cole thought. Heaven forbid that she would serve plain, simple food.

Beth demonstrated how to use a fork and spoon to eat the pasta. Even so, it took several attempts before Cole managed to get the long, stringy stuff from the plate to his mouth. Once he had the knack of it, Beth scooted up in her chair, waiting for his praise. She wasn't sure whether he liked it or not. "Well?"

Prepared for the worst, Cole had steeled himself for the first unwanted bite. Therefore it took a moment for him to realize the food was messy but quite good. He smiled and nodded appreciatively. Not until Beth clapped her hands with glee did he realize the importance of his approval. She quickly filled her own plate.

Remembering that last time Beth had said there was to be no business discussed during the meal, Cole settled down to a delectable supper. Before long he found himself wondering who the real Bethany Alexander was. It seemed that every time he was around her, she acted like a different person. Minutes ago her face had mirrored the delight of a child. Howard had once mentioned something about her being lonesome. Perhaps he had been right.

When his appetite was satisfied, Cole leaned back in his chair and sipped the black coffee that had been served. For the moment he was at peace with the world.

"How much farther will we be traveling before the train robbery?"

Apparently supper was over and business could now be discussed. "Three days," he replied. "I haven't had a chance to thank you for changing our traveling routine. I know it must be a considerable inconvenience for you. It's because of the extra hours of travel that we'll make final camp so soon. Tomorrow we'll pass within four miles of a town." Her excitement was apparent. "However, I don't think it would be wise to stop."

"Why? There are things—"

"I thought the purpose of all this was so you could find out about train robbers? Believe me, they don't make a habit of announcing their presence to a sheriff and a town full of people. If at all possible, they avoid easy identification."

"So we'll just travel on?"

"You and the caravan will travel on."

"What does that mean?"

"It means that Doolan and I are riding to town."

Beth leaned forward, any trace of humor gone. "Are you planning to return?"

"Don't worry. I could have left you any time I wanted. But as long as everything continues to move smoothly I have no intentions of going anywhere. I want my money. It will help buy land when I go to California."

Beth remembered him mentioning that before. "Why can't we all go? I'm sure the others would enjoy seeing a town for a change."

"Come, come Beth. Don't you think a caravan like this one would be a bit conspicuous? Bruster is a small town."

"I'll go with—"

"I'll take Doolan. We can pick up any supplies needed and make sure there aren't any Pinkerton men about. I also need to check on the train schedule."

"I thought we had already established who is in charge here."

Cole rested his elbows on the table. "And I thought you wanted to know what it was like to rob a train. All this traveling and staying out of view is exactly what a bandit would do. The only difference is the manner in which he would travel and the way you're doing it. Have you devised a plan for robbing the train and figured out how many men you're going to need?"

"I'm working on it."

Cole knew she didn't have the slightest idea how to address the situation. "Permit me to offer some advice."

"I'm the robber—the one who is supposed to figure everything out." Nevertheless, Beth watched closely as Cole creased lines on the tablecloth with the blunt edge of his knife.

Cole made crisscrossed lines in several places. "This is your train. You are going to need someone to get to the front—" he pointed to it "—and get the engineer to stop. While he's doing that, others have to enter by the back. There will only be one passenger car. Naturally you'll want guns to be drawn in case someone wants to put up a fight."

Beth's face became ashen. "Are you saying we may have to shoot someone?"

"When you're an outlaw, there is always that possibility. Some people don't take kindly to being robbed."

"But I really don't want to rob anyone. I just want to see what it's like to do it."

Cole shrugged his shoulders. "I hope the people on the train understand that. Now, you're also going to need someone to stay with the horses and have them ready when you exit the train. You don't want to get shot while leaving."

"You've left out one very important detail. How do we get on the train?"

"That's the simplest part. You ride your horse up alongside and climb on."

"You can't be serious!"

"Dead serious."

"While the train is moving?"

"How else do you plan to stop it? You might consider getting a man's saddle and some britches. You could get your foot caught up in a skirt hem and kill yourself. Of course, if you want to change your mind about this..." He raised a dark eyebrow and waited.

"No, I'm not going to change my mind. I always finish what I set out to do. I don't want to hear any more. As I told you, this is my holdup."

"But of course. You will have several days to work it out. I'm curious why a lady of your financial standing would even want to do any of this."

"Research. Purely research. Besides, money isn't everything. It is time for me to start doing something constructive with my life."

Cole stood and made a slight bow. "The supper was excellent, my lady. I thank you for all the trouble you went to." He snatched up his hat before exiting the tent. Yes, sirree, the woman did talk a good story. Of course, come time to commit the crime, the lady would undoubtedly change her mind.

As Cole drove the farm wagon down one of the back streets of Bruster, he kept scanning the area for any sight of the bald-faced nag the traveling sheriff rode. How long had it been? Six years since he last visited the town? Something like that. It wasn't a large town, but it was sufficient for the surrounding farms. He brought the horses to a halt in front of a large saloon.

"Why are we stopping here?" Doolan inquired.

"I figured we could both use a drink."

Doolan jumped from the wagon and followed Cole inside. It was only around ten in the morning, so there were few customers. As he sidled up to the bar, Doolan was feeling more like a man than he ever had. There was something about being around Cole that made him feel different than when he was with the others. Maybe that was because Cole didn't treat him as if he were still in short pants.

"A couple of whiskeys," Cole told the bartender. He pulled a coin from his pocket and slapped it on the bar. "Is Dahlia still here?" he asked when the bartender had filled the shot glasses.

"Yeah, I'm still here. Who wants to know?"

Cole downed the shot, then turned toward the voice. Dahlia had to be in her early fifties, but very little had changed. She was overweight, her hair was dyed a gaudy bright red and her two-layer-deep makeup did little to hide the wrinkles. Nevertheless, she'd always been a fair woman and treated her girls well.

"Cole?" Dahlia pulled her wire-rimmed glasses from between her large breasts and took a harder look. "Son of a bitch! Cole Wagner. It is you!" She hurried forward and threw her ample arms around him.

"You haven't changed," Cole said fondly.

Dahlia released him and stepped back. "Well, I sure as hell can't say the same about you. Why are you dressed like that, you handsome devil? Look at that stupid hat. And that beard. I ain't never seen you with a beard." She laughed with delight. "You aimin' to braid it?"

Cole grinned good-naturedly. "Dahlia, I'd like you to meet a friend of mine. Doolan, this is Dahlia, the best woman for miles around."

Doolan blushed at the brazen way Dahlia looked him over. He wasn't sure what to think about all this. How had these two come to know each other?

"I'll be damned. You brung me a green one."

Cole chuckled. Dahlia knew her men. "Doolan is fixing to become twenty. I figured it was time he learned a few things about women."

Doolan didn't know whether to laugh or cry. "You mean..."

"Knowing you have the best girls in the county," Cole continued, ignoring his young friend, "I knew you would pick him out someone special."

Doolan licked his lips. Was he honestly going to get to be with a woman—naked and everything?

"I got just the one," Dahlia crooned. "Bill," she called to the bartender, "call down Credence."

Doolan was feeling as skittish as a turpentined cat. "Can I talk with you a minute in private?" he asked Cole.

"Sure thing." Cole winked at Dahlia and moved several feet away. "What is it, Doolan?"

"What if I ... I mean, you know ... can't do it."

"Why would you say that?"

"Well, you know I've never ... Don't you need me to help get supplies?"

"Are you telling me you don't want to go through with this?"

"I just don't want..." Doolan forgot what he was about to say. His eyes were fastened on the tall blonde coming down the stairs. The only thing she had on was a girdle that pushed her creamy white breasts up, and a gossamer thing that reached the floor and hid nothing. He'd never seen anything so beautiful.

Cole laughed. "You'll do just fine, Doolan. I'm sure you haven't a thing to worry about." Cole doubted that the boy had even heard what he'd said. He saw Dahlia's slight nod, indicating to Credence which man was her customer.

Credence walked up to Doolan, who looked as if he were frozen in ice. "Oh," she said as she ran her fingers through his hair, "you're a handsome one."

Doolan grinned like a sick puppy.

Credence took his hand. "Why don't you come upstairs with me?"

Cole reached into his pocket and pulled out some money. "It will be a while before I return," he stated as he handed Dahlia the money. "See that the boy has a good time."

"I can't take your money, Cole. Hell, if it wasn't for you I wouldn't have this business."

Cole gave it to her, anyway. "Tell me, has Sheriff Biggs been in these parts lately?"

"No, he tried shootin' it out with some young kid. They buried him nearly a year ago. The new sheriff never comes here 'cause nothin' ever happens. You're free to go where you please."

Cole grinned. "I'll see you later."

As Cole drove out of town, Frank Doolan couldn't stop talking about how well Credence had said he'd performed. "She told me she'd never had anyone who could keep doing it time after time. Damn! I sure do feel good!"

"I hope she showed you how to please a woman, because you'll come to learn that it's a lot better when a woman is enjoying it as much as you are."

"Credence showed me what women like."

"All women aren't the same."

"Why, once I went a whole ten minutes before I... Well, you know what I mean," he said proudly.

Cole chuckled. "Is that so? Then I guess the next thing you have to learn is not to go around bragging about how good you are, because, I assure you, there is always someone better."

"Maybe you can teach me more," Doolan said, still unable to contain his excitement.

"No, you're on your own."

Doolan shook his head. "I never knew it could feel so good. If I had, I'd of done it a long time ago. You have to be the best friend a man could ever have to go and do something like this for me.'' He slapped his leg. "Damned if I don't feel like howling.''

"Then by all means, go right ahead.''

It was a good two miles before Doolan's voice gave out and the howling ceased. It seemed as if the boy now had a permanent smile plastered on his face. Cole welcomed the blessed silence. He was remembering a long time ago when a woman had taken him to her bed for the first time. Like Doolan, he'd thought he had just been handed the world.

Chapter Five

Large drops of rain were already striking the ground when Cole raised his hand for the caravan to come to a halt. It had been a dreary day, but at least they had arrived at their destination before the storm broke. The dark clouds rolling overhead left no doubt that they were in for a downpour. He guided his horse beneath a tall tree, then swung from the saddle.

"Is this it?" Beth asked as she came alongside him.

"Yep. This is where the caravan will remain camped while you play train robber." He reached down and loosened the saddle girth. "You might want to tell the men you picked to go with us that we'll be taking off first thing in the morning."

"Where is the railroad?"

"About a day and a half ride due north. We'll be camping overnight on the way there and on the way back, so we'll need provisions."

Beth reined the feisty mare around until she was again facing Cole. "Aren't you going to help me down?"

Cole pulled on his duster. "That's not my job. However, I can be bribed."

Beth laughed. "With what?"

Cole was sorely tempted to tell her that for a night in bed together she could have just about anything she wanted. "One of those pasta suppers tonight?"

Beth's face lit up with pleasure. "You have a deal. But maybe I should have Magda fix—"

"Please, the pasta will be fine." Cole stepped to her black mare's side and reached up. His hands easily spanned Beth's tiny waist as he lifted her from the side-saddle. Common sense told him not to play with fire, but it amused him to see the smug look on her face disappear as he slowly lowered her down the length of him.

Realizing the outlaw was showing interest in her, Beth's heart leapt. There was something about this man that definitely attracted her. When their faces were only inches apart he held her still, her body molded against his. She was staring into a pair of fathomless dark eyes. Passionate eyes that... "Are you thinking about kissing me?" Allowing her curiosity full rein, Beth closed her eyes and waited.

Cole smiled. Tempting. Very tempting, but it would only lead to trouble. "I was inhaling your perfume."

Beth's eyes flew open.

"I've never smelled anything like it." Cole stood her on her feet. "It's pleasing to the nostrils."

"I gave you an invitation!"

"An invitation to what?"

"To kiss me!"

"Oh. I didn't realize." Cole leaned over and gave her a quick peck on the lips.

"That's it?"

Cole shrugged.

Beth glared at him while unconsciously slapping her quirt against her thick skirt.

"You'd best get beneath some shelter." Cole saw Doolan running toward them. "The rain is worsening and you'll catch your death if you get soaked."

"I don't melt like sugar," she seethed.

"But I do."

Doolan quickly gathered the horses' reins. "The men will have your tent set up in no time, Mrs. Alexander." He took off running, with the horses in tow.

Cole pulled Beth beneath the limbs of the tree. "Looks like you're going to have to wait here."

"Why didn't you kiss me properly?" Beth asked as she brushed away the droplets of water that clung to her green velvet riding gown.

Cole grinned. "I think you overestimate men. Why don't you put that in the journal you're keeping?"

"What do you mean, I overestimate men?" Again Beth became lost in the depths of those dark, penetrating eyes. She had to force herself to turn away and watch the others hurriedly setting up camp. The rain was heavier now.

"I think the average man is shy, or maybe I should say cautious. He has only had a few female encounters before marrying and settling down. He spends a lot of time around other men and he's not nearly as experienced with the opposite sex as he would like women and other men to believe."

"Are you describing yourself?" Had she misread the passion in his eyes only moments ago?

"Probably, but I never married."

"Did some woman break your heart?"

Cole broke out in a hearty laugh.

"What is so funny?"

Suddenly the wind kicked up, causing the rain to come in torrents. Cole could no longer see the wagons parked some thirty-odd yards away. Within seconds the water had worked its way through the thick leaves and branches of the tree and was dripping on both of them. Lightning cracked and danced about. It had all happened so quickly.

Cole removed his duster and draped it over Beth. "We're going to have to make a dash for that shallow ditch!"

The thunder was deafening and Beth didn't hear what he'd said. As Cole started to move her from the protection of the tree, she balked. "I'm not going anywhere!"

Lacking time for explanations, Cole picked Beth up and ran. Raindrops hammered his face. Having to slosh across muddy ground made the distance seem twice as long. He didn't see the ditch bank until he stumbled over it. He toppled forward, landing in a muddy pool with Beth beneath him.

"What are you trying to do?" Beth tried scrambling out from under him. "Drown me?" Seeing that the outlaw was making no effort to move, she frantically twisted and shoved, desperately needing to draw fresh air into her lungs. "Dammit, get off me!" Furious at being held down, she gathered all her strength, braced her back against the muddy bank and shoved. Cole rolled off her, but her legs were still pinned beneath him.

"Is this some way of getting even?" Beth yelled. "If you wanted me dead, why didn't you just shoot me?"

Finally able to sit up, Beth tried wiping the mud from her face. It took the rain pouring down to clear her vision. It would take forever to get her hair, body and clothes clean!

Just then lightning struck the tree they had been standing beneath only minutes ago, followed by a crack of thunder that put Beth's nerves on end.

"Oh, Lord," she whispered.

The tree made an eerie sound as the thick trunk split in half, then burst into flames.

Beth's body was shaking. She could have been killed had Cole not forced her into this ditch. She hated being in the wrong, but even more, she hated apologizing. She looked down at the man beside her just as another bolt of lightning crackled through the air. It allowed her a momentary view of closed eyes and a cut on Cole's forehead. She was sick with guilt. He had to have hit a rock when he fell. Was he unconscious or...dead? She untied the wet silk scarf from her neck and placed it around his wound, hoping to stop the bleeding. As if decreed by God, the rain began to subside.

"Decker!" Beth yelled. "Jeff!" Hearing nothing, she called again. And again...and again. Finally she thought she heard voices. "Here!" she hollered. "We're over here!"

Cole was aware of his head pounding as he slowly awakened. Two things were certain. Night had fallen and he had a knot the size of a goose egg on his forehead. He sat up and winced. The movement made his head pound twice as badly. Where the hell was he? In a wagon. He was on a bed in a wagon. His bandage told him Tucker Washington had tended him. How long had he been here? Hearing no noise, he had to assume everyone was bedded down for the night. He swung his legs over the side of the bed and banged his big toe on something. "Damn!"

"Are you all right?"

Cole tried seeing through the darkness, but it was impossible. "Who is that?" Cole called. "I didn't realize there was someone else in the wagon."

"George. You want me to go fetch the doc?"

"No, I'm all right. Go back to sleep." Cole lay back down and commanded himself to relax. The blacksmith wasn't the only one who needed sleep.

Cole awoke the following morning to the smell of coffee and the mouth-watering aroma of cooking bacon. He was alone in the wagon. Perhaps it had been George's departure that had awakened him. He suddenly realized his body was clean of mud and he had on fresh long underwear. Who had bathed him and changed his clothes? It wasn't likely to have been Beth. That left the good doctor to perform the task as well as the mending.

On the arm of the chair shoved against the bed were his saddlebags, bandanna and a new set of clean clothes. His suit, hat and shirt were nowhere in sight. He grimaced as he slowly sat up. He had a feeling he'd never see the suit again. In truth, he was glad to be rid of the greenhorn outfit. It was out of style, he hated plaids and the damn thing itched. He looked in his saddlebags. Someone had rifled through them. There was little doubt as to who that someone would be. Beth hadn't even bothered to put things back the way they had been. So having seen the Wanted poster, now she knew there was a five-thousand-dollar reward for him, dead or alive. That should satisfy her need for a real outlaw.

The trousers, blue-striped shirt and gold-threaded vest he put on were far more to Cole's liking. The clothes fit surprisingly well, which brought up a question. Where did they come from? Most of the men in the caravan were shorter except for Doolan, and he was too thin.

By the time Cole climbed out of the wagon the sun was bright and the sky devoid of clouds. Except for the puddles scattered about, all traces of the storm had vanished. Feeling hungry, he went straight to the big table.

Once he had some coffee and food under his belt he'd be able to think more clearly.

Standing in the doorway of her tent, Beth watched Cole get his coffee, sit down at the table and fill his plate. She could hear the others inquiring about how he felt, and his assurance that he'd be fine. She turned and went back inside. He looked a lot different in his new clothes. He not only looked more like an outlaw should, he also seemed bigger, taller and dangerous. Maybe she felt that way because of reading that Wanted poster in his saddlebags.

"Is this all you're going to eat?" Esther asked.

"I'm not hungry."

Esther shook her head in disapproval. "Did you find anything of interest in the outlaw's belongings?"

"A Wanted poster. I'm not sure if the face was or wasn't Cole's. The drawing wasn't too good. There was also a set of well-used .45s. You know, Esther, I have a hard time picturing Cole robbing a bank, or anything, for that matter. He seems too even tempered and easygoing. It no longer matters what he is or isn't. He saved my life and I'm indebted to him."

Beth glanced down at the black trousers and black boots she was wearing. Suddenly she sprang forward, leapt over the back of the sofa, landed on the cushions then jumped onto the floor.

"Is there a purpose to this?" Esther asked.

Pleased with her efforts, Beth smiled. "I just wanted to be sure my pants weren't too tight to prevent me from leaping onto the train."

"Doing what?" Esther gasped. "You'll get yourself killed with all this foolishness. Why must you partake? Why can't you just observe?"

"It's not the same." Beth squatted and stood several times, still testing her mobility. She had no intention of telling Esther that she was determined to prove to the outlaw that she had salt.

Beth snatched up the gun belt hanging over the back of the chair and buckled it just below her waist. With lightning speed she drew the Peacemaker from the holster, spun it around and flipped it back into its resting place. "Cole is going to be in for a big surprise," she muttered, more to herself than to Esther.

"What difference does it make what he thinks?"

Beth glanced at her friend. "It's important to me."

"Mrs. Alexander?"

Beth looked toward the tent opening. "What do you want, Frank?"

"Cole was wondering if you're ready to go."

Beth walked toward the young man. He seemed so different lately. More grown-up. "Go? Go where?"

"To where we'll be robbing the train," Frank said excitedly.

"But Cole is in no condition to ride." Beth looked several yards behind Frank and saw Cole gathering his gear.

"Cole said he was feeling fine. He's reminding everyone that we were supposed to leave this morning."

"What about the others?"

"They're ready and waiting."

"Oh. Well . . . I've been waiting, also." Beth heard Esther click her tongue at the outright lie. "Naturally I want to get this over as quickly as possible. There are still so many things for me to do and see."

Beth hurried back into the tent and yanked her vest on over her shirt. A silk bandanna was quickly tied around her neck, the thick braid lifted and pushed under the wide-brimmed hat she jammed on. She looked at her image in the full-length mirror. Perfect. She was ready to rob a train.

* * *

As they sat on their mounts waiting for the train, Cole wiped the perspiration from his forehead. He was still having some trouble from that blow he'd taken. Another day's rest the doc had prescribed would have probably been to his benefit, but he'd had to make sure this was the train Beth and her cohorts robbed. He glanced at each man. Excitement and anticipation were mirrored on their faces as well as Beth's. They were all fools. He'd tried convincing himself that Beth's plan would probably go without a hitch, but that was damn hard to swallow when no one knew what they were about.

Though Beth's clothes were meant to give her more mobility, she probably thought they hid her female attributes. He was certain he had never seen so dainty a man. The only men he knew who wore such tight pants were vaqueros.

Cole had chosen this particular train because it had only one passenger car, but, more important, the incline was steep. By the time the train arrived at this point, it would be going considerably slower. There would be less chance of something happening when Beth and her gang boarded it.

The train whistle was loud and clear, as was the sound of wheels and steam as the train started its ascent. Doolan took off down the track ready to catch the horses. Minutes later the engine chugged past them. The plan was for Decker to stop the train and for George and Wilber to enter the car from behind the coal bin. Beth would get on in the back.

Cole watched Beth pull her hat down firmly on her head, then lean forward, her horse charging into a gallop. As the steed gained its full speed, the passenger car came alongside her. Beth reached for the steel rails so she could swing onto the steps, but missed, almost falling out of the saddle. She wasn't in close enough.

Cole dug his heels into his buckskin's sides. He yelled for Beth to wait, but she had already moved her mount in closer to the railroad tracks. He watched her reach out again. This time she was able to grasp the rails. But before she could get her balance, the train's momentum jerked her from the saddle. It looked as if her hands were slipping, yet her face showed no fear. Only determination.

Cole urged his horse to a faster speed. She was going to fall beneath the grinding wheels! As the distance between them lessened, he leaned to the side and reached his arm out, ready to snatch Beth from her perilous position. But at that moment she raised her foot onto the step and pulled herself up. Finally on her feet, she moved forward, disappearing inside the railroad car.

Not wanting to have anything to do with the crazy scheme, Cole pulled back on the reins. In the next instant he was again urging his buckskin forward. He cursed himself for being an even bigger fool than the others. But he had no choice. He had to make sure the "boss lady" got out of this alive. He needed her to find Tex. Besides, his gut was telling him that this whole mess was about to go awry.

After pulling himself onto the car, Cole unbuttoned his duster, giving him access to the twin Colts bulging under his coat. Why was the train still going? It should have already stopped.

Wondering the same thing, Beth stood staring at the seated men and women stretched out in front of her. Where were Wilber and George?

Feeling she couldn't wait a minute longer, Beth drew her gun. Even though the excitement and danger of robbing a train was shooting adrenaline through her veins, the words she'd practiced stuck in her throat. She took two stabilizing breaths. "This is a holdup," she announced loudly. "I want everyone to toss their money in the aisle. Don't try anything and no one will get hurt."

A woman screamed, several men disappeared behind the seats and others started digging into their pockets. A shot suddenly rang out, barely missing Beth's ear. The men who had ducked behind the seats were shooting at her!

"I have other men on this train," a deep voice boomed from behind Beth. "Fire once more and everyone in this car will be killed."

Beth turned and looked at Cole. He had to be insane to make such threats! He hadn't even drawn his guns!

"I'm not going to say it again! Drop those weapons and stand so I can see you."

To Beth's shock, the men did as they were told.

"We're getting out of here now!" Cole whispered in Beth's ear.

"No. I came to rob a train!"

"Dammit, this is no time to argue."

An arm of steel suddenly wrapped around Beth's waist. He was too strong. She couldn't prevent herself being pulled backward.

"We're getting out of here now, lady." Cole snatched the gun from her hand and shoved her out the door. With her revolver pointed at the passengers, he ordered Beth to go down the steps and jump away from the wheels.

Beth stared at the ground quickly passing beneath her and was immediately overcome with a sickening sensation in the pit of her stomach. "No."

"Either I throw you off or you jump. What's it going to be?" One of the men reached down for his gun in the aisle. Cole knocked it out of reach with a perfectly placed shot. "Now!" he yelled at Beth.

Beth sucked in her breath and jumped.

Everything happened so fast. Beth was aware of hitting the hard ground and felt sure her insides were smashed, but then she was rolling down a steep hill, trying unsuccessfully to stop. She released a loud gasp when a sturdy sapling finally brought her to an abrupt halt. Everything had suddenly become so quiet that her heavy breathing sounded loud in her ears. Every bone in her body had to be broken. Still, she could only feel aches and pains, probably from stones and the blessed tree. She squeezed her eyes shut, gritted her teeth, then carefully moved her right leg. The sharp, unbearable pain she had anticipated didn't happen. Feeling nothing more than an aching throb, she moved the left leg.

Having determined she wasn't going to die, Beth pulled herself to her feet. Her concerns were quickly replaced with anger. How dare Cole order her to jump? And just where were Decker, Wilber and George? Doolan was supposed to be waiting with the horses!

"So you survived."

Beth spun around and saw Cole walking toward her. The caked dirt and grass on his body indicated his landing hadn't been any softer. "No thanks to you."

"You've got that a bit backward, my dear. You would have been dead if I *hadn't* made you jump."

Beth was surprised at his apparent anger. His dark eyes were flashes of glassy obsidian, and his hands rested firmly on narrow hips. She was about to make a tart reply when he suddenly grabbed her to him, covering her mouth with his hand. She didn't even get a chance to plant a kick on his shin. He was pulling her farther down the hill.

"Don't say a word," Cole whispered when he brought them to a halt.

What did he think he was doing? Then Beth heard the voices. "They jumped off somewhere around here. They haven't had time to get away. Spread out." The people on the train were coming after them!

Cole took his hand from her mouth. "I'm going to boost you up this tree," he whispered.

Beth's eyes followed the tall, thick trunk upward. It looked as if it was touching the sky.

Cole cupped his hands in the same manner one would help a lady to mount a horse. Beth raised her foot and placed her heel in his hands.

"Climb as high as you can, then be still. No matter what happens, don't say a word." He raised her until she was high enough to climb onto a heavy limb.

Beth didn't see where the outlaw went. She was too busy getting as far from the ground as possible. Fortunately, she'd never had a fear of heights.

When Beth heard voices again she hugged the trunk, not daring to move as much as a finger. From her vantage point she could see the railroad track and the train sitting waiting. The female passengers had remained inside while the men searched. For some utterly unexplainable reason it occurred to her that everything she'd done in the past had been under controlled circumstances. Even when she'd studied bullfighting in Spain there had been several matadors ready to jump into the arena should something happen. This time she was breaking the law and if she got caught, she was on her own.

"I haven't heard any horses takin' off, so they gotta be nearby."

Beth looked down. Three men were standing directly under her. She could even smell the cigar one man was smoking. She couldn't get a good look at the men because of the thick foliage, but it also prevented them from seeing her.

"Hell, they had to have horses," another man said. "No one would be stupid enough to travel on foot so far from a town."

"Max!" a third man called to someone else. "Any sign of them robbers?"

"Nope," a gruff voice called from her left. "I can't even find where they jumped off the train."

"Let's get goin'," the first man ordered. "They didn't get anything and we'll catch them when they try again."

The men were already walking away, and Beth could no longer hear what was being said. She released a shaky sigh. In one of the dime novels it said train robbers were hung on the spot. She hadn't believed it then, but she believed it now. This was the second time Cole had saved her life.

It seemed like hours before Beth finally heard the train chugging on its way.

"You're safe now. Come on down."

Beth couldn't see Cole, but she had no trouble recognizing his deep voice.

Beth discovered that climbing down was far more difficult than going up. She reached the limb the outlaw had put her on and started to jump, but quickly changed her mind. It was higher than she'd realized.

"Jump. I'll catch you."

"But what if you don't?"

"Woman, is there anything you won't argue about? Surely you don't expect me to climb up after you?" Seeing a look of hope cross her face, Cole tried again. "It's not going to happen. Now, do you want to get down, or do you intend to stay up there for the rest of your life?"

Ever so carefully Beth sat on the limb, her hand pressed against the tree trunk for balance. "Are you sure you'll catch me?"

"I said so, didn't I?"

Without any warning Beth jumped, catching Cole off guard. He caught her, but her awkward position knocked them both to the ground.

Beth rolled over him and climbed to her feet. "You call that a catch?" she asked as she tried brushing the dirt from her clothes. "Any of the other men could have done a better job."

"But they're not here, are they?" Cole asked between clenched teeth. He stood, commanding himself not to wring the woman's neck. "Those were lawmen shooting at you. Didn't you see their badges when you gave orders to throw their money in the aisle? And just what the hell were you doing? You were there to experience a holdup, not to actually rob the damn train!"

"How could I experience it if I didn't do it?" Beth snapped back at him. "What was I supposed to do? Just stand there? Not until that moment did I think about needing a bag to put my booty in." Seeing she was making an even bigger mess of her clothes, she gave up the effort of trying to brush them clean. Where was her hat?

"Booty? Is that what you call it? You could have been taking someone's last cent. And furthermore, if I hadn't come after you, you'd still be standing there—or lying on the floor dead!"

Beth flinched. She knew he was right, but she wasn't about to admit it. "You're acting awfully pious for a man with a reward hanging over him!"

"And where are your cohorts? You insisted on planning this robbery, and more than once you stated you didn't want my thoughts on the matter because you knew exactly how to handle everything. Since you're so good, perhaps you'd like to tell me what we do next."

"Do real outlaws ask for recommendations on how to perform their jobs?" she asked belligerently. "I can't learn if I don't do it." She started walking back up the hill, glancing in every direction for her hat. "I'll do better next time."

"What?" Cole roared. He started after her.

"Tomorrow. We'll do it again tomorrow, that is if I can locate the rest of my gang."

Cole caught her by the arm and spun her around. "You can count me out."

"Just as I thought. You really are a coward when it comes to such things, aren't you?" she taunted, needing to take her frustration out on someone. "I'm surprised you came into the train car with me. I'll bet you wet your pants when those men started shooting. I wonder if that really is your picture on that Wanted poster you keep in your saddlebags?" She wasn't prepared for his cold grin.

"Pray you never find out just how bad I can be, lady." Cole had decided Beth would never admit to going through his things. He had second-guessed her. He had deliberately kept the poster there as proof that he was wanted. Knowing her curiosity would eventually come into play. "I consider it common sense to give it up when those lawmen said they'd be waiting for you next time. But you go right ahead with what you feel you need to do. And who knows? Maybe the boys will hold up their end next time."

Beth started up the hill again, every muscle suddenly protesting. She refused to complain or give way to the ache in her hip, leg, even her foot! Each step seemed to bring more misery.

"You don't look so good. Do you think you can make it to the dead tree where we're supposed to meet the others?"

"Don't you worry about me." Beth picked up her pace. Cole was right on her heels. She hated the way he always brought up facts that forced her to rethink her plans. That was exactly why she hadn't told him how she intended to rob the train.

"I was just wondering if I was going to have to go for help." He knew she would resent any help he might offer.

Beth bit down on her bottom lip. "Don't you worry, I can hold my own. Why don't you spend your time looking for my hat instead of nagging me?"

Beth could never remember such relief as she felt upon sighting the dead tree in the distance. Convinced her feet couldn't carry her another step, she was tempted to have Cole send someone back to fetch her. But she refused to give him the satisfaction of knowing she hadn't made it. They hadn't even spoken for the past couple of hours. The way things had gone today, she wouldn't be at all surprised if the others weren't waiting for them.

It was Decker who spotted the two first. He yanked his horse about and met the pair halfway.

"You might give the lady your mount," Cole commented dryly when Decker joined them. "She's ready to fall on her face."

Beth was too exhausted to argue.

Decker leapt down, then helped Beth up.

When they finally reached the dead tree Beth and Cole were greeted by a group of sheepish faces. Beth picked up a canteen and took a long drink of water before trying to make herself comfortable on the ground. "Well," she finally said, "what happened?"

The men started talking at once.

"Stop!" Beth ordered. "Doolan, you start."

"The horses went in every direction, ma'am. I had a hell of a time catching them, especially yours."

"So if we *had* robbed the train, we had no means of escape?"

"I guess that's the truth of it."

Cole lay down on his back a short distance away and pulled his hat over his face. As the men explained their lack of success at trying to climb onto the train, it was difficult for Cole to maintain a sober face. But when Wilber described how he had managed to board, only to be met with the engineer's gun pointed in his face, it was all Cole could do to keep from rolling with laughter. It was a wonder none of them had been seriously hurt. He did notice the scrapes on Wilber's face and that the front of his shirt was torn from when he'd jumped just in time to keep from getting shot. But that wasn't the only injury. Decker had a definite limp, and George kept rubbing his arm. And though she wouldn't admit it, Beth was in no shape to go anywhere.

Cole could never remember seeing a more inept group. But Beth had been right about one thing. She was the best of the lot, whatever that was worth. Yep, the woman had guts. And he had realized something else about her today. Beth never seemed to really get close to people. For the first time, tonight she seemed to be at one with the others. Was she trying to seek acceptance from people?

Cole rolled onto his side. The arrangements he'd made by telegram when he and Frank had gone to Bruster had turned out just as he had planned. The men with the adges had played their parts well. At least this segment of Beth's plans had been completed. There wasn't any possible way this bunch could try it again tomorrow. He closed his eyes and drifted off to sleep.

Chapter Six

Still in a state of disbelief, Cole again sat on top of his horse watching the others. He'd been wrong. Beth and her gang of ineptness were ready to give the whole thing another try. They had all sat up most of the night working out what they had done wrong that day. Cole had remained on his bedroll, refusing to give any input. Not that he'd been asked. This time he'd made no arrangements for their safety. If Beth persisted in pulling such stunts, she would be constantly jeopardizing everything he needed to accomplish.

He still couldn't believe they were going to turn around and rob the same train the very next day. And each one had that look on their faces that said no matter what it took, they were going to get it right this time. They were all tired and bruised. He'd even heard Beth whimper when she had climbed into the saddle. Once he'd realized what they were up to, he'd tried every way he knew to dissuade them. Besides the group wanting to prove their own mettle, the extra money Beth had promised was the seal of death.

"If we're going to be outlaws we can't make any mistakes," Beth said when they reached the railroad tracks.

Cole rolled his eyes at her rallying words.

"Because we didn't get it right last time, there could be even more danger this time. The law may be expecting us. Let's look professional!"

Professional what? Cole mused. Criminals? The two wagon builders, blacksmith and groom nodded simultaneously before riding off to their designated spots. Cole had already concluded that one had to be mighty damn versatile if one wanted to ride for Mrs. Alexander. Beth wasn't the first person Cole had seen become inflamed with the passion of running against the law. It wasn't until being an outlaw became a burden that one grew to regret the path one had taken. Then it was too late.

They all heard the train whistle.

"Cole, be ready to ride when we return," Beth called as she positioned herself. The biting words were muffled by the black silk bandanna hiding her face.

Cole released a fatalistic sigh. This morning Beth had had an interesting way of excusing the lawman's comment about catching her next time. She was convinced they would never think her foolish enough to pull the same robbery again—and certainly not back-to-back. They were bound to expect her to pick another time and place. He nudged his horse forward. Her highness had left him with no choice. As before, he'd have to make sure she didn't get herself in trouble. He pulled his horse up behind the big roan.

Beth wondered why Cole hadn't remained hidden in the trees, but she didn't have time to pursue the thought. The train had topped the hill.

This time Beth wasn't yanked from the saddle when she climbed onto the passenger car's ladder. Once on the platform, she stopped a moment to glance over her shoulder. To her surprise, Cole was behind her. It flashed through her mind that calling him a coward yesterday hadn't been justified. In truth, he probably couldn't handle a woman being braver than he.

Just as Beth opened the car door and stepped inside, the train came to a screeching halt. People lunged forward in their seats, and Beth would have fallen had the outlaw not braced her with his arm.

"Everyone raise their hands," Beth ordered loudly as soon as she had her footing again. "This is a holdup!"

Beth's chest swelled with pride when George and Wilber entered through the door up front. Why, with a little practice they could become really good at this. And she had been right. There were no lawmen. She glanced behind her, wanting to gloat. Cole Wagner was nowhere in sight.

While George and Beth kept their guns pointed at the passengers, Wilber tugged at the burlap bag tucked beneath his belt. It had been the only thing they could find to put their loot in.

Beth remembered Cole's comment about taking someone's last cent. To her aggravation, she couldn't do it. Even if she left the sack outside, there was no guarantee that everything would be properly returned to the rightful owners.

"Put the sack away, Wilber. We've accomplished what we came for."

The two men looked at her questioningly.

"Let's get out of here." She turned and went out the door.

As she descended the stairs Beth found Doolan and Cole waiting with the horses in tow. She climbed into the saddle and they rode to the end of the car, where George and Wilber holstered their guns and mounted their horses. They took off at a gallop, with Doolan bringing the last riderless mount alongside the train engine. With one big leap, Decker, who had kept the engineer at bay, landed in the saddle.

Interesting that the men seemed to be treating Doolan more like an equal, thought Cole. Since his indoctrination into manhood there was more of a self-assurance about him that the men had apparently picked up. They had even started including him in their conversations.

Not until they had returned to the dead tree did the gang start celebrating their accomplishment. They yelled and patted each other on the back as they tied their bedrolls behind the saddles. When the camp area was picked up, they all mounted and headed back to where the wagons waited.

"I told you we could do it," Beth bragged to Cole as they rode a short distance behind the four men. They were still teasing and bragging about how good they were. "You weren't much of an outlaw, were you?"

Cole's gaze remained straight ahead. "Why do you say that?"

"Ha! You wore that suit and looked nothing like an outlaw—"

"You don't even know what an outlaw is supposed to look like."

"I've read about them. Fortunately I take care of my people, and I had purchased traveling clothes for you prior to leaving on this quest. How come you've never worn a gun until this trip?"

"Maybe I didn't feel the need for one."

"All outlaws wear a gun. One of these days we're going to have to see who can outdraw the other. I'm quite fast."

Cole made no comment. His determination not to let Beth rile him was rapidly fading. He was tired of her trying to point out ineptness. The woman was definitely feeling cocky after pulling off the robbery. And, like it or not, he was experiencing a sense of pride at how she had handled her men as well as herself. Many men would have panicked during that first try, and innocent people would have been shot. And though she didn't show it, he knew she was in pain from having to jump from the train yesterday.

He glanced at her out of the corner of his eye. He rather liked seeing that thick braid again hanging down her back, bouncing with the horse's gait. And at times like this, there was a tomboyishness about her that he also liked. Maybe it was the way the sun had brushed the tops of her cheekbones due to lack of a hat for shade, or the small smattering of freckles that had popped out across the bridge of her nose, or even her billowed shirt that gave no hint of a full bosom. Her tight-fitting trousers were an entirely different matter.

"So, you have a lady friend waiting for you somewhere?"

"Does it also say in your book that an outlaw is supposed to be . . . good with the ladies?"

"Yes, it does."

"Perhaps I should read it so I can learn proper mannerisms. No, there is no lady in particular waiting for me."

Somehow Beth was quite pleased at hearing that bit of information. Of course, the only reason she felt that way was that should anything happen to Cole, she would not need to inform a loved one. "You haven't complimented me on today's success."

"Is a compliment in order? May I remind you that *I* made sure you had a train that was at it lowest speed, had plenty of cover and had only one passenger car? And still the first effort to hold it up was a disaster. And, if I remember correctly, I am the one who gave the clues as to how it could be accomplished. But how would you have handled four...eight...twelve cars? How would you keep all those people at bay at the same time? And, last but not least, what would you do when the men with firearms decided to shoot it out?''

Peeved at Cole for belittling their accomplishment, Beth nudged her horse forward to join the others. At least *they* were in a proper mood. How *would* she hold up a train with lots of passengers? One thing was certain. She'd need a lot more men than she already had.

It was early afternoon the following day that the group rejoined the caravan. Excitement surged through the others as all recounted his or her part in the ''great train robbery.'' Everyone except Cole.

Beth watched him go off by himself, lay out his bedroll, then tend to his horse. Though he was a solitary man, she hadn't failed to notice how her men treated him with respect while at the same time allowing him plenty of space. Why? Did they see or sense something she didn't?

When food for the trip had originally been packed, they hadn't counted on spending an extra day and night. They had foolishly thought they would do everything right the first time. Knowing the men were hungry, Beth had Magda start supper early, while the stories were being retold and questions were being asked.

''Molly Dee, Lizzy,'' the heavy woman called out, ''let's feed these weary travelers.''

Esther followed Beth to her tent. ''I have water heating for your bath.''

''While it is fresh on my mind, I want to write everything that has happened in my journal. Then I want to take a nap. I'm not used to sleeping three nights on the ground, and I'm exhausted.'' Esther went to close the tent flap, but before she succeeded, Beth caught a glimpse of Molly Dee heading toward where Cole had bedded down.

''You don't seem as excited as the others about robbing the train.''

Beth went over to one of the trunks and pulled out her ledger and a pencil. She was already on a second volume. ''I was until Cole pointed out that we would never have been successful if it hadn't been for him.'' She collapsed onto the brocade sofa. The abrasions and bruises she'd tried to ignore now ached fiercely.

Esther straddled Beth's leg and tugged at a boot.

''I keep wondering what it would take to wipe that stoic look off Cole Wagner's face.''

Esther sneered. ''With that hair on his face you wouldn't know it if you did.''

Beth went to the tent flap and peeked out. Cole was on his bedroll, but Molly Dee wasn't anywhere in sight. She smiled as she dropped the flap back in place. ''Don't wake me until Magda has the food ready.''

Beth sat on the bed, delighted at the feel of the fine feather mattress. She sat with her legs folded beneath her, journal and pencil in hand. A thought suddenly occurred to her. She looked up just as Esther was about to step out of the tent. ''Inform Molly Dee that she is to stay away from the men.''

Esther knew what that was all about. She had also seen Molly Dee headed toward Cole. She smiled. While the others had been gone, she and Howard had discussed Cole. Perhaps Howard had been right. Maybe Bethany had finally met a man whom she couldn't control, and the dear girl wasn't taking it well at all.

* * *

After a good rest Beth felt completely revitalized— until she joined the others at the big table for supper. Was it her imagination, or had Molly Dee deliberately sat beside Cole Wagner? As the meal progressed, Molly Dee did indeed center her conversation on the guide. And later, when they went for a walk, their laughter floated back with the soft breeze. Though Beth tried ignoring the situation, she quickly found herself wondering what the two found so interesting to talk about. It had been apparent from the beginning that George had an eye for the girl. Though not as tall as Cole, the blacksmith was certainly a fine figure of a man. Even with pockmarks on his face, he wasn't bad looking. More important, he even worked at an honest profession instead of running about robbing banks. It wasn't right that Molly Dee would turn her eyes toward an outlaw.

Beth took off in search of Esther.

She found her two old friends playing cribbage together. "Esther, did you speak to Molly Dee about leaving the men alone?"

Esther glanced at Howard and smiled. "No, I didn't realize there was any hurry."

Beth folded her arms over her breasts. "I need to have a talk with her."

"She sure seems to have taken a liking to Mr. Wagner," Howard commented. He laid his cards down and moved the appropriate number of pegs.

Beth raised an arched brow. "Mr. Wagner? Aren't we becoming formal."

"I respect the man." Howard shuffled the cards.

"Why?"

Howard paused a moment. "I don't know. Maybe it's the way he carries himself, or—"

"Since when did a useless outlaw become so important?"

Howard smiled affectionately at Beth. "A man sees a lot in another man that a woman would miss."

"I can see right through him. By keeping to himself, he fools you into thinking he's somebody." Beth moved behind Esther so she could see the cards the stout woman was holding.

A distant noise caused Beth to look in the direction Cole and Molly Dee had taken. She told herself it was doubtful anything would happen, but she didn't believe it. Molly Dee was a pretty girl and had a persuasive way with men.

Beth tried to return her attention to the game. Why was she so concerned? After all, they were both grown and Cole was old enough to know how to take care of himself. Beth sneered. Cole had never asked her to go for a walk. He never seemed to listen to her orders, either. He always acted as if he were the one running everything. He didn't even acknowledge her as a woman.

"How did you come to join up with the caravan?" Cole asked. They were standing beside a small stream watching the golden sun disappear behind the horizon. Molly Dee was tall, well arranged and not at all hard to look at.

"I didn't want to stay in Independence the rest of my life, so I answered an ad in the newspaper for men and women willing to travel. Beth interviewed and hired me. Do you have a woman, Cole?"

"I'm too much of a drifter. I don't know of a woman who'd have me."

"I would." Molly Dee moved closer. "I've taken a real fancy to you."

Cole chuckled. "Honey, why would you want some-one like me when you could have your pick of any man you want, including a rich one? Especially as pretty as you are."

"Rich?"

He had her attention. "There are at least twenty men for every woman in Kansas. Now, if I were in your shoes..."

"Yes?" Molly Dee dropped the pebble she had started to toss across the stream.

"I'd take my money and find a place to live. You won't have long to wait until every man from miles around knows there's an available woman. Your problem is go-ing to be which one to pick. Of course, that's assuming you want to settle down on your own land with cattle and that sort of a thing."

"But where?"

"In Wichita, sweetheart. That's where we'll pick up the next supplies."

"Oh, Cole! I never dreamed... I mean... I'm already excited. I owe you a favor."

"I'll take that favor right now. You've gotten to know the men traveling with us pretty well. Who would you say was the least trustworthy?"

Molly Dee giggled. "I wouldn't trust a one of them. They've all tried to get me in their bed, except Howard. I have a lot of respect for Howard."

"I was talking about a sneakier nature—a meaner dis-position than the others."

"Why would you want to know that?"

"I need to know if a man is going to take off running if trouble should arise. If there is an Indian attack, I'll need men I can rely on."

Molly Dee paled. "Are you expecting an Indian attack?"

"No, no. I just like to know the type of men I'm working with."

"Oh. Well...they all got their tempers. But, like Howard says, everyone gets into tiffs when people are thrown together for a long period of time." She thought a minute. "I don't think any one of them is worse than the other."

As before, Cole was getting nowhere. He'd just have to keep his eyes and ears open. "If you see one of them showing a mean streak, would you let me know?"

"I sure will."

"Beth isn't going to appreciate you leaving the caravan, but I'll keep your secret."

"Thank you, Cole. Are you sure you wouldn't like to—"

Cole ran the backs of his fingers along her soft cheek. "The offer is tempting, but I know you won't feel put down if I say no."

Molly Dee looked up at him. "You're a hard one to figure, Cole Wagner." She put her arms around his neck and kissed him full on his lips.

Cole gently pushed her away. "You need to be saving those for your husband."

Molly Dee giggled as she hurried off. She was already dreaming of riches and even the possibility of becoming the matriarch of Kansas.

Beth had been on her way to see what was taking the pair so long to return when she caught a glimpse of Molly Dee kissing Cole. Furious, she marched forward, but the brunette had already taken off in a different direction. Cole had his back turned to her when she reached the small clearing.

"Mr. Wagner," Beth acknowledged as she came to a halt beside him. He continued looking at the night sky instead of her. "I do not allow promiscuity. You will stay away from Molly Dee!"

Cole finally glanced down at the small bit of fire. She reminded him of one of those little dogs that was convinced he could lick the biggest cur around. The result usually wasn't pleasant, and one day the same thing was going to happen to the duchess. "I saw nothing in my contract that stated that."

"Your contract states that you will take orders from me. This is an order. And there is another I'm giving."

Cole rubbed the back of his neck. It amazed him the things she could come up with. "What is it this time?"

"Tomorrow you will shave."

"Says who?"

"I say so. I will have you tied to a chair if necessary. Maybe now you will see who is the boss around here."

"Well, now, I never questioned you being the boss." He rubbed his beard. It was too long. "But it seems to me a man's facial hair is his own business. How come you don't tell the others to shave their mustaches?" He looped his thumbs beneath his gun belt. "And what is to keep me from shooting anyone who tries to tie me to that chair? Then what would you do, boss?" He turned on his heel and walked away.

Beth was speechless. His words had been spoken quietly, but there was a cold undertone that she couldn't ignore. He had never spoken to her in such a manner. Would he really shoot the others? After all, he was a wanted man. No, he was just trying to scare her. Well, it wasn't going to work. She would not let him make her back out of this.

* * *

It was a kick in the rear that awoke Cole the following morning. He was about to grab his pistol from under his saddle when he spied a familiar pair of boots. His gaze traveled upward and came to rest on the pistol pointed down at him.

"Get up, slowly," Beth ordered.

The woman meant business. She had Jeff and Evan standing right behind her. From the looks on their faces it was obvious they didn't like this one bit, but they were obliged to do what Beth ordered.

As Cole stood, he saw the chair and Esther waiting with shears. Molly Dee stood beside her holding a mug of shaving cream and a straight razor. The girl was on the edge of breaking out in tears. Apparently the others were still sleeping.

Cole really wasn't against shaving, but he damn sure didn't like being forced into it. He tried holding his temper, but this time it didn't work. With the litheness of a cat he moved to the side, one arm wrapping around Beth's waist and the other hand snatching the gun away. A harmless shot hit a tree trunk.

Before the two men had a chance to even move, Beth found her back pinned against Cole's hard chest. This time he was holding the gun and she was completely at his mercy.

"Next time try asking, my dear. You get better results with honey than vinegar."

To Beth's shock, Cole released her, tossed her gun to the ground and walked to where the women waited. Molly Dee's face was alight with joy, and even Esther was sporting a wide grin. *Just whose side are they on?* she wondered.

"Try not to nick me," Cole said dryly as he sat down.

Beth squared her shoulders, refusing to show the fear that she had just felt. "It doesn't matter how it gets done, just as long as it is done," she stated, determined to save face. "I've done you a favor. You won't look like your poster now." She turned and headed for her tent.

"How gracious of you. I didn't realize this was all for my benefit."

Beth kept walking, refusing to be baited by his sarcasm. One advantage to keeping a journal was the ability to put in it what she pleased. This incident would most certainly be her version, not his.

Chapter Seven

Cole had had the caravan on the move ten days. Unfortunately for Beth, after leaving Missouri the terrain had become grassy, treeless and uninteresting. Though the ground cover and shrubs were still green, when she went riding now, she had to remain well off to the side to avoid the dust easily churned up by the wagons. It was hard to believe anyone would want to homestead any of it, and easy to understand how the hard land could turn men into outlaws.

Though Beth looked out the window of her carriage absorbing all this, it was Cole who continued to capture her thoughts. She still hadn't recovered from the shock of seeing him without his beard. She found herself regretting her determination to have him shave. His strong features now held a certain sensuality that made her feel vulnerable. His face . . . even his lips looked as if they had been sculpted in stone, and he showed a visible strength that she hadn't noticed previously. She would have been far less inclined to make accusing remarks had she seen it sooner. True, he wasn't the handsomest man she had ever known, but there was little doubt that any woman would want a second look—including herself. To put it simply, pure virility was leading her caravan. And after the shaving episode she could even add the word *danger* to describe him. A combination that definitely caused a trickle of excitement to run up her spine.

Beth thought about the several times she had tried to strike up a conversation with Cole since the shaving incident, but it was always one-sided. He was even more aloof than before. She tried telling herself he was pouting, but she didn't believe it for a minute.

Beth stuffed a small pillow behind her head and tried to take a nap. Unfortunately, her thoughts again drifted to the broad-shouldered outlaw leading them to who knew where. She'd never known a man who completely ignored her as Cole did. Even Jeff and the others in the caravan were always showing interest in one form or another. But with Cole there was never so much as a hint of flirting, and absolutely no innuendos about lovemaking. She knew she was pretty, had an enticing body and could be genuinely charming. But he seemed to bring out the worst in her.

Worrying over the man wasn't going to solve anything. It only served to make matters worse. Beth closed her eyes and finally drifted off to sleep.

Several hours had passed when the carriage wheel hit something, awakening Beth and knocking her off the seat onto the floor.

"Howard! Are you asleep? Watch where you're going—"

Again the wheels ran over something.

Beth tried to grab the seat for support, but the carriage suddenly careened, throwing her to the side. The vehicle righted itself, jarring her body.

"Howard!" Everything came to an abrupt halt. It was the dead silence that made her hesitate to get out. The door suddenly swung open and for a brief moment she didn't recognize the beardless man with his hand extended.

"May I help you out?" Cole asked.

"What is going on?" Beth demanded as she took his hand. "Was Howard trying to kill me?"

"Howard wasn't driving the carriage. I was. Never having driven such a worthy vehicle, I had trouble handling the horses," he lied. "They pulled the wheels over a couple of low tree stumps before I could bring them to a halt. I'm afraid I broke one of the wheels."

Beth placed her hands on her hips. "Where is Howard?"

"He's butchering a hog."

"He's what?" Beth exploded.

"When we arrived, you were still sleeping. He didn't want to wake you. It was I who decided the buggy needed to be moved."

"He went off and left me alone?"

"Only for a short time. Mrs. Bethany Alexander, allow me to introduce Mrs. Norma Gurley."

Beth turned and found herself facing a plainly dressed woman, somewhere in her late forties. Beth was about to ask what they were doing here when Cole spoke up.

"Norma has graciously permitted us to stay with her for a short spell. It will allow you an opportunity to get the feel of how people live on the plains."

"This is not what I had in mind. I—"

"You said you wanted to see the real West. Believe me, it doesn't just consist of outlaws."

"I can't begin to tell you how pleased I am at having guests," Norma exclaimed, her broad smile showing white, even teeth.

In one quick sweep Beth took in the corral with a couple of plow horses and her black riding mare, Seeker, a good-sized barn, chickens pecking about, and a shed of some sort with grass growing on the roof. Toward the river was a partially built house. Her gaze returned to Norma Gurley.

"Cole said you'll be staying a whole week."

Not likely, Beth thought. She forced a smile before looking back down the road. Where was the rest of the caravan? She felt a sense of panic. There were no wagons! Nothing! Her brown eyes became orbs of mahogany when she turned to Cole. "Where are my people?" The question was barely more than a whisper.

Cole wondered if she had read that phrase from the Bible. "On their way to Wichita for supplies."

Her eyes locked with his. "And just who authorized them to go on without me?"

"I did."

"You had no authority—"

Cole smiled at Norma. "Please excuse us a minute." He took Beth by the arm, ready to lead her to where they could talk privately. When Beth balked, he tightened his grip. "If I have to carry you, what will—"

"I don't give a damn what anyone thinks." Beth finished the sentence for him. Nevertheless, she went along peacefully. "How dare you threaten me? And just who are you to give orders?"

The minute he stopped, Beth spun about ready to face the infuriating man. Instead she found herself slammed against a hard chest, and immediately stepped away. "What do you think you're grinning at?"

"I'll be damned." Cole tipped his hat back. "I do believe I've found a vulnerable spot."

"I don't know what you're talking about. Now, I want—"

"You're afraid of men."

"Afraid? Don't be ridiculous. I've been married three times." Beth impatiently wiped away the sleep that still clung to the corners of her eyes.

"Only to old men. Being so close never bothered you before, but without your army—"

"That's a pack of lies."

Cole stared at her, then broke out laughing.

Mortified at being laughed at, Beth pulled her foot back, then brought it forward with all her might. The toe of her boot connected perfectly with his shin. He grimaced, but to her aggravation he refused to dance about in pain. She returned to her hostess, ignoring the concerned look on the older woman's face.

"Is everything all right?" Norma asked.

"Everything is just fine," Beth lied sweetly.

Norma clapped her hands together. "We seldom have visitors, and never a woman unless she's from a nearby farm!"

Beth still wanted to know how she had ended up here. But seeing the joy in Norma's eyes, Beth didn't have the heart to say the stop hadn't been planned. Where was Howard? "I hope we won't be an inconvenience."

"Lord, no. Come along and I'll show you where you'll be sleeping."

Beth followed, still glancing about. Cole was already unhitching the horses from the carriage. That meant he wasn't planning on leaving anytime soon. And what about the broken wheel? Decker and Wilber could have fixed it in no time. Where had Howard disappeared to?

"I just have to tell you that your dress is the prettiest thing I've laid eyes on in a mighty long time." Norma self-consciously smoothed the bodice of her worn gown.

Beth couldn't help but notice her hostess's rough hands. "Why...thank you." She was starting to feel guilty. The woman was being friendly, yet Beth hadn't given anything in return other than a brief acknowledgment. Now this compliment had been issued. The dress had been bought just for the trip, but it was indeed much better than the homemade gown Norma wore. It was easy to see that Norma had once been a true beauty, but hard labor had taken its toll. Her face had become leathery from working hours in the sun.

"It looks as if you and your husband were able to get an early crop planted," Beth said, looking at the tilled fields.

"I lost my husband three years ago. It's my three boys who've done the plowing and kept the bank from nipping at our heels. Last year the grasshoppers ate up everything we had."

Beth could hear the sadness in the woman's voice.

"If the weather holds and the grasshoppers don't invade us again this year, we'll have a fine crop."

They climbed the three steps leading into the house.

"How old are your sons?" Beth asked. There appeared to be only one large room with three beds and a large fireplace.

"The twins are eighteen and the younger boy is seventeen."

Norma led Beth to a door on the far side. When Norma opened it, Beth discovered there were actually two rooms, this one being much smaller. It contained only one bed and one chest of drawers. "You will sleep in here. You'll have plenty of privacy. Cole and Howard can sleep in the other beds.''

Beth had a sudden feeling that Norma had expected them. Everything seemed to have already been planned. But how could that be?

''Joseph—that was my husband—didn't get to build the rest of the house, or even a 'parson's room' before he died.''

''Do you plan to have a preacher stay here?''

Norma laughed. ''No, no. I don't know how it came to be called that, but it's a place for visitors. A farmer seldom has company, and they're mighty pleased when someone stops by. So they have accommodations and food, hoping their guest will stay a spell and tell what's happening around them.'' She tugged at the corner of a bedspread to smooth a wrinkle. ''That door over there opens to the outside.''

''Is Howard really helping to slaughter a hog?''

''Yes. As soon as he found out what the boy were doing he insisted on joining them.'' Norma pushed a swatch of gray-streaked hair behind her ear. ''You seem surprised.''

''Why would he do that?''

''He said he was raised on a farm and hadn't realized how much he missed it.''

Howard on a farm? That was a piece of information he had never revealed to Beth. He'd always seemed too cultured. ''I'm sorry you're being put to all this trouble. Where will you and the boys sleep?''

''The boys will sleep in the barn and I'll stay in the sod house. Now, don't look like that. We don't mind at all. That's where we stayed until this was built.''

''Norma, do you know how to get to Wichita?''

''The town?''

"Yes." Beth could picture the look on Cole's face when he discovered she'd gone on without him.

Norma shook her head. "I have no idea, but I do know Joseph said it was quite a spell away."

Unless one of Norma's boys could help her, Beth was stranded. She didn't want Cole managing where she went or did. As soon as she didn't need him, he'd quickly discover who was boss on this venture! Something she intended to discuss with Howard when she saw him. At least *he* hadn't deserted her, which was more than she could say for Esther.

It wasn't until after supper that Beth finally managed to get Howard to herself. As they walked in the moonlight, Beth looked up at the multitude of stars and listened to a coyote howl somewhere in the distance. The air was still and the quietness was almost deafening.

"Just look at this place, Beth! There is a nobility about living on the frontier and working the land." He reached down and picked up handful of dirt. "Have you ever seen anything better? A person could grow just about anything in this soil."

"Nonsense. I would never be content in such depravity. How could five people have ever lived in that small sod house? Norma told me that rain constantly seeped through the roof, leaving the floor and sides a muddy monstrosity. Then there are the snakes that work their way down and fall inside. She said that in the summer it's almost unbearably hot. Howard, can you tell me where all the confounded trees have gone? I saw some toward the river, but that's about it." Beth slapped at an insect that had landed on her cheek.

"That's exactly why people build soddys. While you were talking to the boys, Norma told me it's accomplished by stacking thick, wet slabs of prairie sod and straw on top of each other. She's lucky she has trees by the river. At least there will be enough wood to finish her home and give fuel. She also said the farther west you go, the fewer trees there are, until finally there are none to be found.''

"I don't believe that. If there is no wood, how do they keep warm in winter?"

Howard smiled. "Buffalo dung. Dried buffalo chips."

"You're joshing me."

"Not at all. It makes excellent fuel."

Beth no longer wished to pursue the topic. "How did Cole Wagner manage to split us from the caravan? Of all people, I thought you would at least know better than to listen to someone else."

"Your outlaw can be very persuasive, my dear Bethany. You would do well to remember that. He appears to be one way, but I sincerely suspect there is a man beneath that facade we have yet to meet."

Beth remembered Esther expressing a similar feeling. "Would you mind telling me how a trunk of my clothes made its way to the carriage boot?"

"I can only surmise Esther or Molly Dee put it there."

"Which means Mr. Wagner had already talked to someone about us leaving the caravan."

They continued down the dusty path, while Howard attempted to explain what had happened. "You were asleep when we came to a junction. Cole announced that was where we were to divide up. The others were to go on to Wichita and replenish the supplies. As soon as you had learned about prairie farming, we would follow. He even said this would allow you to see the lay of the land, something that was important to writers." He shrugged his shoulders. "We split and came here."

"Didn't Esther question him?"

"Not that I know of. She seemed to think it was all right. She's becoming quite fond of your outlaw."

"She has been acting strangely as of late." With the full moon shining down on the land, Beth did see a certain beauty to it. "And what is your excuse? I can't believe that you didn't wake me."

"Think about it, Bethany. You knew I was against going on this trip. I told you it would be too dangerous."

"What does that have to do with anything?"

"Knowing how I felt, you haven't exactly been confiding in me. Esther appeared to know about the split, so I assumed the two of you had discussed it."

Beth knew Howard was right about not revealing her plans to him, and in all fairness she couldn't blame him for what had happened. "I have a plan. I will buy a horse from Norma, and you and I can ride away from here and join the caravan in Wichita."

"Norma and the boys need the horses, Beth. Another thing is we've traveled this land long enough for you to know how easy it would be for us to get lost and stranded. And Cole does have a valid point about you getting to know how people live out here."

"You're on his side?" Beth again swatted at the pesky bug.

"It's not a matter of being on his side. We have no choice but to wait until he is ready to leave. He's only doing what you hired him for, Bethany."

Again Howard was right. Other than telling the others to go on to Wichita, Cole Wagner hadn't done a thing wrong. Then why did she sense she was being manipulated? "When you're alone with one of the Gurley sons, ask them if they know how to get to Wichita. And don't say anything to our guide."

* * *

Cole stood in the open doorway of the soddy listening to crickets serenading the moon. "It's been four days now, Norma. What do you think?"

Norma walked over and joined him. Everyone had gone to bed except the two of them. "I'm attracted to him. Very much. But he's . . . he's much too fancy for the likes of me."

"Nonsense." Cole put a protective arm around her shoulders. "Norma, remember when I came to see how you and the boys were faring? I asked if there was anything I could do for you. You said, 'Find me another husband.'"

"That was two years ago, Cole."

He shrugged. "I never found a man I thought was good enough. I think Howard is a good man. He has to be, after putting up with Bethany for so long. But you're the one who has to decide if he's what you want. I will say that some weeks ago he told me he has had a yearning to return to his roots. He said he wanted again to feel the freshly tilled soil in his hands and watch the crops grow. He claimed it was something you never outgrew. There is another thing to consider. He has worked for Beth for a good many years and she pays handsomely. He can furnish needed money."

Norma rested her head on his chest. "Three years since your brother died. Three years without a man is a long time, Cole."

"I know, honey."

She patted him on the chest then moved back into the room. "What do you have to do with these people, Cole? They're not your kind. Is it the woman? She's mighty pretty, but delicate."

Cole raised a dark brow. "True, she's small, but I certainly never thought of her as being delicate. Anyway, it's business."

"And just like your brother, you can't tell me what that business is," she stated knowingly. "I hated Jim being a government agent, and it cost him his life."

Cole removed his hat and ran his finger around the inside of the brim. "You know, Norma, nothing has changed. Remember that is why you had to use the last name of Gurley. It's for your and the boys' safety. You can never tell anyone we're related."

"I know."

"Not even Howard, should he decide to stay."

She sat in the rocking chair and looked helplessly at her brother-in-law. "If I... Suppose I was interested? How could I get him to stay? It's been so long, I'm not sure I am capable anymore of..."

Cole turned, looked at her and smiled. "You had no trouble charming my brother. As I remember, he took one look at you and his bachelor days came to an immediate halt."

"I'm not as pretty as I used to be."

"You're still an attractive woman, Norma. You've just had hard times. You need to find pleasure again. I don't think you'll have any trouble in this matter. If Howard is interested, you'll see the signs. Just don't discourage him unless you decide you want him to go. I'll understand."

"We've known each other too long for you to fool me, Cole. I also know you have no scruples when it comes to matters pertaining to your work. There is something else behind this besides getting me a husband. You want to get rid of him, don't you?"

Though it was the truth, her next question would be why. "What makes you think that? Your imagination is running away with itself."

"I can't believe I'm even considering this." Norma broke out laughing. "Why I'm deliberately..." She laughed all the harder, causing even Cole to start chuckling. "This is about as cold a way to pick a husband as I've seen," she finally managed to say.

"It's not as bad as being a mail-order bride. At least you're getting to see and try him out."

Norma waved her hand at him. "Get out of here so I can go to bed." She couldn't stop giggling.

Cole started to leave.

"Cole," she called.

He turned and faced her again.

Norma grew sober. "Thank you for all the money you've sent us. Oh, and the boys said Howard was inquiring about directions to Wichita."

Cole smiled. "Did they tell him?"

"No."

He nodded and continued on his way. He'd sleep in the barn with the boys. As it was, he was never able to spend as much time with them as he would have liked.

Cole thought about the situation he had set up. If everything turned out the way he had planned, Norma would have her man and he'd have one less from the caravan to think about. This would make three men he'd culled so far: Doolan, the groom; Howard, Beth's close friend and caretaker; and Tucker, the black doctor. He'd deliberately first picked those men he least suspected. The Jones brothers would be next. He tended to discount them, as well. Neither had the hardness of a criminal. He was more inclined to lean toward George Higgins, Evan

White or Jeff Dobbs. They all had cold eyes that one man would easily recognize in another.

What face is Tex Martin hiding behind? Cole wondered as he neared the barn. He had finally dismissed all the women from having any attachment with the outlaw. The only one that might have been involved with him was Molly Dee. However, Molly Dee was a smart lady. She wouldn't have been foolish enough to openly flirt with others if she was Tex's woman. Cole wasn't sure which would come first—his discovery of which one was Tex, or Tex becoming sure of himself and finally showing his hand. Either way, Cole would have his man. Then it would be a matter of sitting back and waiting.

The following five days passed amicably. Cole spent a good deal of time fishing, hunting and visiting with his nephews. Howard joined them on several occasions, but he seemed to prefer staying around Norma. During an evening meal Norma had looked toward Cole and had given him a very brief nod. He knew she was giving her approval of the striking gentleman.

Cole was pleased and surprised at how the women were getting along. Beth had taken Norma under her wing. He'd thought the copper-haired beauty too self-centered to pay attention to another woman's appearance, but as before, he'd been wrong. Just having company had brightened Norma considerably, but Beth had made her blossom.

After giving Norma several dresses, Beth had insisted on washing and styling the woman's thick, gray-streaked hair.

At the back of the house Beth had Norma remove her worn blouse, then bend over a shallow washtub. Beth dipped water from the rain barrel, poured it over Norma's head, then added shampoo.

"How long have you known Cole?" Beth asked casually as she began scrubbing.

"That's a strange question to ask. It was the same day we met you."

Norma was lying. Beth had felt the taller woman stiffen when she'd asked the question. By the time her hair had been washed, rinsed, combed, dried and styled, Beth had managed to ask all sorts of questions, including directions to Wichita. Norma had proven to be very good at avoiding answers. Even so, Beth had enjoyed the afternoon and especially the camaraderie.

A new dress and a touch of face coloring turned Norma into an entirely different woman. Still, Beth was shocked when she found out her new friend was only thirty-six. Just eight years older than herself. Beth suddenly realized how much easier her life had been in comparison.

For Beth, the time passed quickly. To her surprise, she was thoroughly enjoying being with the family. There was love and caring among them that she had never been privy to before. She delighted in their teasing and compliments. The boys had openly declared their love and each wanted to marry her. When she wasn't busy with the others, she spent a good deal of time sketching on the paper she kept in her saddlebags. She not only drew the prairie homestead, she recorded the bodies and faces of the people around her. Norma and the boys were quite taken with her drawings.

After a while, however, other than the few times she and Norma were alone, Beth began to feel odd man out. Everyone seemed to have paired off, and she wasn't in one of the groups. On more than one occasion she found herself with nothing to do. Loneliness was again creeping up on her. It did, however, allow her time to contemplate.

Something strange was happening to Howard. There was a contentedness about him that Beth found to be most disconcerting. He had his eye on Norma. They needed to leave this place as soon as possible, she thought. If only they could leave right away. But Cole wasn't letting that happen. And what about Cole? There was an easiness about him, as well. A warmth...a caring for these people. She could see it when he looked or talked to Norma or one of the boys. Beth was becoming convinced that he had known this family prior to their arrival. That it would cause too much of an inconvenience to the family would explain why he hadn't brought the caravan. Why hadn't he said something to her instead of acting as if they were strangers? Even more curious was the way Norma and the boys acted as though they hadn't known Cole until his arrival. Did being an outlaw make them act the way they did? Maybe Cole didn't want the law to come here looking for him? Or had he and Norma been lovers in the past?

Something else was happening that was making Beth fidget. On more than one occasion she had caught Cole raking her with those dark, sensual eyes, warming her entire body. When he realized she'd caught him, he immediately looked away. Had leaving the caravan been nothing more than an attempt to get her alone so he could make love to her? How did he plan to do that with Howard and all the others constantly about? But Beth didn't feel nearly as sure of herself as she had when she was with the caravan. She found herself giving Cole a much wider berth.

All of Beth's concerns seemed to fade away each night when everyone gathered for the evening meal. There was a wonderful closeness and happiness that enveloped her. She felt a part of this family, and she cared what happened to them. When they rejoined the caravan, she'd find a way to send them money.

Chapter Eight

The following night Beth wasn't sure what had awakened her. Because the spring was unseasonably warm, she decided it had to have been the heat. She tossed the covers off, left the room and headed for the outhouse.

By the time Beth returned she was yawning and ready to go back to sleep. She quickly removed her slippers and dressing gown and was about to plop back down on the stiff mattress when she heard something. It was talking. It took a moment for her to realize the sound was coming from the other room. Was Howard mumbling in his sleep?

Her curiosity eating at her, Beth tiptoed to the door that separated the two rooms, and listened. The words were muffled. Maybe Cole had come to talk to Howard about something he didn't want her to know.

Carefully, Beth turned the knob and eased the door open.

"Oh, Howard, I've needed a man so badly."

Beth's hand flew to her mouth, stifling any noise she might have made. She had recognized Norma's voice.

Norma giggled. "I'd almost forgotten what it felt like to be made love to."

"You're beautiful," Howard replied huskily.

"We're making too much noise. Bethany might hear us."

"She sleeps soundly."

Beth closed the door quietly, though with the couple in the throes of passion, it wasn't likely they would have heard a thing.

Hearing Norma's moans of pleasure had caused Beth's own body to react. Her skin became heated, and moisture had already formed between her legs. She returned to the bed, tossing the quilt to the side. The door and walls didn't shut out the sounds of passion. She turned onto her side and placed the down pillow over her face. Like Norma, it had been quite a while since she'd been made love to, and knowing what was happening in the other room was stirring suppressed desires. She closed her eyes, willing herself to sleep, but sleep wasn't forthcoming. She envisioned Cole making love to her, a thought that surely would never have entered her mind were it not for what was going on in the other room.

Beth tossed the pillow aside and climbed off the bed. Perhaps the air would help cool her fevered flesh. She shoved her slippers and dressing gown back on, went outside, and began to walk, trying to erase the raw ache playing havoc with her mind and body.

Beth hadn't realized she'd gone so far until she found herself standing in the middle of a field. Holding open her dressing gown, she allowed the cool breeze from the Cottonwood River to penetrate her chemise and caress her heated body.

"Is something wrong?"

Beth sucked in her breath. The deep voice made her skin tingle. Cole. "No, I'm fine." She couldn't turn and face him. She was vulnerable. Too vulnerable. She had always tried to abide by her first husband's rule never to mix business and pleasure. He had said it only confused matters. But at this moment she could think of nothing she wanted more than to have Cole draw her into his arms and make love to her. She wrapped her dressing gown back around her. "Don't you ever sleep?"

"Being attentive almost becomes second nature when you're a wanted man."

"Oh. I hadn't thought of that."

Even standing a short distance behind her, Cole could smell her musky female scent and could see the moonlight shimmering on her damp skin. Her hair had been released from the braid and hung wildly about her head. It would take so little to remove her clothes. She was a temptress, and he was definitely tempted. To make sure he kept his hands to himself, he hooked his thumbs in his belt and waited for her to say something.

"Doesn't it bother you seeing me here with little but my nightclothes on?" Beth bit her bottom lip, trying to get control of herself.

Damn! She was baiting him again. The woman was certainly dead set on making his life miserable. "Not particularly. I have three sisters." The lies were mounting.

Finally feeling more secure, Beth turned. His comment had piqued her curiosity. "Bit by bit I'm starting to learn to know you."

"If you want to know anything, you have but to ask."

"If you were so used to being around women, why do I make you nervous?"

"I wasn't aware you did." She looked to him as if she'd been lowered from heaven. "I doubt that we have anything in common."

"What do you mean? Are you saying Molly Dee is more your type of woman?"

It was plain to see his comment hadn't sat well on the lady's shoulders. "Molly Dee does most of the talking, and being around family is a lot different."

"I see." Was he saying she was too good for him, or not good enough?

"Well, since you're all right, I'll go back to the barn."

Saddened for a moment, but in control of her emotions, Beth raised her chin. "Cole, why did you really bring me here?" She wanted to hear him admit his desire.

"I had to be sure no one was following me. Have you forgotten that I'm a wanted man?"

Beth could feel her disappointment all the way to her toes. "No, I hadn't forgotten. When do you plan to leave?" she asked, a bit too sharply. Beth rubbed her arms. She was becoming chilled. "I've seen all there is to see here. Time is wasting and we need to be getting on to other things."

"We'll leave the day after tomorrow, bright and early in the morning."

Beth stared at him a moment before turning and going back to the house. Was it his aloofness that made him so appealing? He was still watching her. She could feel his eyes boring into her back. Should she throw caution to the winds and find out exactly what was under that untouchable exterior? This was all so unbelievable. She'd always had to shove men away. Marrying older men had seemed safer—they couldn't break her heart, which was what had happened to her mother. To this day she could remember her mother and father constantly fighting. Yet even knowing that, she had actually contemplated being the aggressor. She needed to stay away from Cole Wagner—she was beginning to believe that he was the type of man who would claim a woman's soul.

Beth didn't fall asleep until the wee hours of the morning. At least there weren't any more sounds coming from the other room.

After what had happened the night before, Beth found it difficult to talk to Norma the next morning during breakfast, unlike the slender woman, who was quite talkative after her night of pleasure. All during the meal she and Howard constantly stole glances and touches. Beth soon grew tired of it. Good heavens, one would think they were in love, if there really was such a thing.

When everyone had finished eating, the women tackled the dishes while the men went out to do chores.

"Howard is such a wonderful man," Norma commented when the dishes had been put away in the hutch.

Beth knew Howard too well. The forty-two-year-old man had never wanted for a woman. "Yes, women have always been attracted to him." Seeing the older woman blush bothered Beth. Nevertheless, she refused to let Norma build false hopes. Lord a-mercy. The woman had three grown sons.

"Bethany."

Beth looked toward the door and saw Howard standing there. "I thought you were feeding the chickens," she said to him as she placed her cup towel on the kitchen board. "We were just talking about you."

"Yes, I heard. Bethany, could we go for a walk?"

Beth glanced at Norma. The woman avoided her gaze. Did this have to do with last night? "But of course." She brushed the folds of her printed skirt before walking out the door.

They had gone only a short distance before Beth confronted the attractive older man. Though his dark hair had receded considerably, the gray at his temples made him look quite distinguished. "Has Cole told you we will be leaving the first thing in the morning?"

"That's what I wanted to talk to you about. I won't be going with you."

"Come, come, Howard. I know what happened last night—"

"What?"

"I do have ears, and the two of you weren't the quietest lovers. I can't imagine why she came to you instead of the other way around."

"She was afraid one of the boys might return to get something from the soddy."

Beth pulled the gold watch from his vest pocket. "Remember when I gave you this? I believe it was a Frenchwoman that time. And I was right. You quickly forgot all about her."

"I'm staying here, Bethany."

"That's ridiculous. We've only been here a few days. You can't possibly have real feelings for this woman. I assume that is what this is all about." She started walking again. "You know this isn't any different from the others you were convinced you loved."

"You're wrong. I fell in love with Norma the moment I first saw her."

"There is no such thing as love. In a month you'll be ready to move on."

"I don't think so. Not this time. Decisions have to be made quickly out here, Priss. It's not just Norma, though she's the biggest portion of it. It's the land and wanting to be part of the frontier. This isn't a life you're used to, Bethany, so I know you don't understand. It's hard, but rewarding. I'm going to stay."

"No! Howard, what about me? Who will watch after me? I'll be lost without you. You're my family!"

"I've been your father figure long enough. I want to be where I'm needed."

"I need you."

"No, Beth. It's time we made a life of our own."

"You can't do this," she said desperately. "How can you leave me alone with Cole? He's underhanded. I wouldn't be surprised if he hadn't planned on you remaining here."

"Now who's spouting nonsense?" Howard gently ran his hands down her arms. "Your arguments are futile. You're not going to talk me out of staying. You're a strong woman, and you'll get along just fine. In a couple of days you'll have joined the others in Wichita. Don't look so sad. When you decide to settle down, write me. I have a feeling it's going to happen sooner than you think." He tilted her chin up with his finger. "Come on, be happy for me."

They had been together ten years and she didn't want to think about their parting. But she knew she wasn't giving him much of a life, and she cared too deeply for him to prevent his happiness. "If it doesn't work, promise you will go back to Boston and wait for me. Whatever you do, please let me know."

"I will." He pulled her to him and they hugged.

The pair walked on for some time, talking about the past and allowing Beth the opportunity to regain control of her emotions. It hurt her to know she might never see Howard again, and it had been difficult to hold back the tears. But seeing him glance toward the house, she knew his thoughts were with Norma. She had never seen him so immovable in his decision.

As they rode away, Beth turned in the saddle and took one last look at her carriage parked by the barn. Cole had insisted that from here on they would be traveling over unmarked territory and that the vehicle wouldn't be able to withstand the conditions. Besides, there was no one to drive it for her. Her eyes traveled on to the corral, the unfinished house, the boys standing off to the side and, lastly, Norma and Howard holding hands and waving goodbye. She waved back. She was leaving part of her heart behind. Howard had been the closest thing to a father she'd ever known. Even though he had mellowed over the past few years, he had always had a mind of his own. If this didn't work out, she knew he'd leave.

Beth straightened in the saddle and looked at Cole, who rode beside her. He was leading one of the two carriage horses, which served as a packhorse. Ahead were plowed fields, and she could even see green sprouts already peeking through the sod. She still wasn't pleased at having to leave her trunk of clothes behind. Not even Norma would have any use for most of them. They were too fancy to wear about a farm. Her demands to take a change of clothing on the trip had fallen on deaf ears. Cole had insisted she could make do with a riding suit until they reached Wichita. "Why change clothes?" he'd said. "They'd only get dirty." The man knew absolutely nothing about women. At least her journals were safe with the caravan.

Because of Cole's attitude and insistence that she ride astride, Beth had had to forgo her riding suit for comfort's sake. She had replaced it with the buckskin trousers she'd bought at a trading post outside of Topeka. At the time she'd thought of it as her first representation of the West. There had been no intention of wearing them—until now. Wearing britches—as Cole called them—was going to take some getting used to. A white shirt and several others packed in her saddlebags was all she had for the trip to Wichita. She fingered the silk crimson scarf tied around her neck. At least she had something feminine.

Beth reached down and touched the gun at her side. Howard had given it to her, along with the Winchester rifle resting in her saddle scabbard. Now it was going to be just her and Cole all the way to Wichita. If they should run into trouble, she'd at least be able to defend herself.

"How far do we have to go?"

"Don't know," Cole answered. "Never measured it."

"Do you at least know what direction we'll be going?"

"Southwest."

"But that could be anywhere. How do you know we're going in the right direction?"

"Lady, is there nothing I do that you don't question?" Her distrustful nature had aggravated him many times, but somewhere along the way it had also become a challenge. "I've gotten you this far, it only makes sense that I can get us the rest of the way." He nudged his horse into a canter.

Beth glanced at the arrogant man's rugged profile. All she could see was undeniable sensuality. Why wasn't he letting his beard grow back? She looked ahead, her thoughts suddenly on Howard. Though it hurt to know she might never see him again, for some reason Cole was now supplying her with those needed feelings of security. In her heart she knew he would take care of her.

Chapter Nine

"Look!" Beth called excitedly. "Aren't those bison?"

Cole pulled back on the reins and sat staring ahead at the small herd. "Used to be one could stand on a promontory and see the great herds stretched across the entire horizon. Take a good look, Beth. This may be the last you'll ever see of them."

Beth leaned forward and stroked Seeker's glossy neck. "You sound angry."

"The slaughter of buffalo means the starvation of Indians."

"You're being a bit dramatic. Who could possibly destroy all the buffalo?"

"It's already being done. You've never seen what a man with a buffalo rifle can do. He puts his cartridges in his hat beside him, makes himself as comfortable as possible, aims his Sharps .50, then methodically shoots down an entire herd. If he's good, he can kill a hundred fifty to two hundred a day, keeping a force of skinners steadily busy."

"What would be the purpose of that?"

"The hides were worth four to five dollars each. But the slaughter has been so rapid that they've dropped to a dollar a hide. Perhaps you'd like to hear about the pile of forty thousand hides or the mountain of bones—"

"That won't be necessary." Beth remembered seeing a dime novel that had something to do with killing buffalo, but she hadn't bought it. It was hard to believe such devastation could take place. But not for a minute did she doubt what Cole had said. His set face and cold eyes told its own story. "You said the Indians would starve. Do you also have empathy for them?"

"Yep."

"That's not a popular opinion."

"This was their land, not the other way around." Cole kneed his horse forward.

Beth followed behind the packhorse. She had never considered herself lacking in intelligence, yet she had come to realize how little she knew about this vast land. And though she had professed to know all about outlaws and how they dressed and acted, Cole was proving that even that had been wrong. It had never occurred to her that an outlaw could have empathy for anything or anyone, and certainly not Indians.

As they drew closer to the herd, Beth could see that the shaggy bison were shedding their winter coats. They seemed much larger than the one she'd seen at the taxidermist's in Boston. The bulls were particularly ferocious looking, and she was glad when Cole turned in a different direction.

Beth's gaze fell on the guns holstered at Cole's sides. Ever since this trip had begun, she had been itching to test her draw against someone. How fast was Cole? What would it feel like to challenge someone? Admittedly there was a bit of a problem she needed to work on. Though fast, she still wasn't particularly accurate. More than one tree limb had been shot off accidentally during her practices.

Less than fifteen minutes had passed when Cole raised his arm. Beth was about to question why he wanted her to stop when she spotted buzzards circling. She brought Seeker alongside Cole's horse for a better view. Ahead, the big birds were hopping about on the ground, while others were feasting on something dead.

"Wait here," Cole ordered before continuing on.

"Who are you to give *me* orders?" Beth muttered. Refusing to be left behind, she followed. The first thing she noticed was the tall lance decorated with feathers and paint, its metal point buried in the ground. There were arrows everywhere. It took a moment before she realized they were embedded in the bodies of cavalry men.

"I told you to wait!" Cole barked out.

Beth didn't even hear him. Though she wanted to turn away, her eyes were fixed on the grisly sight. Bile filled her throat as she stared at scalped men, their heads caved in and their brains exposed to the buzzards. Then there were the men who appeared to have been burned alive.

Cole was furious at himself for not making sure Beth had waited. But it was too late to prevent her from seeing the carnage. Her face was as white as alabaster and it was plain to see she was fighting to keep from vomiting. He considered offering kind, reassuring words, but decided against it. Instead he turned back to the unpleasant scene. Maybe this would finally convince Beth that the West wasn't just a place to entertain a spoiled, unthinking wildcat whose only reason for being here was to write some damn dime novel. And maybe next time he told her to stay put, she'd do so.

After tying the packhorse's lead to the pommel of his saddle, Cole dismounted. He needed to find out how long ago the slaughter had taken place. Several rocks had to be thrown before the buzzards moved away. They didn't go far. They stood on the outskirts, waiting.

Beth gritted her teeth when Cole grabbed the hand of one of the cavalry men and pulled him off to the side. With the toe of his boot Cole kicked at the dirt that had been beneath the unfortunate soul, then squatted.

"Why are you doing that?" Beth managed to ask, hoping to dispel her nausea.

"Indians are very good at building a slow, adequate fire." He reached out and felt the dirt. "There is still heat. This didn't happen more than three hours ago. Kiowa," he muttered.

Beth was no longer listening.

Cole noted the missing ear on one of the scalped soldiers, a common mutilation ascribed to the Kiowa. There was also an eagle-bone whistle partially buried in the dirt.

"What did you say?"

Cole looked up at the small woman. "I said Kiowa. That's the name of the tribe that is responsible for this. As mean and as fierce a fighter as man could have the misfortune to run up against. Their hatred for the white man runs deep."

After a quick check of hoofprints left by unshod ponies, Cole swung back up in his saddle. "We have to get the hell out of here." For once, the lady offered no protests.

Cole's loud "Yaw" put his horse into action. Beth was right behind the packhorse. Cole moved them in the opposite direction to where the unshod ponies had gone. Not only did he need to get Beth away from the hellish scene, they were now faced with a problem of survival.

Once they had crossed a long ridge and moved down a ravine, Cole finally brought the horses to a halt near a shallow stream. Though they could ill afford to stop, the animals needed water and he needed Beth to be alert if they were to make it to the town of Hicks. They could stop only a few minutes, but he'd give her that time to calm herself. Death was never a pleasant sight, and especially devastating when the Kiowa had done their handiwork.

Again Beth held her tongue when Cole lifted her to the ground. Her face was still chalk white. He removed his bandanna and quickly soaked it in the water. He wasn't fast enough. Beth fell to her knees, humped over and retched.

Not until Beth sat back on her heels was Cole able to place the wet cloth on her forehead. She held it in place as he helped her to her feet. She was wobbly as he led her to a rock where she could sit. At least color had started to return to her cheeks.

"I guess I should have listened when you told me to wait." Her attempt at humor fell flat. She gave the bandanna back to him. "How could they do it?" she whispered. "How could Indians be so cruel?"

Cole tied the scarf back around his neck. "I'm not saying it's right," he said softly, "but if you try to understand, it simplifies matters. The Indians feel justified in what they do. The white man was first to take their land and slaughter their women and children, then they took away the buffalo." He removed his hat and raked his fingers through his ebony hair, pushing back the strands that had fallen forward.

"How can you defend them after such atrocities?" Beth asked bitterly. She leaned forward and rested her head in her hands. "A white man would never scalp or burn people to death. They're beasts. I don't blame Colonel Chivington for wanting to eradicate them. The colonel was right when he said, 'There is no good Indian but a dead Indian.'"

Cole slapped his hat back on. "The Indians' barbarism is nothing compared to what that religious hypocrite did at Sand Creek," he stated harshly. "And I suggest you get off that righteous podium and stop spouting nonsense about what white men don't do. They not only can, but have done every atrocity you accuse the Indians of. A man's color doesn't have a thing to do with savagery."

Taken back by Cole's sudden burst of anger, Beth looked up at the austere man. His eyes were like black ice. He reminded her of pictures she had seen of... How could she have been so blind? With his coloring, he had to have Indian blood. No wonder he was talking that way. He'd warned her about the others, but he was the one she should have been the most concerned about.

"If you're so interested in writing about the West, do the readers a favor. Learn to tell the truth." Cole walked the few steps to where the horses stood nipping shoots of grass. "We need to get going. I have no desire to be cornered by a bunch of bloodthirsty Kiowa on the warpath."

Beth drew her gun and pointed the barrel directly at Cole. "You defend them because you're one of them!" she accused. "That's why you have such black hair and eyes."

"Woman, where do you come up with these ideas?" Cole looked toward the sun, trying to keep his temper in check. Yes, he had some Indian blood, but that was several generations back. It had, however, come in handy when he'd had to deal with them. "Be careful with that gun. One shot will bring those braves back."

Beth stood, never taking her eyes off her enemy. "At this moment I'm more worried about you. Now, move away from the horses."

"You're making a mistake." There was no doubt in Cole's mind that he could disarm her without getting shot, but he couldn't risk having her pull the trigger. "You've just had a bad experience, and you're not thinking straight."

"I said move away from the horses."

Cole managed a warm, humorous smile, trying to repress her suspicion. "You would indeed make a good author. You have the imagination needed for writing. Stop and think a minute. If you were right about me being an Indian, wouldn't you already be dead?" He stepped aside, bowed at the waist and made a dramatic wave toward the horses. "But if you no longer trust me, then be my guest."

Cole watched her cautiously make her way around him. "If you're really interested, my coloring came from my mother's side of the family. They were from France." He waited for her to mull over what he had said. They had to get out of there. Time was wasting.

Beth grabbed Seeker's reins. Had the terror of seeing those dead men made her addled? She *had* seen Frenchmen with the same color hair and eyes. And hadn't Cole kept her safe so far? Most important, where would she go?

Beth sighed. "Well... perhaps I did jump to conclusions." She holstered her gun. "I may have overreacted." Pictures of the slaughtered men flashed in her mind, making her feel sick to her stomach again.

Seeing the flicker of anguish on Beth's lovely face caused Cole to relent. He went to her and pulled her into his arms, offering comfort. His hand moved up and down her back, calming her trembling body. She was probably going to have bad dreams in days to come. At this moment she seemed so small and helpless.

She had no idea how close she'd come to trouble had she put one foot in the stirrup. Traveling in harmony was a hell of a lot better than having to secure her, but he wouldn't have hesitated a minute if she'd tried to ride off. Playing hide-and-seek with the enemy was hard enough without her pulling this sort of thing. At least he'd learned to be careful. He would never have suspected her to be as fast a draw. If she ever tried drawing on him again, he'd be prepared.

Beth tried to comprehend the haze of emotions she was going through. Right now, held in Cole's arms, she felt safe and protected. Yet only minutes ago she had been ready to shoot him if he'd tried to prevent her escape.

"We have to go," Cole said gently.

"I'll try to help you bury the men." Beth backed away and squared her shoulders. She hated weak, prissy women. The time had come for her to stop feeling sorry for herself. After all, she was the one who had chosen to come west. "I assure you, my fit of nausea will not happen again."

Cole gave her a half-cocked grin. "Then I guess that makes you better than a lot of men who do the same thing under such circumstances." He saw her mouth twitch. "As for the cavalry men, we'll have to leave them."

"But—"

"If the Kiowa return and find the men buried, they'll come looking for us. They would find our horse tracks and come after us."

Beth nodded. Cole was very good at logical reasoning. Too good. "Do you think anything has happened to the caravan?"

"I don't know," he replied. He'd been wondering the same thing. "They should have already passed through here before the band of warriors went on the warpath." Cole went to his horse, grabbed the pommel and swung himself up into the saddle. As soon as Beth was mounted, he continued following the ravine. At least for the time being, they were hidden by the steep sides.

After a half hour Cole moved them back onto the open prairie. They were unprotected now, but he had no choice except to make a wide half circle then go due west. He kept their horses at an easy canter, not wanting to stir dust into the air for some Kiowa brave to spot.

From the moment they had come into the clearing, anxiety and apprehension had been growing in Beth's chest. And when she saw the smoke curling into the air directly north and south, she was attacked by stark fear. Pictures of the dead cavalry men kept flashing in her mind.

Cole closed the short distance between them, until they were riding side by side. "Listen to me, Beth," he said, his gaze shifting here and there for any signs of the raiding party. "I'm going to try to get us out of this alive, but I'm going to need your help. Should we meet up with the Indians, I don't want you trying to outrun them. Most likely, other braves will be positioned to cut off any escape. We'll pull up and wait for them to join us."

Beth's panic exploded. It rang in her ears and diminished all sensible thoughts. "I'll not give up without making a run for it!" She leaned forward, ready to plant her heels in Seeker's ribs, but Cole grabbed the bit and yanked the black's head toward him.

Beth could do nothing as long as Cole held on to the bit. She whipped unmercifully at him with the ends of the reins. He still held on.

"Stop it, Beth!" Cole commanded.

Beth didn't care that Cole's voice was hard and his expression dangerous. No one was going to take her hair without a fight. She wasn't going to die like the others.

Beth went for her revolver, determined to shoot if Cole didn't release his hold. But before she could point the barrel at him, he'd reached over and grabbed the gun, easily forcing the barrel toward the sky. But he wasn't able to wrench the weapon from her before she squeezed off two shots. Still holding on to the bit, Cole snatched Beth from the saddle with his left arm. Frantically she sank her teeth into his shoulder. He didn't drop her as she'd hoped. Instead, the hard muscle in his arm tightened, sending pain along her ribs.

"Dammit, Beth, stop fighting me!"

Beth continued to struggle. "I'll never listen to you again...you yellow-bellied—" All other accusations were left unsaid. Her mouth was suddenly dry, and she became very still.

Five mounted Indians in full plumage were riding toward them. They, as well as their horses, were splashed with all the colors of the spectrum. Cole lowered Beth to the ground. He had also seen the intruders.

"I don't give a damn what you may be going through," Cole stated coldly, "but if you intend to get out of this alive, you'd better get hold of yourself and do as I say. You wanted to see scalpings and you wanted to see Indians. Well, here they are in all their glory."

"That was an unfair comment."

"Unfair? That hasn't a thing to do with it. We're not playing some kind of game, lady. This is the real West you wanted to see. Now, you climb back in the saddle—slowly—and under no circumstance show fear. I want you to smile and appear happy to see them. If you try to bolt, you're a dead woman. A bullet travels a lot faster than a horse.''

Beth was furious at Cole but frightened by the approaching Indians. She could think of nothing she wanted more than to run as fast as her legs would carry her. Instead, she slowly mounted Seeker. Cole had finally let go of the bit. She forced a smile.

As the Indians brought their horses to a halt, Beth cautiously twisted the reins around her hand. She couldn't just sit there. Cole wasn't going to do anything. She would have to protect herself. She looked down at the ground where he had dropped her pistol. The gun was no use to her now.

When Cole began speaking with the apparent leader in the man's own language, Beth was convinced she had been right all along. Cole had Indian blood. He pointed to the ground, then to her. What was he saying? He moved his horse closer, leaned over and lifted her thick braid. The others jumped when he let the hair fall back in place. Beth couldn't imagine what he was saying, but it certainly involved her.

Beth squeezed the reins tighter. The war paint made the Indians look like demons risen from the depths of hell. The grotesque paintings drawn on the horses added to the hideous scene. The one talking to Cole had a blue face with white dots, and wore a headdress of feathers and pointed buffalo horns. The natives she had seen in Africa had dressed similarly.

Beth's gaze traveled down the leader's horse's withers with a yellow handprint on them, and to the thick legs. She was assessing the paint's speed. Her mare had long, powerful legs, and she was certain it could outrun every one of the Indian ponies. Wouldn't it be better to die immediately rather than be tortured? Whatever was being discussed was irritating the braves. She fought not to squeeze her eyes shut and plug her ears when they shouted something and raised their rifles and lances in the air. She looked past them to the flat, open land.

"If you make a move to run, I'm the one who will have to shoot you, and I don't miss."

Beth jerked her head around. The look on Cole's face told her he wasn't bluffing.

"Dead, there is no hope," Cole added.

Beth forced herself to relax her hands.

The tall, lanky man Cole had been talking to turned his pony around and took off in a northeasterly direction. Cole followed. Beth quickly guided her horse alongside him, needing his strength. She swayed in the saddle.

"Don't you dare pass out on me, Mrs. Alexander," Cole snapped at her. Soft words would only cause her to break down more. Right now, anger was the only tool Cole had to keep her from crumbling. "When you hired me you said I could rely on you to hold up your end."

His harsh words brought Beth back to reason. "If you'd had any guts, we could have escaped."

"We'd be dead. Remember, sweetheart, I didn't fire the bullets that brought them to us."

"Being dead is better than being tortured! Where are we going?"

"To the buffalo herd we saw earlier."

Beth gasped. "Why?"

"I told them you were a spirit—that's a god to them. I said your red hair captures the sun and that you were a seer."

"I'm a what?"

"I said you can see the buffalo and you are taking us to them."

Maybe he should be the one writing the book, Beth thought after hearing such an outlandish tale. "And they believed that?"

"They have doubts, but it's enough to keep them from harming us. After all, I might be telling them the truth. They've never seen anyone with your hair color, so that helped, as did the buckskin britches you have on. However, you also have to act like a god. Do not show fear, and sit straight in the saddle. You must appear alert." He smiled faintly at seeing the way she was quickly regaining control of her fears. "While you're at it, you might try saying a prayer that I can relocate that herd."

They rode on in silence. Beth acknowledged that Cole had been right, as usual. Her actions earlier had been un-called-for. She should have listened to his warning about shots drawing the Indians to their location. All she could do now was do what he said and get control over her mis-givings. Since Cole had so far managed to prevent their demise, she had to believe he could perform other mira-cles.

Beth took a quick glance at her outlaw. How could he appear so relaxed? If he wanted to point a finger, none of this would have happened if he hadn't insisted they stay with Norma and her family. Beth was suddenly horri-fied. What if other Kiowa had attacked the farm? Would she never see Howard, Norma, or the boys again? She couldn't stand to think about it. She stiffened her back. She would not give up hope. They *would* all survive. The irony of all this was that after fortifying her caravan with men and guns, there was only one man standing between her and death. An outlaw with a five-thousand-dollar re-ward on his head. And while she was on the subject of Mr. Wagner, just how had he learned to talk to savages?

* * *

Beth's mouth hurt from smiling so often, and the least noise made her jump. They had been searching for the buffalo for what seemed like an hour. Was Cole ever going to find the herd? Because Cole had said the Indians were fascinated with the color of her hair, she had considered releasing it from the braid—until she realized those were scalps fluttering from the braves' shield rims and bridles. Her hair wasn't going to hang from anything except her head.

"Beth, spread your arms out wide and make strange noises!" Cole called back.

Past the point of arguing, Beth tied a loose knot in the reins, spread out her arms and began jabbering. "Now what do you want me—" Laughter burst forth. Cole had found the buffalo! The shaggy beasts were beautiful! Apparently her spread arms had been Cole's way of playing up the part about her being a god. Maybe now they would be released.

The braves yelped in jubilation. Beth watched Cole ride up to the one wearing the buffalo horns. The quicker they got away the safer they'd be. But something wasn't right. The two men were arguing.

Beth knew the minute one of the warriors grabbed her horse's reins that she and Cole would remain prisoners. They moved on at a fast pace. Cole continued to ride alongside the chief. Why didn't he tell her what was happening? She should have followed her first instinct to make a run for it, but it was too late now. They had been joined by others and were surrounded by painted faces and painted horses. They turned directly south—not the direction she and Cole had been heading.

Chapter Ten

⟪≈≋⟫

There wasn't a place on Beth's body that didn't ache. Trying to follow Cole's instructions to remain straight in the saddle had become the most demanding thing she had ever done. Shortly after finding the buffalo, the Indians had stopped long enough to clean themselves and their horses at the river. Shields were carefully placed in hide pouches and other equipment stored.

After the brief pause the Indians remained on the move through the night and the following day, continuing their southerly direction. Only on occasion did they walk to rest the horses. Even so, she continued to wonder why the animals didn't drop from exhaustion. But like the savages, they pushed on.

Everything seemed to pass in a haze, but Beth did spend a good deal of time thinking. She must have appeared very callous—or downright addled—when she had told Cole she wanted to rob a train, watch a scalping, see Indians, outlaws, killings and so forth. No wonder he had looked at her with a frown. Yet there she had sat, acting so pompous, knowledgeable and fearless. It was embarrassing to even think about it. And though she had wanted to belittle him by thinking he had Indian blood, she had to admit it was only the need to feel superior. After all, he had saved her life again. It was beginning to become a habit.

Weary to the bone, Beth had reached the point of not caring what the Indians might think of her. She wasn't a god and she was tired of trying to look and act like one.

They were racing across the floor of a large valley when Beth suddenly realized the scenery had changed from flatland to trees, tall grass and mountains. How could she have been so lost in thought to not have noticed? She inhaled deeply, hoping the crisp, fresh air would provide a resurgence of energy. Just as she made up her mind that she could still go on, for no apparent reason the band of Kiowa came to an abrupt halt.

As the others slid to the ground, Beth moved Seeker to the stream. After dismounting, she dropped to her knees. Dousing her face in the water, she drank. She hadn't taken more than ten gulps when unexpectedly she was yanked to her feet. Furious, she swung around, ready to fight whoever had dared to take her from the water she needed.

Cole grabbed Beth's fist before it met his jaw. "Whoa, there! If you drink too much you'll become sick."

"I don't care!" She brushed away the water dripping from her face.

"I didn't say you couldn't have any more," Cole said in a softer tone. "Just wait a few minutes."

Cole's devilish grin helped relieve some of Beth's tension. Amusement flickered in her eyes. "How many minutes?"

"I'll let you know when," Cole gently bantered. He would have been willing to bet a year's wages that the woman before him had never been this disheveled in her entire life. Her britches and shirt were covered with dirt, her hair was in total disarray, and though she had put her face in the water, there were still streaks of dirt on it. Even so, she was still one of the prettiest women he'd ever laid eyes on. "I thought you might like to know that we will soon be riding into a Kiowa camp. Our trip is about to come to an end."

Beth sobered. "Are they going to kill us?"

"Not if I can help it." Cole's respect for the woman's courage continued to grow. Though she was frightened, it hadn't even occurred to her to beg for mercy. "I know all this hasn't been easy for you, Beth, and I have to tell you that you are without a doubt the bravest woman I have ever met."

The praise was like being fed sweet cream. It bolstered her strength. Somehow he knew how hard she had worked to overcome her fear.

"I won't lie to you. I've been in better predicaments and I've been in worse." Cole raised his finger and removed a drop of water from the end of her nose. "We have no choice but to wait and see what happens. I can't guarantee anything. We're still alive and we'll stay that way if I have anything to do with it."

Beth felt guilty. Cole was so brave, and she could at least show the same valor. Something moved, causing her to look past Cole. "What are the Indians doing?"

Cole glanced over his shoulder.

"Oh, no!" Beth gasped. "They're painting their faces black."

Cole took her by the arm and walked a short distance from the others. "They are getting ready for their victorious ride into camp. Late afternoon and tonight *A-dalde-guan,* or scalp dance, hair-kill dance, whatever you want to call it, will take place. It is to honor the triumphant warriors. This has nothing to do with us, so don't let it worry you."

"Why are they painting their faces again?"

"To show they have killed an enemy. It goes with the ritual. They will ride into camp in full dress, including their war bonnets. We will be riding toward the back. Don't make the mistake of thinking we can ride off. We are being watched at all times. For now, we just do what we are told." He winked. "I think you can drink now. Just take it slow."

Beth watched him stroll away, appearing to not have a care in the world. She had felt alone, and hadn't expected his kind words.

When they rode off a few minutes later Beth held herself proudly. She wouldn't disappoint Cole again.

The first sign of humans was the smoke Beth saw curling into the sky. When the raiding party rounded a stand of trees, she was awestruck. At least eighty tepees were spread across the valley. An uncountable number of horses were grazing by the river and everything appeared so tranquil.

The serenity was quickly broken when the warriors kicked their mounts into a full gallop. Beth drew her horse up next to Cole's and watched as the braves rode into camp firing their guns and discharging arrows, apparently demonstrating how they had met and struck down the foe. Friends and families ran out to meet them, shouting *"Imkagy'a gya!"* The warriors lifted the women up behind them on their ponies' rumps and rode around in a circle singing, while the scalps were carried on long poles.

It was a joyous occasion to all but Beth. She could find no pleasure or forgiveness in her heart. She had seen where some of those scalps had come from.

A young brave with a clubfoot who seemed to come out of nowhere spoke to Cole.

"What does he want?" Beth asked.

"For us to follow him."

They dismounted and followed the limping boy. "Why can't we ride out of here?" Beth asked. "You've hardly said a word to any of these savages. Did you tell them the part about me being a god?"

"There will be a council meeting to determine our fate."

Beth was almost having to run to keep up with him. "What do you mean by a council meeting?"

"A group of men make a council. White Horse will tell his side of the story about our being captured, then I will be permitted to tell my side of the story."

"Then what?"

"Then our fate will be decided."

When they came to what appeared to be an empty tepee, the boy again spoke to Cole, then hurried off.

"Well, my dear," Cole said as he tethered his buckskin to a stake, "this is to be our home while we accept our hosts' hospitality."

"Whose place is this?"

"I have no idea, but for the present, it is ours. The Kiowa are very cognizant of making guests comfortable." Cole turned and looked at Beth. She hadn't moved. "Well, don't you want to take a look inside?"

Beth stared at the paintings of animals, rattles and various other drawings that decorated the tepee. There were also glass beads, feathers and other decorations. "This is supposed to be for both of us?"

"That's what I said."

"But we can't do that. We're not... I don't want you to think... I never... how long will we be here?"

Cole's laughter floated from his throat. "Don't tell me you never, not after being married three times," he teased.

"That's not what I meant and you know it." Under normal circumstances she would have demanded a tepee of her own. Now it was undoubtedly safer to remain by Cole's side. As if he could read her thoughts, Cole added, "We have no say in the matter. I assure you there is no need for concern. I don't make a habit of attacking unwilling females." She still hadn't budged. "Well, stand there if you like, but we could be here for days, and I'm worn-out."

Beth's mouth dropped open. "You mean we'll be..." She refused to say what she was thinking.

"Sleeping together," he finished for her. "That is exactly what I'm telling you." He took the reins from her hand, looped them over the post, then led her inside.

Beth was amazed at the warmth. There were furs of all types scattered about. In the center was a circle for cooking. The smoke went out the hole at the top.

"My, my, my," Cole commented as he looked about. "I do believe we have a good chance of making it through this alive."

"Why do you say that?"

"We have an eleven-pole tepee. A poor Indian only gets nine poles. It escalates from there, eleven being the highest position. Apparently my tale about you being a god is bearing fruit."

"But how would anyone know about that?"

"A brave was sent ahead to inform the big chief that we were being brought in. Undoubtedly the brave also told of the buffalo and my claim that you are a god."

Beth felt her stomach rumble. "What are we going to do for food? They took the packhorse."

"We won't have to worry about tonight. I'm quite sure we're going to be invited to the ceremony. Get some rest while I go check out the camp."

"You can go anywhere you want?"

Cole grinned. "As long as I'm a good boy and don't try to sneak away."

Even after Cole left, Beth hesitated to lie down. She wasn't comfortable with something she had no control over. No, that wasn't exactly right. Her discomfort came from knowing she and Cole were to be cloistered together. It was all a bit confusing. The passionate feelings she had experienced since she'd met Cole were foreign to her.

Beth suddenly thought about the horses. Why hadn't Cole tended them? She walked over and looked out of the tepee. The mare and buckskin were gone, but the saddles and saddlebags were lying on the ground. Had Cole taken them to water or did the Indians have them?

Beth moved back inside feeling a bit safer. Cole might want to move about, but for the time being she'd stay right where she was. She sat on the furry side of a large buffalo hide. She was going to have to change her attitude. Cole had said they had a chance of surviving. Arguing with him wasn't going to accomplish that. From here on, she had to do whatever Cole told her.

Her eyelids had become heavy and she had to blink several times to keep them open.

More than once she had told him she could hold her end up, no matter what happened. She remembered when she had almost made a dash for it when he was negotiating with one of the Kiowa. It was no wonder he had become angry with her.

Beth's head bobbed. She stopped fighting her weariness and gave in to sleep.

Cole quietly entered the tepee a few minutes later. As he had suspected, Beth was sleeping. He tossed his hat on the floor, then boldly stared down at her. Lying on her side with her lips slightly parted, her eyes closed and her face relaxed, she showed a softness that wasn't often displayed. With such a look of pure innocence, no one would ever suspect how much trouble so small a woman could be.

Her dark, thick lashes fluttered, bringing to his attention how they rested on her cheeks and curled at the ends. Most women with her hair color had trouble with the glaring sun burning their skin. Not Beth. The sun wasn't her enemy. It served to give her skin a golden hue. Yes, Beth had the best of everything. Looks and money. Then why wasn't she content? Well, it wasn't his concern. He had a job to do, nothing more and nothing less. He had been in this business long enough to know a man in his position didn't get involved with others around him. His brother had been a good example. It had made him less attentive, vulnerable, and eventually a dead man.

Cole leaned down and gently moved the tangled hair that had fallen over her eyes. Beth had no idea what the Kiowa could do to her should they decide not to let them go. He had seen women who had been raped and tortured, or used as a slave. It wasn't a pretty sight. He could handle whatever they dished out, but she couldn't. He had to get her out of here soon.

He moved to the other side of the tepee and lay down. While walking around camp and observing the preparations for the dance, he had briefly chatted with some of the women who would talk to him. He had discovered a very important piece of information. Say-tine-day, or Santanta as the soldiers called him, was in camp. The very same man whose Kiowa lurked about the base of Pawnee Rock and had swept down on unwary stagecoaches and emigrant trains. He had all but destroyed traffic on the Santa Fe trail at the start of the war. He was notorious for his hatred of the white eyes, and was the leading spirit for the Cheyenne and Kiowa raids. The great chief was highly intelligent and crafty and would undoubtedly be on the council.

Cole had two slight advantages. While staying with the Cheyenne several years back, he had met Say-tine-day. The big man would not be able to deny that Cole was indeed a brother of the Kiowa allies. Also, Cole knew Say-tine-day was a strong believer in the spirits. Now it was a matter of convincing the council that Beth truly was a god. If he could do that, he and Beth would get out of this alive.

Cole placed his arms under his head. Like Beth, he needed sleep.

Beth fought opening her eyes, but the nudges on her shoulder became too persistent. She rolled over and looked up. Cole was standing over her.

"We have been invited to the dance."

Beth rubbed her eyes. For a short time she had been able to forget where she was. "I don't want to go anywhere. I want to know what has happened to Seeker. Have you seen if she is being properly taken care of?"

"Your mare is fine."

"I do not want anyone riding her."

"Neither you nor I have any control of that. Also, the invitation didn't come with an option of refusal."

Beth looked down at her soiled blouse. "Am I still supposed to be a god?"

"Yep."

"Then don't you think I should change my blouse and try to clean up?"

Cole chuckled. Beth was starting to recover from her ordeal. There was no sign of fear in her eyes, just determination. "They won't know the difference, and with your hair in such wild disarray, they'll probably be more inclined to believe you have special powers."

Beth tried to smooth her hair. "You mean a witch."

Cole's grin spread. "Something like that."

Beth stood. Though her body felt sticky and dirty, she wasn't going to say a thing. "I won't let you down again, Cole."

Cole nodded. "At least we're going to be fed. Let's go."

When Beth left the tepee she was surprised to see that night had fallen. She would have sworn she had been asleep less than an hour.

"Cole, promise me you will see that Seeker is all right. I would go myself if I could."

Cole nodded.

Beth and Cole were motioned to sit where they could partake of the food and watch the celebration. A quiver ran up Beth's spine as she sat among the men who had rained death and destruction across the land. The men who had engaged in the war party and all the women were dancing around a fire in the center of the circle.

"Act happy," Cole whispered.

That wasn't easy to do, especially when Beth realized the hoops the women were carrying in the dance had scalps stretched over them and had been painted red inside.

The old man sitting next to Beth said something to her. She looked to Cole for an interpretation.

"He said, 'Everybody very happy time.'"

That's a matter of opinion, Beth said under her breath. However, with the food, drink and merriment surrounding her, she was soon able to relax. With that came a sudden revelation. Cole had been right. She was getting to see

Indians, and given a hundred years, it was doubtful she would ever see such a dance performed again. Feeling less intimidated, she could even move her head and look around.

"How long will the dance last?" Beth asked Cole. She stuck meat into her mouth and followed it with another drink.

"The afternoon and night dance might last for days or even a month."

"But... when will the council be held?" Her gaze suddenly settled on the Indian who had brought them here. He was sitting next to a huge man, and boldly staring back at her. She averted her eyes.

"They'll have the council when they decide to."

Beth took another bite of meat and washed it down with a drink. "The man wearing the buffalo horns that brought us here is staring at me."

"His name is White Horse. Don't let him see that it bothers you."

Beth took another drink from the gourd. At first she had turned her nose up at the taste, but she had now decided it wasn't bad at all. By repeating to herself over and over again that these people weren't going to hurt her, Beth began to feel less and less intimidated. And when that happened, she became oddly fascinated with the view. Other than the old men with deep wrinkles, the braves' bodies were strong and their movements lithe as they danced, their ornaments of beads and silver flashing in the firelight. They were absolutely splendid and absolutely terrifying.

"Watch how much of that stuff you drink," Cole warned. "Cactus firewater is powerful and you're not used to it. It'll get you drunk."

Beth looked at him wide-eyed. "This will probably come as a shock, but I've drunk whiskey." She deliberately took another long drink.

"I'd be more surprised if you hadn't."

Beth tilted her chin just enough to let him know she was ready for battle. "I suppose you think women shouldn't drink."

Had they been anywhere else, Cole was of just the right mood to give her the argument she was looking for, even if she was just letting off steam. "What you do is your business."

"That's right. I don't need anyone to tell me what to do." Beth was fighting her emotions. The dance being performed seemed powerful and strong...and very erotic. Her skin felt as if it were on fire. Was it due to the warmth inside or was it caused by the throes of passion she found herself caught in? Never had she wanted a man as strongly as she wanted Cole at this minute. Her desire was so overwhelming she glanced around to see if anyone had noticed.

Cole hadn't realized the drink had already taken effect until Beth suddenly stood. Before he could stop her, she had moved away to dance with the other women. There was absolutely nothing Cole could do about it. His Kiowa brothers would never accept a mere mortal dragging away a god, and that is what it would take to get her seated again.

Though Beth's dance was entirely her own interpretation, Cole relaxed when he realized the others were actually enjoying her performance. Especially the war party. In their eyes, she was celebrating their victory with them. He looked toward White Horse. The man was practically frothing at the mouth. Cole had seen that same look of hunger when the warrior had first set eyes on Beth.

Knowing he had to do something, Cole was about to stand when Beth returned. As luck would have it, she tripped and landed right in his lap. That was followed with a full kiss on his lips. Everyone started laughing and pointing. Beth joined in the laughter.

Cole stood, picking up the contrary woman with him. He smiled, nodded and left the circle. Not a man or woman doubted what would happen next. Only Cole knew differently.

"Cole," Beth purred in his ear, "are you good at making love?" She wrapped her arms around his neck and nuzzled his cheek. "You need to shave. Well?"

"Well, what?" He continued walking in the direction of their tepee.

"Are you good at making love?"

"Nope. You would be very disappointed."

"I think you're lying. Why don't we find out?"

"It wouldn't serve any purpose."

"Oh, yes, it would."

Cole entered the tepee and stood Beth on her feet. "Get to bed," he ordered as he moved to the far side of the tent. "Tomorrow I'll show you where you can bathe." Receiving no reply, he looked up to see what she was doing. She had already unbuttoned her blouse and dropped it on the floor. She was now in the process of pulling her chemise off over her head.

Cole hurried to her, preventing the last bit of her upper clothing from being removed. Once the woman had her mind made up, it wasn't easy getting her to change it.

"What are you doing?" Beth asked.

"There is no need to take off your clothes."

Beth tried smothering a giggle with her hand. "Didn't you say we were going to be sleeping together?"

As Cole's gaze took in the long, slender neck, soft shoulders and the outline of desirable breasts pressed against the cotton chemise, he was more than a little tempted to take his pleasure with the half-naked woman. He was saved by the absurdness of the situation. A fatalistic smile spread across his face. Here was a beautiful woman blatantly waiting for him to bed her, and he had orders to keep his hands off. Sometimes the gods just weren't on his side.

"Do I please you?"

Still smiling, Cole reached down and picked up a buffalo blanket. "Oh, yes. You please me more than you know." He wrapped it around her shoulders.

"Are you going to pull my boots off for me? I can't take off my britches until I'm rid of my boots."

"I wonder if you would be so welcoming if you hadn't had so much of that Mexican liquor?" He reached up and brushed her hair back from her face.

"Are you refusing my favors?" Beth tried to be angry, but she couldn't even remember what she was supposed to be angry about. Her eyes closed then snapped back open. "I thought... You said I was pleas—" Everything went black.

As Beth's body went limp, Cole swung her up in his arms. Thinking of Grant's order, he wondered what his commander in chief would have done had he been younger and in the same situation.

After laying her on the soft furs, he proceeded to pull off her boots. He tried telling himself that everything had turned out for the best, but the words didn't ring true. He took his place beside her, keeping his back turned to temptation.

Chapter Eleven

Wearing only a buffalo robe, Cole left the sweat lodge and headed for the river. For two hours he had sat in the small lodge, occasionally sprinkling water over the hot rocks. For the Indians, a sweat bath was for purification, to rid the body of disease, or to exorcise evil spirits. For Cole, it had an entirely different purpose. He had wanted the Kiowa to remember he was a Cheyenne brother and deserved to be treated as such.

When he reached the river, Cole dropped the robe and jumped into a deep pool. He emerged feeling like a new man. All of this had served another purpose. When he awoke this morning Beth had been curled up against him, one arm stretched across his chest. He had managed to slip away without awakening her, but it was becoming increasingly difficult to turn his back on something he definitely wanted. He considered himself an honorable man, but he *was* a man.

As Cole swam toward the bank, the young brave with the clubfoot appeared from behind a tree. Cole treaded water, waiting to hear what he had to say.

"The council will meet when the sun is overhead," he called to Cole.

Cole nodded. He had approximately four hours. He already knew what he needed to say. However, another matter had to be taken care of before the council convened. While in the sweat lodge, he had realized he'd overlooked something very important. To make sure his willpower wasn't tested beyond its limit, he had made a point of keeping away from Beth as much as possible. That had to change, and no matter how he looked at it, he was digging a big hole for himself.

Fully dressed in clean clothes, Cole returned to the tepee. Beth was sitting with her head resting on bent knees. He noticed she had her blouse and boots back on. "Good morning," he greeted her.

Beth looked up. Her head was pounding unmercifully.

"How would you like to bathe?"

"Do you mean it?"

"I do, but first we have to talk." He sat in front of her Indian style. "The council will be meeting in nearly three hours." He had the beauty's full attention. "Last night—"

"Don't mention last night." Beth rubbed her forehead.

"Last night I noticed White Horse watching every move you made." He couldn't resist adding, "Especially when you were dancing. I'm certain that he is going to claim you as his woman."

Beth's eyes became stony with anger. "He can't have me!"

"Try to remember where we are."

"You have to do something."

"Not just me, we."

Beth leaned forward. "What are you saying?"

"We are going to have to prove him wrong. There are hundreds of eyes in this camp and they have to see that you have chosen me as your mate."

Beth leaned back. "Mate?"

"Only until we can get out of here. Perhaps I should explain a woman's position in Kiowa society. They are menial. They take no part in tribal government and are subservient to the men. They care for the tepees—setting up, packing and moving them and the household articles. They harness and pack the dogs and horses. They prepare food, care for the children, and cut and carry home the meat and hides obtained from the buffalo. They tan the hides to make clothing, care for the household and herd the horses, unless children—usually boys or slaves—take over this duty under their supervision. They fetch firewood and water unless they have captives to do it for them. They—"

"Enough! Why are you telling me all this?"

"I want you to understand what your duties would be if you became White Horse's woman."

"And what would be expected of me if I am your woman?"

Cole paused and stared at her. "Do you mean while we're here, or after?"

"Of course I mean while we're here. We both know that if we get out of this, we will continue on with our journey as before."

Cole felt considerably better. "As a god, you wouldn't be expected to perform all the women's tasks, but you would have to cook the meals, and show affection."

Beth didn't remember everything about last night, but she clearly remembered her failure at trying to seduce Cole. She had been thinking about it when he had entered the tent, and now found herself quite embarrassed.

She had never acted that way around any man. She had never had to. "Can I go bathe now?"

Cole had expected an argument. "Of course." He stood, then offered his hand to help Beth up.

Beth walked over to her saddlebags and pulled out the single bar of soap Norma had given her. It was the only toilette provision she had. Angry at Cole for not letting her bring any gowns, she had mindlessly left the farm without a comb, brush, or any other necessities for grooming.

When they stepped out into the fresh air, Beth took hold of Cole's hand and looked up at him with loving eyes. "Am I doing this right?" she asked. She watched the muscles twitch in his firm jaw. What was he angry about? He had been the one to tell her to act this way. She suddenly wondered if she had misread the tall man. Was it possible that he was drawn to her but had kept his distance through sheer willpower? "Didn't you say we were to appear loving?"

Cole headed for the river with Beth right beside him. As he had expected, he had given her an opening, and she had every intention of using it. If he had guessed right, she would taunt him from this day forward. She was paying him back for his aloofness. "Do you know how to swim?"

"Yes. I do quite well in the water."

Is there nothing the woman can't do? Cole wondered.

Beth made a point of remaining by Cole's side as they followed a well-worn path. She still didn't trust any of the Kiowa people. It was all she could do to keep from glancing about to be sure some brave wasn't coming at them with a raised knife.

"Relax," Cole said softly.

It hadn't occurred to Beth that Cole could detect her nervousness. What else had he observed that she wasn't aware of?

Beth soon heard water running, but the river remained hidden from view by thick brush, undergrowth and trees. She soon tired of being poked, stabbed and whipped by limbs and branches. However, when they stepped into a small clearing she was awed by the beauty before her. The pool was clear and inviting, and farther out the swift water cascaded over and around large boulders. At one spot there was even a rainbow. On the far bank were trees and small patches of grass. Wildflowers of every color had blossomed. It was a fairyland. It was little wonder the Kiowa had chosen this place to make camp. Beth quickly returned to reality. "How am I supposed to bathe? Didn't you say we were being constantly watched?"

"You're protected here. No one can see you. The ground drops off quickly and the pool is well over your head. You *were* telling the truth about knowing how to swim, weren't you?"

"And what about you?"

"Of course I can swim."

"That wasn't what I was talking about." Nervous at possibly exposing herself to the tribe, Beth took a long look at their surroundings. Cole was right. The place was completely secluded. "Do you intend to turn your back while I bathe?"

"Of course."

"But what if someone should happen to pass by on the other side and see me in the water and you looking the other way. Wouldn't they find that a bit strange?"

Cole scowled down at the wily woman standing before him. "Don't play with fire unless you're willing to face the consequences. I will sit and wait."

Beth began unbuttoning her blouse. She hadn't swum naked since she was a girl. She managed to pull off her boots, and as she removed her britches she glanced toward Cole. He had positioned himself against a tree trunk with his eyes averted.

After removing her clothes, Beth was overcome by a sudden sense of wickedness. Here she was, buck naked in broad daylight, with a handsome outlaw sitting no more than ten feet away. She wanted to be a seductress. She wanted just once to taste the danger of a forbidden love. She wanted to face the consequences Cole had mentioned. Instead, she stepped into the water, her toes sinking in the soft bottom. As Cole had said, the ground quickly gave way.

The cool water against Beth's hot flesh caused her to shiver. But as she became accustomed to the temperature and let the water caress her body, the tightening clutches of desire returned. Maybe it was where they were, or it could be that having faced death made her feel brazen. She wanted Cole to make love to her, and in her heart she knew there was only one way to accomplish it.

In a euphoric state, she swam forward until her feet again touched the bottom. Then, with the deliberateness of a big cat, she moved forward.

Cole was thinking about the council meeting when he felt water dripping on the sleeve of his shirt. He turned and looked up. Beth was standing beside him. Her wet skin glistened in the sun, her full breasts were high and her nipples pointed. Her stomach was flat and the triangle between her legs was a declaration of her womanhood. He rose to his feet and stepped away. "Do you know what you're doing?" he asked harshly.

"I'm helping you save our lives. You said I was to act as your mate. Some things can't be pretended. Other things can clearly be seen in the eyes. According to what you said, if we do not do this, we die.''

Cole couldn't believe how a slip of a woman was successfully turning his guts inside out. He had never been in a situation like this and he didn't like it one damn bit. She made it sound as if they were embarking on some business transaction. Even so, his willpower was rapidly fading. What made it so bad was that whichever path he took, he was going to be in a lot of trouble.

''Of course, this will all cease when we get away from here,'' Beth assured him. Though she had managed to sound calm, her nerves were in a state of chaos. How long could she continue to stand there, waiting for him to do something? The prolonged anticipation was unbearable. She had made him an offer. If he refused she'd positively die.

''You are probably right. It is indeed a matter that needs handling.''

Beth's heart thundered in her ears as she watched Cole undress, inch by inch. His muscles stood out on his gigantic frame like knots of whipcord, and his powerful hips and thighs made swallowing difficult. She'd had no idea Cole was so... well equipped. He was standing so close she could feel the heat from his body.

His eyes raked boldly over her. ''Until we leave,'' he muttered, his voice already husky with desire.

Beth nodded. She would have agreed to anything. It couldn't have been just her insistence that was making him do this. A man couldn't be forced. He had to have already wanted her.

A hard lump formed in Beth's chest as her eyes locked with his. A sense of urgency drove her to touch his chest. Then his mouth covered hers, and she was certain she would swoon from the thrill of his kiss. As his hands glided down her back, he brushed kisses on her nose, her chin, the curve of her neck, sending her pulse pounding.

Cole gently laid Beth on the ground. He suckled her breasts, and Beth's sensitive skin felt like fire. "You're perfect in every way," she heard him whisper as his tongue trailed past the flat of her stomach. She gasped as he showed her ecstasy she had never experienced. Then he rose back up and entered her.

Beth stroked his body in shameless abandonment. She had become a woman possessed. She arched her back, eagerly accepting each thrust. Her fingers raked through his thick hair as his mouth teased her aching breasts. Soon a silken gleam of sweat covered her body.

She kissed his mouth, his chest and dug her nails into his flesh as she eagerly neared that moment of absolution. Suddenly she arched her back, nearly lifting herself off the ground. He pushed deep within her, causing a delirious explosion. One wave of ecstasy cascaded over another and another.

Satiated, Beth finally lay quietly beside Cole, still unable to believe what had happened. Cole had given her far more than just a romp on the grass. She still didn't quite understand it, but he had made her feel like a woman. A real woman. But she had indeed paid the price. She had once thought that Cole was a man who would settle for nothing less than a woman's very soul. She had been right.

Cole rolled over on his side and looked down at the wildcat who had come alive in his arms. He'd known too many women to not realize that Beth had been awakened for the first time. Undoubtedly her husbands had not provided her with what she needed. He gently ran his knuckles across her cheek. "You were right. It is in the eyes. If the Kiowa can't see we've made love, they are blind." He leaned over and brushed a kiss across her swollen lips.

Beth smiled. She had never felt so completely whole.

As one, they went into the water to bathe. Cole was the first to climb back out. As he dressed, he thought about how displeased Grant was going to be about what had happened. He pulled on his boots, then sat watching Beth wash her hair. He had never met a woman quite like her. He chuckled. Nor had he ever been so perfectly seduced. Sleeping next to the minx was going to be quite pleasurable. "By the way," he called, "I went to see how your mare is faring. Her coat is shiny and she's as frisky as ever. The boys watching the horses swear they have never seen an animal as fast. I was told no one has been given permission to ride her."

Cole puffed on the pipe that had been passed to him. Though the tepee was large, it seemed crowded, as though every brave in camp was seated behind the council circle. The chief whom Cole was the most concerned about was Say-tine-day. The man himself was intimidating. He was well over six feet in his embroidered moccasins, with immense shoulders and a gigantic frame. His braided scalp lock was adorned with one eagle feather. Like others, he was naked except for his breechclout and leggings. Cole knew he and Beth couldn't be in more dangerous company.

Cole looked back at White Horse, who was speaking. "I would have had this one's tongue cut out had he not spoken our tongue and said he was brother to Dog Fang, the great Cheyenne warrior. Knowing our Cheyenne brothers would be displeased should we destroy one of theirs, I came for your council."

Santanta nodded. "Wolf Eyes spoke the truth. I saw him sitting with Dog Fang at a powwow when my number-two wife was with child."

"Is it so that Sun Bird is a god, Wolf Eyes?" the shaman asked Cole.

"She delivered buffalo," a hawk-nosed brave testified.

"The buffalo grow scarce. Why did she not deliver them here?" the wizened old man persisted.

This time all looked in Cole's direction.

"The powerful spirit, *Gadombitsouhi,* Old Woman under the Ground, has sent her daughter to her people." Cole raised his hand toward the sky. "She came in human form so she could travel the land and see what is happening to *the people.*" He waved his hand. "Have you not seen how she draws the sun to her hair and how it dance on her shoulders?"

The braves began whispering to one another.

"You must let us go."

"The woman is mine!" White Horse bellowed. "I captured her!"

"White Horse did not capture Sun Bird," Cole stated calmly. "We did not give battle, nor would I war with my blood brothers. Sun Bird knew her friends, the Kiowa, were near. She had me deliberately fire my gun to attract them. She wanted to present them with a gift. A fine herd of buffalo. Now we are being held like slaves and prevented from continuing our travels. Because of this, she refuses to bring the buffalo here. She asked, 'Have my people become so lazy that they depend only on the white man for food and can no longer hunt?' She showed you the herd, now you must go after it. I ask if this is the hospitality to be shown to a god and a Cheyenne brother?"

"I claim my right to the woman!" White Horse's eyes flashed with anger as he looked toward Say-tine-day. "Do not listen to his lies. He did not fight because he is a coward. He is not deserving of such a one. She will become mine when I kill him.''

"It is not wise to incur her wrath," Cole warned.

White Horse's smile was twisted. "If she is a god, I will keep her so our people will once again have food and clothing. And if she is a god, why can she not speak our language?"

Santanta looked at Cole. "White Horse's claim is justified. What would you want with such a god and why can she not speak our tongue?"

Cole gave no sign of being disturbed by the unexpected question. "It is the same reason why Sun Bird's face is white. Gadombitsouhi wants her to go to the great chief of the white man to demand he free *the people* from the reservations and return their lands. I have been provided to speak for her."

"You said she came to see her people!" White Horse hissed.

"How else can she tell the white chief of your plight?"

Santanta nodded. Friend of Dog Fang was a good speaker for Sun Bird. "We will think on this. Your answer will be given in three days."

"And White Horse?" Cole asked.

"He will wait also."

"Why must she be permitted to remain with the white eyes?" White Horse asked angrily.

"Because she came with him," another of the council answered.

Cole was disappointed. He had hoped for an immediate answer. He stood and left the tepee. Now the council would deliberate on whether Beth was or was not a god, something he had hoped to avoid. Cole knew the Kiowa could ill afford to incur the Cheyenne's wrath. They were needed to help destroy the white eyes who wanted them on reservations so they could take their land. There was no longer any doubt that he would be allowed to leave. What was being decided was Beth's fate.

As Cole neared the tepee he and Beth had been given, he was surprised to see Beth sitting on the ground, surrounded by four small children. He stopped and watched. She reached out and tickled one, then made a funny face at the others. They were all laughing, and Beth's face gleamed with pleasure. Then, to Cole's surprise, she made a coin seemingly appear from nowhere. Others began to gather as she did several other simple tricks. Her finale was making it appear that she was pulling a crimson scarf from her ear. Everyone gasped, including someone standing behind Cole. He turned and discovered Say-tine-day standing there. Though his bravery was renowned, he probably had no desire to displease one who could pull colors from within her head. He released a grunt, looked at Cole, then walked away. The others also left.

Cole smiled. Beth's show couldn't have happened at a better time. Would she never cease to amaze him?

"Where did you learn to do all that?" Cole asked when he had joined Beth.

Beth stood and followed him into the tepee. "Howard used to teach them to me when we would sail to Europe. For a short time he had worked as a clown in a circus."

"Say-tine-day watched your performance. You may have convinced him you really are a god. He is a great warrior and can easily be the one who will determine our fate."

"I get the feeling you respect him."

Until now, Cole hadn't given it much thought. "I guess I do."

"But he's a killer."

Cole's grin was humorless. "Aren't we all?"

"Apparently we are still not permitted to leave. Did they ask questions?"

"They wanted to know why you do not speak their tongue if you are their god." While he told Beth what had been discussed at the council, he watched her stir the coals in the center, then place fresh fish on the hot rocks. "This has gone too far," he finally said. "Are you going to tell me you caught, cleaned and scaled those fish?"

Beth smiled. It wasn't easy to hide the passion that had flared the moment she had seen him watching her. "The children brought them to me." After spending time with the children, she could no longer think of the Kiowa as only killers. They had families, worries and heartbreaks just like white men. Only their cultures were different. Because of this realization, she didn't want to leave. Not right away. She wanted time to relish her newfound sensuality. She needed Cole to keep alive her lascivious nature so her memories wouldn't fade in the years to come, because when they left, it would all end.

"The food is cooked," Beth announced. Like Cole, she could hardly wait to taste the succulent fish. She could also hardly wait until nightfall when they would be lying together again.

After eating, Beth left to fill the water canteens. When she returned, Cole was nowhere in sight. Undoubtedly Cole was watching the scalp dance that had started up again some time ago. She laid out the bedrolls, then took paper and pencil from her saddlebags and went back outside.

Picking the spot that would give her the best view of the encampment, she sat on the ground and began to sketch. It was a perfect opportunity to record what was stretched out before her. Beth had been drawing for less than a half hour when she started getting peeks of someone riding between the tepees. She recognized the horse before she recognized White Horse. She tried to act as if she hadn't seen him, but he was making her very fidgety. She could feel his eyes watching her. Then, out of the corner of her eye, she saw him galloping his horse directly at her. She wanted to jump to her feet and run, but there was no time. Terrified, she remained sitting, the horse's sharp hooves missing her legs by inches.

White Horse jerked the paint around, then in a haze of flying dirt rode circles around Beth, causing her to become dizzy. His horrible screeching rang in her ears. As he rode by the next time he leaned to the side of his horse and with one quick stroke of his knife, he cut a lock from her hair. As quickly as he had appeared, White Horse rode away.

Coughing and eyes watering, Beth tried to fan the dust away from her face. Was White Horse finished with his show? Her eyes narrowed, trying to see if he was waiting to make another charge. He was nowhere in sight. Beth expelled the pent-up air from her lungs. Cole's words rang in her ears. *Never let an Indian see that you are afraid.*

With shaking hands Beth waved her paper in the air to get rid of the dust that had settled on it. With what she hoped was a show of nonchalance, she continued her sketching. She was drawing White Horse as he had appeared to her.

Beth continued drawing until it was too dark to see. The moment she was inside the tepee she collapsed onto the floor. She was shaking so badly that her teeth were chattering. Never again would she scoff at fear.

Beth looked at the low fire, her gaze fastening on the red embers. Suddenly she felt very alone. Too easily she had forgotten just how precarious their situation was. How could she have so quickly forgotten the torture of the cavalrymen?

Beth was disappointed when she awoke the following morning and found Cole gone. She eagerly ate the food he had left on one of the cooking stones. She had been asleep when he had returned last night, but she vaguely remembered him pulling her into his arms. Finally she had felt safe, but she had been too tired to tell him so.

Chapter Twelve

Beth watched the children scatter toward their tepees, the pictures she had given them clutched firmly in their small hands. Their round black eyes had almost doubled in size when they had watched their faces come alive on her paper. Some had even become frightened.

Beth scanned the busy camp, hoping to see Cole. It was noon and he still hadn't returned. Had White Horse killed him? No. She couldn't allow herself to believe that. She squeezed her eyes shut. This time fear was not going to be her conqueror. "Use your head," she muttered to herself.

Beth welcomed the warm breeze that fanned her cheeks. The weather here seemed inconsistent. The days were especially hot and the nights cool.

Beth stood. With nothing to do, this would be an ideal time to wash clothes. She was about to go gather her laundry, but hesitated. Overcome by an instant warmth, she knew Cole had to be near. She was even convinced she could feel their hearts beating as one. Automatically she turned to the left. With the sun in her eyes, the figure her gaze settled upon was still nothing more than a dark shadow. But it didn't matter. She would have recognized that easy stride anywhere. There was also a way he carried himself. Tall and erect.

As Cole drew nearer, joy bubbled within Beth. How could she have been too tired to make love last night when that was nearly all she could think about? Or had Cole lacked interest? It suddenly occurred to her that she was taking a lot for granted. They had made love. That was all. No commitments, nothing. She had gone into the situation with her eyes open. Making more of it would only end up hurting her.

Seeing Beth waiting struck an unfamiliar chord of sadness within Cole. It was as if he had missed something in his life. He thrust the thought aside. After little sleep last night, he wasn't in the best of moods. He'd kept his hands off the voluptuous woman in a foolhardy attempt to convince himself he was at least trying to follow Grant's order. This morning he had decided it hadn't been worth the discomfort. Beth knew that when they left camp their romantic episodes would end, so he needn't concern himself with the possibility of it continuing. But there was another reason behind his decision not to act the celibate. While making love, she had forgotten her fear. She had become calmer and was already starting to recoup that fiery disposition. If she did nothing but sit around, she would dwell on the horrors she had seen and become withdrawn. Should that happen, their situation would turn more precarious than it already was. He couldn't afford that.

Cole stopped in front of her, and Beth was surprised when his mouth covered hers hungrily. His lips created heady sensations, and she wanted more. Slowly his hands moved downward, skimming either side of her body, and she was beginning to wonder if he planned to bed her right there. Her concerns ceased when he raised her in his arms and carried her into the tepee. Heaven could never be as wonderful as this. When he placed her on the fur robe and began unbuttoning her blouse, she knew she was hopelessly in love.

Cole tucked his shirttail into his trousers. The drums had started beating again and the scalp dance had resumed.

"Are you sure you don't want to go?" he asked Beth.

Beth smiled weakly. "I'd rather not, unless you think it might cause a problem." Though there was nothing to indicate it, Beth could feel Cole withdrawing from her again. He had done the same thing yesterday, but at the time she thought she had imagined it. "Why do you go? To celebrate with them?"

"It serves as a reminder that they have until tomorrow to set us free." He buckled his belt. "Besides, I told them you wouldn't participate in anything until they had delivered their verdict." He stepped to the tepee opening. "I'll bring back some food."

"Cole, there is something I haven't told you."

Cole waited for her to continue.

"White Horse charged at me, and—"

"I know." Cole shoved his hat on. "I'm sorry I wasn't here when it happened."

"You know?"

"He rode straight to Say-tine-day, who was talking with the elders. White Horse waved your lock of hair and bragged of his bravery at testing a god. He stated quite proudly that you were unable to inflict harm on him. The shaman was especially pleased to hear the news. It could be he is jealous and doesn't like a white woman usurping his position in the tribe. Of course, if you are a real god, that's an entirely different matter."

Beth sat up on her knees. "How did you know all this?"

"I was sitting with the others when White Horse rode up." Cole smiled without humor. "At the time, the elders were discussing the buffalo you had provided. Braves have already been sent to locate the herd."

"Will White Horse's declaration have any effect on the council's decision?"

"I don't know." He left the tepee.

Beth brushed her hair from her face. She should have tried to defend herself when White Horse charged at her. But how?

She stared at the opening of the tepee. Cole had closed the flap. She already wanted to feel him beside her again, holding her as if she belonged to only him. It was strange how she could be so happy and so sad at the same time. When making love, Cole was wild, gentle, attentive, demanding, but never withdrawn. Yet, even after sharing each other's bodies all afternoon, he had just acted as if nothing had taken place. There was no goodbye kiss, no touching, no words of endearment, no emotion, no nothing.

Beth lay back down on her side. Her body was enveloped in tides of weariness. How did Cole manage to remain on his feet with so little sleep? She ran her hand across the spot where he had lain only minutes ago. She had almost thought it would still be warm, but it wasn't. Just thinking about their afternoon together caused her nipples to become taut. He had told her they made a good pair because they shared an insatiable lust for life. She closed her eyes. A picture of White Horse's furious face flashed across her mind, causing her to clench her teeth. Was she living in a fool's paradise? Would White Horse win his demand that she belong to him?

* * *

After a lengthy nap Beth felt as if she could conquer the entire Kiowa tribe and Cole Wagner, as well. She gathered the laundry and her soap. The sun was already dropping behind the horizon and she didn't have much time. She would go to the cove she'd found and scrub her two dirty shirts.

Fingers of fog had already started covering the ground as Beth hurried down the path. A child was crying in one of the tepees and the smell of cooking food caused her stomach to grumble. Hopefully Cole would soon return with food.

Beth hadn't gone more than twenty feet when White Horse rode forward, blocking her way. He raised his fist in the air, then pounded his chest. Beth had no idea what the bear of a man was babbling—nor did she care. The smug look on his face released such a flood of fury that all caution was tossed to the wind. She raised her fist and shook it at him.

"You bastard!" Beth yelled. "It's because of you that all this has happened! I wish I could do to you what you did to those cavalrymen!"

White Horse hit his chest again and bellowed more words.

Beth threw down the soap and clothes she was holding. Her eyes took on the glassiness of a madwoman. As if possessed by the depths of insanity, she waved her arms in a wild manner, while making faces and shouting guttural nothings. She leapt at him, raking her nails down his leg and drawing blood.

White Horse shrieked his anger, causing his already nervous mount to dance about. Beth took the opportunity to again charge forward. This time she delivered a bite to his ankle. A swift kick sent her flying through the air.

She sat up and hissed at him for several seconds. Then she laughed hysterically. The more crazily she laughed the more terrified White Horse became.

White Horse delivered another hard kick, but this time it was to his horse's flanks. Panicked, he galloped away from the madwoman as quickly as possible.

As soon as White Horse was out of sight, Beth's laughing ceased. Hearing giggles, she turned. Several children, a woman and a brave were standing just outside their tepee, apparently having witnessed what had happened.

Beth stood, rubbed her sore bottom, then proceeded to pick up her clothes. Slowly her lips spread into a delighted smile. She felt whole again. She hadn't liked sneaking about, fearful of what could happen at any minute. Quite proud of herself, she continued along the trail.

Cole arrived at the tent with venison, yams and onions for Beth's meal. He was surprised to find the tepee empty. She must have gone to fill the water canteens. He glanced around the small area, taking in the saddles, bedrolls and gear. Of course, the rifles and revolvers were nowhere in sight. Those were now the property of White Horse.

Spying some papers peeking out of Beth's saddlebags, Cole went over and pulled them out. The low fire in the center allowed enough light to see by. As he flipped from one page to the next, he was quite taken with the artistry. Never having seen Beth's work before, he'd had no idea she was so talented. They were perfect depictions of people in camp. She had even drawn a rough sketch of Saytine-day. When Cole saw the drawing of White Horse, he knew she had done it after the brave had charged at her. He studied the last picture, a portrait of the lady's guide. Cole didn't consider it a good likeness. He looked too nice. She hadn't captured the cold-bloodedness of a man who had killed or committed every trickery known to man to get what he wanted—or whom he wanted. He went back to the saddlebags to see if there were any more drawings. He found two. Both were composites—miniature drawings of him in different positions. He released a heavy sigh. Beth was in love with him. He could see it in her drawings.

He squatted and returned the pictures back to where he'd gotten them. He should never have let Beth seduce him. They could have pretended they were mated. He stood. Who the hell was he trying to fool? No woman, man or beast had ever persuaded him to do anything he didn't want to. He pulled off his hat and raked his hair back with his fingers. Beth was only a pawn being used to checkmate a king. Dammit, if she wasn't so curious, high-spirited and stubborn, his search for Quin Turner wouldn't have put her in harm's way. She could have returned to Boston and written her book—until she decided to embark on some new adventure. And if she wasn't so beautiful and willing, her heart would have stayed intact.

Cole went back outside, wondering what was taking Beth so long. He started walking down the trail. Oddly, it was those same qualities he was just complaining about, plus her courage, that drew his admiration. Something he gave to very few women—or men. He didn't want to see Beth get hurt, but there was nothing he could do about it now. He'd made sure she understood there would be no future for them. If he left her alone, perhaps the hurt would soften.

The fog lay like a thick blanket over the river and pebbled beach. Cole could hardly see a thing.

''Beth,'' he called.

There was no reply. Everything in Cole turned to hard, cold steel.

"Beth," he called again.

He heard nothing, and his thoughts jumped directly to White Horse. Had he gone against the council's decree and stolen Beth? Cole was prepared to go back and tear down every tepee if that's what it took to find the woman. But the fog cleared momentarily, allowing him a glimpse of wet clothing stacked on the bank. Looking more closely, he recognized his shirt mingled with Beth's. He stood very still, looking out across the water. Then he heard the voice, faint at first until he centered his senses in that direction. Someone was humming. Was it Beth? There was a pond a short distance away. The fog, water, trees and shrubs could have smothered the sound of his voice when he called her. Before he realized what he was doing, he had already begun to strip.

The humming was all Cole had to guide him through the water. By the time he realized that it was indeed Beth's voice he was hearing, he had an erection that would have put a tree trunk to shame.

Beth finished rinsing the soap off her body. After scrubbing the shirts, she had decided she had enough time for a quick bath. She wanted to smell clean when Cole returned to the tent. But time was passing quickly, and she'd have to hurry.

"When I didn't find you in the tepee, I came looking for you."

The words didn't startle Beth. She immediately recognized Cole's deep voice drifting across the water. "As you can see, I'm fine. I didn't mean to take so long," she apologized.

Cole's emotions were a combination of anger, happiness and passion.

Beth didn't know what to think. His words had been clipped, and now he wasn't saying anything. "You can have a clean shirt after it dries." She didn't know what else to say.

Cole pulled her roughly to him. "I'd rather have you."

His harsh, tempestuous kiss took Beth by surprise. He was angry about something, but she didn't care. For the moment he was all hers.

Cole could never remember wanting any woman the way he wanted Beth. His hands memorized every curve of her body and his mouth tasted her sweet flesh. He raised her and had her circle his waist with her legs. As he slid himself inside her, the tight, moist pleasure caused him to shudder. He smiled when Beth placed her arms around his neck, then leaned back, inviting his mouth to caress her nipples. He had a feline mounted on him and he wasn't about to disappoint her.

Afterward they washed each other, and Cole was the first to head back to the bank. Standing beneath an umbrella of a tree, he donned his trousers. He smiled when a pair of soft arms wrapped around him from behind. Though Beth didn't say a word, he could feel her small, delicate hands gliding down his chest and the firm breasts pressed against his naked back. He was quite sure that he and Beth weren't going to make it back to the tepee anytime soon if she kept this up.

"I make you happy? You want me?"

The unfamiliar voice had the effect on him of falling into an icy lake. He grabbed the hands before they could continue their downward path, then shoved them aside. Had White Horse had a hand in this? He would probably never know. He had just turned to confront the squaw

when Beth came into view. Even in the dim light he could
see her nostrils flare and her eyes flash with anger.

"Get away from him!" Beth shouted. She looked at
Cole. "Did you ask her to join you?"

Cole was about to say no when he heard wood crack-
ing. A large dead limb fell from overhead, just missing all
three of them. The Indian girl screamed and quickly disappeared into the stand of trees.

"Believe me, my dear, you are more than enough for
any man," Cole said, thoroughly amused at Beth's up-
roar. He looked at the dead limb, then howled with
laughter.

Realizing the ridiculousness of the situation, Beth
joined in the hilarity.

Chapter Thirteen

"Cole, wake up!" Beth called.

He rolled onto his back and opened his eyes.

"Come out here. I want you to see something."

He rose to his feet and stretched. "What is it?"

When Cole stepped outside he was as astounded as Beth had been. Besides their provisions having been returned, there were woven baskets in all shapes, clothes, food, blankets, pelts, jewelry, cherished buffalo cloaks and fetishes of every description.

Beth leaned over and picked up something white. It was a hide, but so soft it seemed to caress her fingers. She held it high for a better look. It was a dress!

"Oh, Cole. I must give this back to whoever left it. It's too beautiful to—"

"Nothing can be returned, Beth. You would offend the givers."

Beth fingered the rows of adornments that went across the chest and back and down the sleeves.

"Those are elk teeth. Only two teeth can be obtained from one animal, so you can see how long it took to create that design. Then there is the time spent making the deerskin so soft. Whoever gave this to you thinks you are indeed a mighty god."

"But why are all these things here?"

"I'm guessing these are gifts to the daughter of Gadombitsouhi so she will bestow good fortune. After the episode with the branch last night, the squaw probably spread the word that you were punishing her for being near your man."

Beth threw her arms around his neck and kissed him soundly. "Then we've won?"

Cole looked down and smiled. "There's a damn good chance of it."

Beth's excitement grew when she spotted a delicately carved comb made from buffalo bone. "Cole, remember when you were telling me about the mounds of buffalo hides and bones?"

"Yes."

"What do the white men do with the bones?"

"They're sold for fertilizer or bone china."

"Oh." She pulled out a plain deerskin dress and held it in front of her to determine if it would fit. It was nothing more than a simple tunic but it was cleaner and looked a lot more comfortable than her tiresome britches and shirt.

"Now that we have provisions again, how about you fixing us something to eat?" Cole asked.

Beth nodded, but her joy was quickly fading. Today was the day of decision, and a show of fondness, warmth or even caring from Cole would have helped her nerves. And they had, after all, been asleep only a few hours. The rest of the night had been spent giving pleasure to each other. But there wasn't so much as a hint of affection in his eyes.

Out of spite, Beth considered telling Cole she couldn't cook. No, she was too hungry for that. "I'll fix coffee." She smiled. She'd be damned if she'd let him see her disappointment. "After we eat, I'll go change clothes and comb my hair. Cole, this is the third day. When will the council tell you of their decision?''

"I don't know. They'll send for me."

Beth was determined to shove thoughts of the Kiowa decree to the back of her head. After collecting the supplies she needed, she dumped coffee beans into the pot, covered them with water and placed the pot in the coals she'd stirred earlier. Corn cakes followed. She poured water into the skillet, then cut up chunks of dried meat and added them. A perfect start for gravy. She licked her lips in anticipation.

"Smile," Cole said softly.

Knowing he was aware of her concerns, Beth felt the word lighten her heart. She gave him a brilliant smile. Would there ever come a day when she would tire of seeing him? She didn't think so.

When their stomachs were satisfied, Cole left the tent and Beth proceeded to attend to her toilette. She eagerly stripped off her shirt and britches, then slipped the tunic over her head. It was amazingly comfortable, but it only came to her knees. She couldn't possibly allow herself to go unprotected around a group of male heathens. On the other hand, it didn't seem to bother the Indian women. She decided to leave it on, at least until her hair was groomed.

Beth sat on the tent floor and suddenly wondered how the native women kept men from looking up their skirt. Maybe that was why they sat with their legs crossed.

Finally comfortable, Beth raised the small mirror that had managed to survive in her saddlebags, and looked at herself. There were faint dark circles under her eyes, but she looked surprisingly good after all she'd been through. She set the mirror back down and picked up the comb.

The grooming proved to be a long, arduous task. By the time the snarls were gone, her hair was as puffed out as a lion's mane. She was about to plait it when she changed her mind. A full head of wild, curly hair was perfect for her current image. She would look like one of the witches from the fairy-tale books her nanny had read to her.

Beth let her hands fall to her lap. She and Cole might leave today, or tomorrow. The ramifications of that were shattering. Would they cease to make love, or would what they shared endure? Though she had been terribly frightened by the Indians, she was now grateful for the time she and Cole had had alone. Had they remained with the caravan, she would never have come to know him so well—his movements, his moods, his touch, yes, and even his protectiveness. Lady Fate hadn't dealt her a fair hand. Just when she thought she had her entire future planned, the elusive lady had delivered a tall, husky man.

Beth smiled sadly. She had never believed there was such a thing as love, yet here she was, completely smitten. So Lady Fate had stepped in again. She had allowed Beth to taste the nectar, but she couldn't have the fruit.

A few minutes later Beth went outside to show off her new image. She found Cole sitting at the side of the tepee, whittling on a small limb.

"How do I look?"

Pretending to give the question serious consideration, Cole took his time studying her bare feet, the calves of her legs, the long, shapely thighs that pressed against the hide, the tiny waist presently hidden by the looseness of her dress, and the full, unhampered breasts with pert nipples. He forced his eyes upward, to the graceful valley of her neck and, lastly, the lovely face framed by a full copper mane. Oh, yes. She looked just fine.

"Well?"

"Other than the color of your skin and hair and lack of moccasins, you look like the other squaws."

Beth stared at him in disbelief. "That...that's not much of a compliment."

"What did you want me to say?"

Beth sighed. "Cole, have you ever given a woman a compliment?"

"Oh, maybe one or two." He chuckled.

"Oh? And—" Beth covered her mouth with her hand.

Cole quickly stood. "What's the matter?"

Beth watched the approaching brave, and her hand slid to her throat. "I believe you are about to be summoned to the council."

Time crawled by. It was no longer possible to sit calmly and appear to be some god. Beth paced, worried and fantasized all kinds of terrible things happening. One thing was certain. If they gave her to White Horse, she would kill herself. What if the Kiowa thought a witch should be burned at the stake? That was what had happened at Salem. She wrung her hands, went in and out of the tepee at least a dozen times, sat, stood and paced some more.

Then Beth saw Cole. He had that stoic look again, and she had no idea as to the outcome of the council's verdict. Her feet rooted to the ground, she waited for him to join her.

"Well?" Beth asked as soon as he was within hearing distance.

"Tomorrow morning we will head back up towards Wichita."

Beth ran the short distance to Cole, threw her arms around his neck and planted kisses all over his face.

Cole grinned broadly as he gently pulled Beth free. "The falling limb was the deciding factor." His eyes raked boldly over her. "Did I forget to mention that your dress is most becoming?" he teased.

A peal of laughter escaped Beth's full lips. But as suddenly as she had laughed, she became serious again. "Why can't we leave now?"

Cole placed his arm around her waist and led her into the tepee. "I know you want to get away as soon as possible, but I think it would be better if we left tomorrow."

"The leaders might change their minds."

"No. I guarantee that won't happen. Once a decision is made, it stands. If we leave now, we wouldn't get far. However, if we wait until morning, we'll have the rest of the day to pack supplies, we'll have a good night's rest and a full day of travel."

"And there is no longer any threat of me becoming White Horse's woman?" she asked, needing to put all the pieces together.

"He still claimed that you belonged to him by right of capture. But White Horse has lost face with the braves. Did you and he have another confrontation?"

Beth told him how she had acted like an insane woman, scratching and biting him.

Cole chuckled. "That explains a lot. He ran from you, which made him appear a coward. Also, he believes your fangs pumped venom in his blood, and that he would eventually die. He wanted to kill you for your coup, which he believed would make him well. The elders declared that he had simply delivered you to your people and that you were never his. The council also stated that we were to have a safe journey. Then they looked directly at White Horse. In essence, they were warning him to stay away from us."

"You won." She impatiently brushed away a tear of joy.

"We won," Cole corrected.

"I don't even want to think about what would have happened to me had it not been for you." She wanted to reach out and touch him. She wanted him to pull her into his arms. But when their eyes met, an unspoken understanding passed between them. All intimacies had ended.

"Thank you for saving my life," she said softly. She looked toward the gear stacked at the back of the tepee. "I guess we had better start to work. I'd like to take my gifts with me. Will we have room?"

Cole nodded. "I'll check the food supplies."

As she reached down to pick up her saddlebags Beth heard Cole leave the tepee. The distance that had already come between them made her want to cry. Once again they were just two people. One working for the other. She had thought it would be impossible for them to return to the relationship they'd had before coming here. She had been wrong. Cole would make sure it happened.

She thought she had come to know him over the past two weeks. She now suspected he had allowed only her to see that part of him that he wanted her to see.

Beth awoke and rubbed her eyes. She could tell by the cool air touching her arms that it was still early morning. Sleep hadn't come easily last night. Not with Cole beside her, and having to suffer the pangs of unfulfilled passion. She looked at Cole's broad back. Though she had ached unmercifully for him to ease her ardor, it hadn't happened—nor was it going to. She started to rise, then became very still. Why was it so quiet outside? The women should be tending to their chores by now. And what about the children? She glanced at the deerskin dress lying on the floor. Today she would wear the beautiful white tunic with elk teeth to celebrate their freedom.

Making sure she didn't waken Cole, Beth quickly slipped out of bed then pulled the dress over her head. When she stepped outside her eyes widened in disbelief. The Kiowa were gone! Her mare, Cole's buckskin and the packhorse were hobbled nearby, but other than that, there were no signs that the tribe had even been there. There was only grass, trees and mountains. She hurried forward to see if they had possibly moved to the far side of the hill.

Beth hadn't gone far when something caught her eye. Someone or something was approaching, the top of the hill revealing it only in segments. First she saw the tip of a spear. It grew longer. Then she could see something that looked like... The buffalo horns were as unmistakable as the face that came into view.

As the rest of White Horse's body was exposed, Beth was already running back toward the tepee. The thundering sound of a horse's hooves hitting the ground pounded in her ears. She had to warn Cole. But she couldn't outrun the paint. She screamed just as White Horse reached out and snatched her from the ground.

Cole had just pulled on his trousers. The bloodcurdling scream sent him running out of the tepee. In a flash of a second he assessed what was happening. White Horse had his arm wrapped around Beth's waist, and his horse was in a full gallop. Considering the direction they were headed, they would pass some twenty feet in front of him.

With calculated speed and timing, Cole closed the distance between them. He and the horse crossed paths at the same time. Cole grabbed the lead rope and jerked hard, sending the pony to its knees. White Horse and Beth flew over the top and hit the ground. The powerful brave immediately leapt to his feet, a knife clutched in his hand. He raised the sharp weapon and charged at Cole.

Beth shook her head, trying to clear the fuzziness caused from the hard jolt she'd suffered. Hearing grunts, she looked up. Cole and White Horse were locked in combat, their arm and leg muscles bulging as each tried to down the other. Her heart pounded fiercely against her ribs when she saw White Horse's knife glistening in the sunlight.

Beth looked away, unable to watch, then immediately turned back around. She couldn't bear not knowing what was happening. This was a fight to the death, and Cole had no weapon.

Feeling completely useless, Beth slowly stood. She wanted to help, but she was no match for either of the giants. She could only watch and pray.

The men pulled apart. Beth's throat constricted as White Horse slashed the sharp steel toward Cole. The brave was swift and agile and managed to draw blood twice on Cole's chest. Unchecked tears rolled down Beth's cheeks and she clutched her breast, feeling Cole's pain.

But to Beth's relief, Cole was also agile. The Kiowa wasn't able to put a quick end to the white man he'd come to hate.

Cole grabbed White Horse's wrist and raised it in the air, trying to dislodge the vicious weapon from the Indian's grasp. Their momentum carried them so close to Beth that she had to jump aside.

"Stop it!" Beth yelled. She felt so helpless. However, it wasn't likely either man heard her. Any thought of further protest died. Beth couldn't breathe. White Horse's arm was slowly descending. The point of the blade was headed directly toward Cole's chest. Beth screamed. She couldn't bear the thought of the man she loved being killed. But Cole suddenly shifted to the darker man's back and pulled the wrist in a downward thrust. She squeezed her eyes shut as the knife lodged in the warrior's gut.

A shot rang out, and Beth's eyes flew open. White Horse had apparently pulled the knife free. The bloody handle was grasped in one hand as he stood staring in disbelief at the bullet hole in his chest. He looked at something behind her before falling forward, dead. Beth twisted around to see what had drawn the warrior's attention. Say-tine-day had already turned his horse and was riding away, his rifle hanging at his side.

Beth ran to Cole. He had dropped to his knees and was gasping for breath after the desperate battle. Blood seemed to be smeared everywhere. She would gladly have given her breath to him. She wanted to hug him and make him well, but she didn't. The rules had been laid down and she no longer had any choice but to obey them. "Can you make it to the river?" She was almost afraid to touch him for fear that she would worsen his pain.

Cole nodded.

Beth cautiously placed her arm around Cole's waist to help him up. A useless motion considering he was at least twice her size.

"I'm not going to die, Beth," Cole grumbled. "Do you have a needle and thread?"

"Yes, in my... No, Cole! I can't do it!"

"You can. There's no one else. I assure you, darlin', I'm not looking forward to it, either."

When he had climbed to his feet she saw the gaping wound. She had to fight to keep from retching.

"Come on, Beth," Cole said harshly when he saw how her face had paled. "I thought you said you wouldn't let me down."

He had no idea how she was suffering at the thought of causing him more pain.

"Don't think of it as hurting me, Beth. Think of it as starting the healing process."

By the time Beth had the two deep cuts stitched, and Cole washed, she was feeling more than a little proud of herself. She had even given up a shirt, which had been ripped apart and used as bandages. With Cole's encouragement she'd managed to keep her hand steady, and the stitchery had been good enough for even the finest dress. How Cole could sit quietly and not even issue a groan was another matter.

"Thank you, Mrs. Alexander."

"You're quite welcome, Mr. Wagner. Are you going to be all right?" Beth helped him put on the clean shirt she'd fetched from his saddlebags.

"I'll be fine. How about you?"

Beth smiled warmly. "If I can survive this, I can survive anything."

"Then how about we get away from here?"

"But you can't ride like that," Beth protested.

"I'll manage."

"Cole, why did Santanta shoot White Horse?"

"He had given his word we could leave in peace."

Beth mounted the glossy black mare. It was time to leave. She didn't look back as they rode away. She had her memories. Never again would she view life as she had prior to coming here. It was far too precious to take for granted. Nor would she forget the Kiowa. She had seen them at their best and she had seen them at their worst.

"Where have *the people* gone?" Beth asked.

Cole lowered the brim of his hat to block the sun. "To get the buffalo Gadombitsouhi's daughter gave them."

"And then?"

"Some will go to the reservation, others will raid and *then* return. They will continue to fight a losing battle, but they will try to go in glory."

Beth hoped she could remember those exact words to write in her journal.

Chapter Fourteen

As Beth soaked in foamy hot water, she contemplated her future. Cole had led her to where the caravan waited. As Esther had told it last night, he'd instructed them to make camp on the west side of town. It had been a joyous occasion. When everyone rushed forward with happy greetings and a multitude of questions, she'd felt as if she had returned home.

For three and a half days she and Cole had ridden hard across the unending prairie. It hadn't been a sociable journey. The distance between them had become a chasm. After all they'd been through, she had expected him to at least be friendly. But he had returned to the reclusive man she'd hired in Independence. Even when she had offered to care for his wounds, he had refused.

Thinking about how they hadn't met a solitary soul on their trip to Wichita drew a soft chuckle from Beth. Even so, only once had loneliness nipped at her heels, and then all it had taken to rid herself of it was to look at Cole. Now she believed that somehow, in some way, that terrible feeling she'd lived with all her life was gone. However, because of Cole's attitude, she had decided to discontinue her tour. Having him out of sight would rid her of the desire she felt every time she looked at him.

But now that she'd had time to rest and think about it, quitting her tour of the West had no merit. Look what she had learned and seen already! And if she circled the globe she would never find a better guide than Cole to take her to the sights. No, she couldn't quit now. Once Cole was out of her life, she'd need something to keep her mind off him. Writing novels would come in very handy.

She raised an arm and blew at the bath bubbles. The death of the cavalrymen, the long ride with the Kiowa, the days of not knowing if she was to die or live had all taken its toll, but at the same time it had been the most exhilarating experience of her life. Of course, she could feel that way now that she was safe again.

She released a heavy sigh. Learning to control her emotions could prove to be the hardest thing she had tackled so far.

"Do you plan to remain there all day?"

Beth glanced up at Esther. "What a tempting thought."

As soon as Beth stepped from the tub, Esther wrapped a large bath sheet around her.

"After what you've been through, I would have thought you would want to sleep all day. At least you're now back where I can look after you," Esther fussed.

"Why didn't you show that concern when you left me and headed for Wichita?"

Esther proceeded to rub Beth dry. "Howard was with you, so I assumed the outlaw was telling the truth."

"His name is Cole."

"I still find it hard to believe that Howard would stay at some farm in the middle of nowhere. Are you certain he wasn't a bit addled?"

"I'm sure." Beth slipped into the red silk caftan, then sat in front of her dressing table.

Esther raised the brush to Beth's hair and started counting the hundred strokes necessary to keep a woman's hair shiny.

"I understand Howard's reasoning," Beth said, "but I'm still confused as to why Doolan would even consider leaving, let alone actually do it. I've known him since he was a boy. Perhaps I should send one of the men to fetch him. Surely I can talk him into returning."

"I don't think that would be wise. He told Decker he didn't think it right that he should be expected to do without manly needs."

Beth spun around on the chair. "Doolan?"

"He's not a little boy anymore, Bethany." Esther pushed her back around so she could continue her brushing.

Where had the years gone? Beth wondered. She was reminded of Howard saying it was time he had a life of his own also. Would Esther also eventually want to leave? "I suppose you're right. And didn't you say Molly Dee is also gone?"

"I have no idea who put the bee in that one's bonnet, but after we left you on the trail she started spouting words about marriage and cattle barons. Then as soon as we arrived in Wichita she insisted on getting a room in town. Gracious sakes, if she didn't up and marry some rancher a week later."

"Huh. If we don't watch out the others will soon be leaving to find women."

"Forty-four, forty-five," Esther counted. "I haven't been idle while we waited. I've hired others to take Doolan's and Molly Dee's places."

"I thought I had everything carefully arranged, and I hadn't an inkling as to the enormity of what I intended to accomplish."

Esther wondered at the sadness in Bethany's voice. Did it have to do with the Indians, Cole, or both? She had also noticed a maturity about Bethany that she had never seen before. Esther wanted to ask about it, but if she did, Bethany would clamp her mouth shut. There was no choice but to wait and hope Bethany offered the information freely.

"Ninety-nine, one hundred. It's done." Esther set the brush down on the dressing table and went to the chifforobe. "You're going to feel like a new woman now that you can wear proper clothes again. Do you have a preference in color?"

"No, just pick the frilliest one of the lot." Beth turned on the stool and looked at her companion. "On our way here I had plenty of time to think. Oh, Esther, only minutes ago I was thinking that there are still so many things I want to see and do."

"What things?" Esther pulled out a white affair with yards and yards of lace.

"I want to see Chinese laundries, gold or silver mining, draw on a gunslinger and—" Beth laughed "—see some of the seamier side."

"Surely you don't mean what I think you mean?" Esther asked suspiciously.

"I haven't been in a saloon and watched people gamble, and I haven't seen ladies of ill repute or the inside of a prostitution house."

"Bethany Alexander! Ladies do not speak to 'soiled doves.' You've gone too far this time. Besides, I would think you had read enough about it in those Western books."

Beth didn't want to admit she hadn't read that many of the novels. "It's not the same as actually seeing everything with your own eyes. And you needn't get upset about tarnished women. They don't disappear just because they aren't spoken of. It's an age-old profession."

"Nor does it mean you have to be around such."

Beth pulled on the pantalets the older woman handed her.

Esther laid the dress across the bed, then tied the pantalet strings around Beth's waist. "You've seen too much already."

"As soon as I've finished dressing, I want you to fetch Cole. I need to know what our next destination is to be."

"He's gone."

Beth's heart skipped a beat. "What do you mean, he's gone?"

"He rode to town after Doc examined his cuts. I wouldn't be surprised if he's up to finding one of those women you were just talking about. A man like that would have strong needs, and it has been some time since he's enjoyed carnal pleasures—hasn't it?"

Beth refused to be baited. She grabbed the chemise Esther handed her.

Esther pursed her lips. "I think it is time to return to Boston."

"No. I haven't accomplished what I came for." Beth wanted to say she was in love and she wanted Cole to be near her for as long as possible. But her love was too new and too fragile to discuss at this time. "I think I'll also ride to town. A new bonnet always tends to brighten the day. But before I leave, gather the others for a meeting. Oh, and I won't be wearing that dress you pulled out."

"While you're in town, why don't you purchase me a bottle of elixir?"

Thirty minutes later Beth stood outside her tent, talking to her menagerie of travelers. She quickly informed them that Cole was well enough now to travel, and the caravan would be moving on in two days. Because of that, she wanted everything examined and repaired as was necessary.

The men scattered to perform their duties. They were all anxious to be on the move again.

No one paid any attention to the short, stocky gentleman's departure from the poorly lit saloon—except the tall man who had been sitting with him. Cole poured himself another shot of whiskey and downed it. Another drink followed. He wanted to get drunk, but knew he wouldn't. Unfortunately, Cox had had no new information to give him. Cole was still on his own when it came to locating Tex Martin, and finally Quin Turner. Cole told Cox to let Grant know that when it came to keeping his britches up and hands to himself, there were no guarantees. Cox had given him a quizzical look, but Cole had no intention of explaining the message.

The rickety chair's legs scraped the floor as Cole shoved it back and stood. After paying for the bottle of whiskey, he left the saloon. Feeling the need to stretch his legs, he strolled down the wooden sidewalk. He had always liked Wichita. It was a much quieter town now that the cattle drives had stopped.

Beth had just stepped out of the drugstore with Esther's bottle of elixir when she heard Cole's name being called. She glanced across the street. A charming brunette hurried to where Cole Wagner stood waiting. He had to catch her when she jumped up and threw her arms around his neck. Thinking about the cuts on Cole's stomach made Beth flinch. Seeing him with another woman in his arms made her jealousy flare. She was furious at the blatant way the woman acted, but what bothered her the most was Cole's broad smile. It hurt to know he wanted nothing to do with her yet he could openly flirt with other women. Perhaps she was jumping to conclusions. The woman's husband and Cole might be friends. The two parted, and the brunette returned to the millinery shop.

Beth watched Cole move on. He looked good even from the back. Her gaze traveled up his long legs, narrow hips....

Cole had passed only a couple of other shops when another woman came out of the dry goods store, just as excited as the female preceding her. This time it was an attractive blonde. But it didn't just stop there. He had hardly left the blonde when a brassy-headed woman came rushing out of the saloon. Beth felt like a volcano ready to erupt. The hussy could have at least finished dressing!

Suspicion and curiosity eating at her, Beth crossed the busy street, carefully avoiding the ruts.

A tiny bell attached to the door jingled when Beth entered the millinery shop, which was called Patricia's. It was a small place, but the hats on display were rather attractive. The brunette she'd seen with Cole stepped from behind drawn curtains in the back.

"Good morning. Isn't it a marvelous day?"

Beth smiled. "Yes, and perfect for a new chapeau."

"That's a most attractive one you are wearing."

"I bought it in Paris." Beth picked up a wide-brimmed affair that had satin flowers adorning the crown.

"Would you care to try it on?"

"I believe I would." Beth sat on a small chair positioned in front of a mirror and removed the French creation she was wearing. "Are you the owner of this store? I noticed your store when you were talking to your husband a few minutes ago," she remarked.

"I'm not married." The milliner placed her creation on Beth's head at just the right angle, then inserted a long hat pin.

"Your fiancé?" Beth hedged.

The attractive brunette smiled. "I doubt that any woman could get Cole Wagner to the altar."

Beth studied her image in the mirror. The straw affair looked awful on. "It's lovely," she lied. "Maybe he's too shy."

"Shy?" The milliner laughed. "There isn't a shy bone in the man. Cole is very fond of women, all kinds of women. Did you want to try on one of the other hats?"

A few minutes later she left the small shop. So Cole was a notorious womanizer. Yet she had had to force him to make love to her. Apparently he didn't think she was good enough for him. However, with no other choices, he took what was available.

Beth was in a total rage as she rode back to camp. Never had she felt so used and humiliated. She had thrown herself at Cole, and all the time he had considered her unworthy. The least he could have done was to express his feelings instead of letting her continue her attempts at seduction! He probably found it amusing. The bastard!

By the time Beth reached camp, her wrath from hurt pride was beyond control. She stopped her horse in front of Decker and allowed him to lift her down, then glanced over at the tree to make sure Cole had returned. This was a matter she wanted to handle herself.

Beth went to her tent.

When she came back out, her gun belt was strapped on. She marched toward where Cole had put his bedroll. As always, it was well away from the others. He was standing with his back turned to her.

"Outlaw!" Beth yelled. "Draw!"

Cole spun around, his hand moving toward his holster. Beth had already drawn when his fumbled attempt to yank his .45 free ended with it falling harmlessly to the ground.

Beth sneered. She was so angry that everything appeared blurred. She pulled the trigger.

Fear and regret converged on Beth when she realized the enormity of what she had done. The bullet had hit Cole in the arm. She hadn't meant to shoot him—she had only wanted to scare him. His obvious cold fury, tight jaw muscles and damning black eyes caused her to back away. Her hand was shaking so badly she couldn't return her gun to the holster.

"You needn't concern yourself with me forcing myself on you!" she stated, trying to defend her actions. "You're not good enough for me. And to make our previous agreement final, you are fired. As soon as Doc dresses your wound, I want you out of here."

She spun on her heel and walked away. Not until she had collapsed on the lounge in her tent did she permit the tears. Even Kenneth's mistreatment when they were married hadn't driven her to such drastic measures.

Having heard the gunshot, everyone had come running. They knew Beth had fired because they had seen her go into her tent still holding the gun. Though no one asked, each one's curiosity was boiling over.

Doc Washington ripped the shirtsleeve to look at the wound. Cole clenched his teeth. When he left this caravan he'd be lucky if there was any part of him left. Certainly not if Beth had a hand in it.

"It only nicked his arm," Tucker announced to the others, "but the bullet took a good chunk of flesh with it. He's going to be mighty sore for a while. Lizzy," he called

to his wife, "bring me my bag. And Decker, fetch some
whiskey and a chair for Mr. Wagner to sit on."

"I'll stand."

"Get the chair, Decker," Doc repeated.

Cole was having a hell of a time trying to contain his
temper. He didn't take kindly to being shot by any man,
and damn well not by a crazy woman! He knew exactly
what this was all about. When riding out of town, he'd
seen Beth talking to Patricia. At the time he'd doubted
that he had become the topic of conversation. His arm
was proof that he had been wrong. Because of Beth's
temper, he was now being forced to figure a way out of
this mess.

Did anything ever run smoothly when Bethany Alexander was involved? Having recognized her voice, he'd
deliberately let his gun fall to the ground to avoid a confrontation. Well, he'd paid for it. He had been a damn
fool. How many times had he seen an agent's destruction
simply because he had let his emotions take over? Yet that
was exactly what he had just done. He had chosen not to
shoot the gun from Beth's hand because he knew it would
hurt her. He'd paid for that, too.

He looked toward the tent. It had taken every ounce of
willpower he possessed to keep from going after her and
giving her a thrashing she would never forget. The only
thing that had stopped him was that he couldn't afford to
be kicked off the job. It would ruin everything. And, too,
he wasn't going to have to put up with her antics much
longer. In two days they would be headed for Dodge City.

He sat in the chair provided by Decker and watched
Tucker open the black bag his wife had delivered. How he
hated those instruments resting inside. More than one
doctor had used them on him at different times.

Tucker took a knife to cut away the rest of Cole's sleeve.

Cole wished to hell he could have overheard the conversation between Patricia and Beth. They couldn't have spoken for long, because Beth had ridden into camp just after him. There was no doubt that Beth hadn't intended to shoot him. He had seen her hands shaking and the horror in her eyes. Nevertheless, it was time she learned a gun was meant to kill. She had looked so ridiculous standing there with that hat on, wearing a fine peach-colored town suit, and drawing on him. He'd liked her much better in her squaw outfit.

The doctor poured whiskey over the wound, causing Cole to grit his teeth. It hurt more than the confounded bullet had. While Tucker bandaged his arm, Cole wrestled with how he was going to get Beth to keep him on. After she'd tried shooting him, it galled like hell to know he was going to have to grovel. He had to keep his temper in check. He had a job to do, and getting fired would throw everything into turmoil. He released a grunt. This was the first time he'd gotten in trouble because he *didn't* touch a woman.

"How could you have cold-bloodedly shot a man?" Esther chastised. Her hands rested firmly on her plump waist. "He had dropped his weapon and couldn't defend himself!"

"It was an accident, but he deserves every pain he's feeling," Beth responded.

"What do you mean, it was an accident?" Esther went over and picked up the hat that had been carelessly tossed on the floor. In front of Bethany was the gun belt she'd also discarded.

"I told you I hadn't mastered the aiming part. The bullet was meant to miss his shoulder and put some fear in him."

Esther paused and stared at her ward. "It could as well have been his head!"

"But it wasn't!"

"If you can't shoot what you aim for, you have no business carrying a weapon!"

"I can shoot as well as anyone, and you know it. It's the drawing and shooting I haven't mastered yet."

"Where is my elixir?"

Beth swung her feet over the side of the lounge and sat up. She must have left the confounded elixir at the millinery shop. "I forgot to get it," she lied. "Is Cole all right?"

"He won't be able to use his arm for a while, but other than that he's fine. You went too far this time. You were wrong to do what you did."

"It was wrong for him to make a fool of me."

"And, pray tell, how did he do that?"

"It doesn't matter." Beth began unbuttoning the waist-length jacket of her suit. "Just knowing he did should suffice."

Esther looked keenly at her ward. "Bethany, are you pregnant?"

Beth laughed bitterly. "No." She walked to one of the sea chests and dug out some money from beneath her clothes. After carefully counting out what she owed Cole, she handed the agreed amount to Esther. "Here is what he's earned. Give it to him so he'll have no reason to show his face around us again."

"Why don't you take care of it yourself?"

Both women turned and saw Cole standing inside the tent.

"How long have you been there?" Beth questioned. Had he seen her take the money from the chest? She snatched the money from Esther's hands and crossed to where Cole stood. "Here is what I owe you."

Cole took the money. "Much obliged. Now that that has been taken care of, would you mind telling me why I'm being dismissed?"

Beth remembered the way he'd smiled at the other women. An infectious smile that he certainly had never used on her.

"I've done everything you've required of me...and more."

"Esther, leave us alone."

"But—"

"Make sure there are guards outside."

Esther hesitated.

"That won't be necessary." Cole adjusted his arm in the sling the Doc had made for him. "You should know I don't make a habit of harming women."

"You heard me, Esther, leave."

Esther gathered up the hem of her skirt and hurried away.

Cole chuckled. "You mean after all we've been through together, you don't trust me."

Beth's heart fluttered. It hurt to be so close and unable to touch him. "I trust you to protect me. I trust you to lead the caravan. I trust you to show me the real West. I don't trust you when it comes to women, and I think you are a very practiced liar." She looked down at the rest of the money she was still holding. "And I don't trust you not to rob me. Isn't that what you're wanted for?" She shoved the money into her pocket.

Needing to sit, Cole made himself comfortable on a chair. "My dear Bethany, I rob banks, not widows' purse money. Had I intended to rob you, I would have done so a long time ago. You would never have seen me again.

Anyone with half a brain would know you're traveling with money. How else could you continually purchase needed provisions?"

Beth snapped her mouth shut.

"By keeping me around, you'll know the secret is safe."

"Is that a threat?"

"It's simply a fact." Cole tipped his wide-brimmed hat to the back of his head. He was still furious at what she'd pulled. Her eyes were red and puffy, which meant she'd been crying.

"I want you to leave."

"Have you forgotten the reason for this trip?"

"I haven't forgotten." Though he didn't show it, she knew Cole was still angry at having been shot. She didn't blame him. "A man isn't supposed to be seated until a woman seats herself first."

"I'm injured. Then you're giving up becoming a novelist?"

"No, I intend to hire someone else to take us to Dodge City."

Cole leaned forward. "What is all this really about, Beth? I saw you in town talking to Patricia. It that what brought all this on?"

"No. Of course not."

"You're lying. I've never known you to back away from the truth."

Beth's back stiffened. How could she admit that she hated him for thinking she wasn't good enough for him, and using her when there was no other woman to satisfy his needs? His eyes locked with hers, and she could feel the flame throughout her body.

"I've never known a woman who affected me the way you do, Beth," Cole said softly. "It hasn't been easy for me to keep my distance. But I can never give my heart to any woman, and it's best that what happened ended there. I wanted to be sure you didn't fall in love with me.''

She wanted so badly to believe him. "Me? That's ridiculous. We did what we had to to survive. Nothing more.''

"Exactly.'' Cole leaned back in the chair. His arm was hurting like hell. "Then why were you so angry at me? You know I can take you to Dodge City. Why am I fired?''

Beth was suddenly tongue-tied. How was she going to get out of this without admitting her hurt pride and jealousy? "It's a bit difficult.... I ... ah ... Okay, fine. You still have the responsibility of getting us to Dodge City.''

Cole glanced around the Victorian-style room. Beth hadn't had the practice he'd had when it came to hiding the truth. "You're unlike any woman I've ever met.'' He looked down at the floor for effect. "In years to come I'll still remember you.'' He stood, ready to leave.

Beth shrugged in mock resignation. "Did you bed me only because I forced the issue, or possibly just to convince the Kiowa that we were lovers?''

The corners of Cole's lips slowly curled upward. "Not for a minute. But it gave me one hell of an excuse.'' He left and headed for his bedroll. He was tired. At least he had managed to talk Beth into letting him stay on.

Beth wanted to rush to the opening. She knew she should try to apologize for what she had done, but she couldn't move. Maybe what Cole had told her was true, maybe it wasn't. Maybe her hurt pride had been the result of an overactive imagination. In turn she had shot at a man and embarrassed herself in front of the others. But her anger, worry and embarrassment were of no significance now. Cole's visit had made one thing very clear. They had no future. It was time to overcome the hurt, hide her love and get on with her life.

Chapter Fifteen

Though Tucker Washington had assured her that Cole's wounds were healing nicely and he could ride, Beth had insisted Cole be given a full week to heal. But in only three days she had become antsy. She knew she should spend her time reading Bret Harte's story, *The Outcasts of Poker Flat*. After all, she had brought it with her to gain more knowledge of life in the West, and so far she hadn't even opened the front cover. But then it occurred to her that this was a perfect opportunity to practice her draw-and-shooting accuracy.

Beth continued to have problems. She had seen Cole watching her on more than one occasion, but he kept his distance. To Beth's surprise, it was the blacksmith, George Higgins, who stepped forward with advice. Beth was quite pleased to discover he was accurate when he pulled a gun, though not nearly as fast a draw as she. After he showed her how to position the revolver at her hip, her aim immediately improved. By the end of the week she seldom missed her target.

While Beth was enjoying the fruits of her labor, Cole was brooding. Though he told himself he should be grateful to George for keeping her busy, the thought didn't ring true. Cole resented the time the blacksmith and

Beth spent together, and he sure as hell didn't like the way the other man tended to wrap his arms around Beth's shoulders or waist when he was supposedly giving advice on shooting. In fact, Cole didn't like George at all! For the last week the blacksmith's temper and rude remarks had been directed at everyone except Beth. Cole was beginning to suspect he had finally identified the Turner gang member.

The night before they were due to pull out, Cole and the others sat at the long table enjoying their supper. When they were well into the meal and George still hadn't joined them, Cole wanted to know why.

"He and Bethany are eating in her tent," Lizzy answered. "There is something about that man that—"

"Now, now, Lizzy," her husband interrupted, "you'd be wise to keep your thoughts to yourself. You know nothing about George."

"Tucker Washington! You said yourself—"

"It doesn't matter what I said." He swallowed a mouthful of food. "How are you feeling, Cole? You think you're going to be up to traveling tomorrow?"

"I'll be fine, Doc." Cole's ravenous appetite had vanished. Was Beth entertaining George in her diaphanous bloomers and veils? And would she try to seduce him? George wouldn't have a qualm about accepting, which made Cole all the more aggravated.

For the next half hour Cole picked at his food, half listening to others discuss Molly Dee's marriage and Doolan's departure. Though it was tempting, he was determined not to haul George out of Beth's tent. And why was he getting himself all worked up? Beth was a grown woman and—Esther was with her.

"Why do you think Howard stayed at that farm?" Wilber asked.

Cole's lips spread in a deceptive smile as he muttered something about the gentleman finding the right woman.

When Esther joined them at the table, Cole's gut twisted. George and Beth had been left alone! Moreover, Esther gave no indication of returning.

"Has Bethany told you what she wants to do in Dodge City?" Esther asked Cole as she filled her plate with food.

"Among other things, she has aspirations of drawing against a real gunfighter."

"She'll get herself killed," Lizzy protested worriedly.

"Why would she want to do such a thing?" Decker asked.

"Maybe she'll change her mind by the time we get there," Wilber commented.

"I doubt that." Esther frowned. "She seems more driven than ever before. I'm worried about her. Cole, you have to do something to stop her. I know she's headstrong, but surely..." Esther's words dropped off. She looked pleadingly at Cole.

Suddenly everyone was staring at him.

"I'll think of something," he finally said.

A sigh of relief was heard around the table. It was hard for Cole to believe they all had such faith in him.

"I wonder how much longer that blacksmith is going to be." Wilber stood to light a lantern.

Cole, who was about to leave the table, looked toward Wilber. "If you boys are planning to go into town tonight, remember, we'll be leaving early in the morning."

"Naw, we're not going into town," Decker answered. "George promised to teach us poker. We all have our money ready."

"We?"

"Me, Wilber, Jeff, Evan and George. Tucker said he wasn't interested. Would you care to join us?"

"No, but perhaps I'll watch." Cole stood. "I'll mosey over and remind George that you're waiting for him."

Cole had just reached the tent when he heard a deep groan from inside. "What the hell do you think you're doing?" George roared.

"I invited you to supper to thank you for helping me improve my aim," Beth stated angrily. "Not on some romantic whim!"

Cole shook his head and smiled. Apparently Beth had forgotten to warn George that she could take care of herself. "May I come in?" he called. Not waiting for an answer, he stepped inside. Dressed in a very proper high-necked gown, Beth looked quite the prim and proper lady. Her guest, however, was bent over holding himself.

"The boys are waiting to play poker, George," Cole casually announced.

George gave Beth a scathing look before leaving the tent.

"Did I interrupt anything?"

Beth tugged at the waist of her dress. It had hiked up during her wrestling match with the blacksmith. "As a matter of fact, you did. George and I were about to... He finds me most attractive, but I'm sure you couldn't care less." She shoved back the unruly hair that had managed to work its way loose from the soft bun resting on top of her head.

The little liar, Cole thought humorously. *She's trying to make me jealous.* It would never happen. Jealousy wasn't in his nature.

"All right, I admit he was being obnoxious. He wasn't a gentleman like you," she said sarcastically.

"You might want to go play poker with the others."

"That's an excellent idea. Isn't that the game played in saloons?"

"Right. Everyone is at the long table. I'll tell them you're coming."

The fresh air did little to alleviate Cole's surly disposition. Seeing George in Beth's tent had brought on a cold fury which surprised him. He'd wanted to break the man into a hundred pieces. Then, the smell of Beth's perfume and her nearness had brought him to the brink of pulling her into his arms and telling her to forget about the poker. The night was his. He was furious with himself for allowing a slip of a woman to get under his skin. She had wormed her way into his thoughts and she was tampering with his mind.

Cole headed toward the long table, then changed his mind. Instead he walked to the line rope and untied his horse. A few minutes later he rode out of camp. He'd find relief elsewhere.

Beth stepped outside just in time to see Cole ride off. Her hand flew to her breast. The pain was sharp and deep. Just as she knew God created man, she knew Cole was going to town to be with a woman. Any woman except her.

She refused to cry. She looked at the men positioned around the long table, the lantern casting them in eerie shadows. She raised her chin a fraction and headed in that direction. Staying in the tent bawling wouldn't serve a thing. It was time she started thinking about her self-esteem. She looked ahead and saw George sitting at the table. Hopefully she had put him in his place. She didn't want to have to replace him. He'd been with the caravan from the beginning and he knew the routine. He was also a good blacksmith.

"Is everything ready to go tomorrow?" Beth asked as she paused in front of Esther and the other women. They were busy doing last-minute mending.

"Everything is ready," Esther replied. She had also seen Cole ride away.

Beth continued on to the long table. By positioning herself behind Jeff, she could watch the game. She could also keep an eye out for Cole's return.

"Now, let me get this straight," Jeff said an hour later. "Two pairs beat a pair, but three of a kind beats two pairs? That doesn't make sense. It should be the other way around."

"Why are you having so much trouble with that?" George asked scathingly. "Even Evan remembers what beats what."

Again, George had the winning hand. He raked in the money, adding to the healthy stack already in front of him.

Decker tossed his cards in the center. "I'm out." He spat tobacco juice on the ground. "And broke." He stood.

"Me, too," the others chimed in.

"Wait a minute," Beth protested when George began shoving the money into his hat. "Aren't you going to return what the others lost?"

"Hell, no," George protested.

"But they were only learning the game."

"They're grown men." George jammed his hat on his head. "They knew this was for money."

"No! I will not allow this. Return the money!"

George stared at Beth with cold, unwavering eyes. Finally he took his hat off, dumped the money back on top of the table and left.

When everyone turned in, Beth had no choice but to go to her tent. Sleep didn't come. All night she sat up waiting for Cole's return and trying to cope with the reality of life.

Breakfast was being cooked and the men were already loading everything onto the wagons when Cole finally returned. He rode to where he normally slept, pulled back on the reins to stop his horse, then slid from the saddle onto his bedroll. Everyone stopped what they were doing and stared. Cole Wagner wasn't moving.

"Continue your work," Beth ordered. "We need to get on the trail."

She went to where Cole lay on his side and shoved him onto his back with her foot. He reeked of whiskey, but there was no indication that he'd been harmed. "Wagner," she barked, "get up. It is time to move on."

He didn't open his eyes.

"Decker," she called, "bring a big bucket of water."

When Decker arrived, she ordered him to pour it over Cole's head. He hesitated, then did as he was told. Cole didn't even flutter an eyelash.

"Doc," Beth yelled.

A few minutes later she had Decker and Wilber try to pour coffee down Cole's throat. All efforts to awaken him proved futile. The caravan was going nowhere today.

By eight the following morning the caravan was once again on the move. Other than sarcastically asking Cole if he thought he was capable of leading them, Beth hadn't exchanged a word with the big man up front. She had already found too many excuses for his behavior, but that had ceased. Being with another woman was beyond her willingness to forgive. Henceforth, she would concentrate on the purpose of her being here. Maybe instead of writing dime novels she should write about her travels. The world would come to know and adore her. That was a lot better than loving a no-account outlaw.

Still suffering from a hangover, Cole catnapped in the saddle. He couldn't remember ever being so thoroughly drunk as he had been the night before. He wasn't even aware he'd slept nearly twenty-four hours until he awoke this morning and saw everyone sitting on the ground staring at him. He'd had to forgo breakfast. There wasn't even any coffee. According to Esther, Beth had had what was left thrown out and the pots packed.

Cole raised his arms and stretched. He didn't have to be a gypsy and read tea leaves to know his "boss" was angry. It was something he was starting to get used to.

That night everyone retired early, including Cole. But not before hearing about the poker game. No one was pleased with Beth's interference, especially not George.

The following day Cole told the men to keep their rifles within reach. They would be entering an area that was known as Turner territory, after the ruthless bunch of riffraff who had been terrorizing the area for the past five years. From here to Dodge City they all had to remain alert for any attack.

Even after Cole's warnings and the Indian incident, that afternoon Beth galloped her roan over a hill and disappeared from view. Convinced she needed to rid herself of her restlessness, Cole paid scant attention—until fifteen minutes had passed and there was still no sight of the stubborn woman. How could she continue to be oblivious to danger? This was happening too often.

Thoroughly vexed, Cole ordered Jeff to continue leading the caravan straight ahead, then took off in search of Mrs. Alexander. After topping the same hill Beth had disappeared behind, Cole followed her horse's tracks around a series of oddly shaped rocks. Some balanced precariously on top of others, making one wonder why they didn't fall.

Cole finally spotted his quest headed in his direction, some two hundred yards away. Sitting in the shadow of the rocks, he knew Beth was unaware of his presence. It was the relief of knowing she was unharmed that caused Cole to chuckle. But the sight that welcomed him added to his humor. Apparently justice had been served. Bethany Alexander was quite a sight. Her black riding hat was nowhere in sight, strands of hair either clung to her face or flew about in the soft, warm breeze, and her face and clothes were covered with dirt. The lady was limping and leading her horse, but other than a possible dent in her pride at being thrown, only her ankle or foot appeared to be injured. From the way she was walking, even that couldn't be very serious. Yes, sirree. Quite a sight. He nudged his horse forward.

Beth stopped the minute she caught sight of Cole. "Well," she yelled when she thought he was close enough to hear, "it certainly took you long enough to come to my rescue!"

Cole swallowed his grin. "Come to your rescue? It wouldn't have happened if you had stayed with the caravan." He gave her a reproving look. "You should be grateful that I came. I warned you about riding off by yourself."

"I became fascinated by these rocks. Can you blame me? Just look at them. I even found several places where pictures had been painted. Some were Indians hunting buffalo. That was when a snake made its presence known. Satan reared, and I fell off his back."

Cole's brows furled. "Did it rattle its tail?"

"Do you mean the horse or the snake?"

"The snake, confound it!"

"You needn't get angry. Yes, it rattled its tail. But when I beat the foul thing with my riding crop, it slithered away. Are you going to help me onto my horse or not?"

"Listen to me, Beth, the snake is poisonous. Did it bite you? Is that why you're limping?"

"Of course not. I'm limping because I couldn't get back on the saddle."

Cole was losing his patience. "Beth, what is that supposed to mean?"

"The grass is so high I didn't see the gopher hole. I twisted my ankle and it hurts!"

"Are you like this on all your excursions, or is it just with me? Confound it, Beth, what does it take to make you understand the dangers?"

Beth wasn't exactly pleased with the results of her endeavor. "I get tired of just poking along mile after mile." She suddenly realized something. "You were worried about me."

"Of course I was worried. I hardly want you dead. I told you before that a sidesaddle wasn't made for this type of terrain."

Beth squared her shoulders so as not to show her disappointment.

Cole dropped his horse's reins to the ground. "I'll put you back on your horse. The doc can take a look at your ankle when we join the others." He placed his hands on her waist, ready to lift her onto the sidesaddle. He wasn't sure if it was those large doe eyes staring up at him, the hurt she was so determined to hide, or the proud set of her chin that made him pause. He reminded himself that he couldn't afford to give way to temptation, and that the others in the caravan would be wondering where they were. Nevertheless, he was already lowering his head, ready to claim those lips that were made to be kissed.

"Cole! Is everything all right?"

Cole turned and watched Decker come into view. Cole released a fatalistic chuckle. Maybe Beth was Gadombitsouhi's daughter after all, and the old woman spirit was looking after her. Decker's arrival couldn't have been better timed. He placed her on top of the horse and handed her the reins.

Beth was dazed. Had it been her imagination, or had Cole been about to kiss her? Her gaze shifted to Decker. She wanted to bawl him out for showing his face, but what would it accomplish? He was only watching out for her safety. Besides, the magical moment had passed, and it had probably been her imagination working overtime again. Cole had already mounted his horse. Decker had gone on ahead of them.

"What would you have done if I'd been an Indian or a marauder?" Cole reprimanded as they headed back to the caravan.

"What would marauders be doing in these parts?" Beth asked. "I haven't even seen a farm."

"Nevertheless, this is Turner territory and none of us would want to come in contact with them."

"Then why doesn't someone arrest them?"

"Who? You've seen how vast this land is. It's doubtful a hundred men could locate his camp."

"Very well, I'll stay close to the caravan."

Cole automatically looked across the land, unthinkingly searching for any signs of trouble. He moved his horse alongside Beth's mount. "Before we return to the others, there's something I need to talk to you about."

"What?"

"The poker game the other night."

"What about it?"

"You shouldn't have made George give the boys back their money. No one feels good about it. Men have died because someone accused them of cheating."

"Oh, this is ridiculous. I never accused George of cheating."

"No? How would you take it if you were told to give back the money? Just a word to the wise."

Beth leaned forward and patted Satan's thick neck. "Do you know how to play poker?"

"Yep."

"Don't you think it a bit strange that George won all the money?"

"It happens sometimes."

"When we reach Dodge I want you to take me into a saloon so I can sit in on a poker game." A roadrunner ran by, spooking Beth's horse, but she had no trouble handling the gelding.

"Like I said, men take their poker seriously. They wouldn't be interested in playing cards with someone who doesn't know the game."

"But I do."

Cole rested his hands on the pommel. "Where did you learn?"

"I watched the boys play the other night. It's a very simple game."

"You know nothing."

"I do!"

"Let's see how good you are. We'll play six hands tonight. Five hundred a hand."

Beth sneered. "You're on." She thought about how angry George had been when she had made him return the money he had won. "Maybe we should play in my tent."

"I'll be there after supper."

* * *

That night, after the six hands had been played, Beth sat glaring at Cole. She hated losing to him. "I owe you three thousand dollars."

"That's right."

"You cheated."

Cole leaned back in the chair. It was interesting how Beth made a habit each night of changing from her trail clothes into some fancy gown. He had yet to see her wear the same one twice. Tonight's affair had a deep décolleté that allowed a delightful peek of the wonders hidden beneath the soft material. "Whether I did or didn't is of no consequence. Hopefully it will serve as a lesson not to jump into something you know little about."

Beth rested her elbows on the table. "You took advantage of me. Tell me how you did it."

Cole gathered the cards, trying to ignore the view she presented by leaning forward. "I don't give private lessons and I'm not George. I don't give money back, either." He stood. "Remember this. Out here, a man takes his poker very seriously. More than one good man has met his Maker over the game." He moved toward the tent opening.

"No guts?" she challenged. "I'm beginning to think you only gamble when you know the odds are in your favor."

"You're right."

"No wonder you seldom seem to ever enjoy yourself."

Cole knew he was being baited, but damned if he'd let her get away with her comment. "Very well, I'll give lessons every night after supper."

"Good. I'll be ready."

"The lessons will be held at the long table for anyone who cares to partake."

"But—"

"Good night, Mrs. Alexander."

"Mrs. Alexander?" Beth jumped to her feet and hurried forward, putting herself between Cole and the tent opening. "Wait just one minute! I didn't deserve your sarcasm."

He looked down at her creamy white shoulders. "I believe *you* were the one throwing the accusations."

"Did I call you Mr. Wagner?"

Cole stared down at her quietly.

Beth was both angry and hurt by his sudden coolness. "When we get to Dodge City I want you to find me a gunfighter. I want to experience what it feels like to outdraw someone of importance."

"Be careful, Beth," he warned angrily. "What you're wanting becomes an addiction. First it could be one, then two and so on, assuming you don't get killed. The obsession grows to prove to the next one and the next one that you're the best. Then one day you meet a man who is better than you, and as you lie dying, you realize none of it was worth a damn thing."

Beth gulped loudly. "I meant a draw down. I said nothing about shooting."

"When a gunman draws, he shoots to kill! You already drew on me. Wasn't that enough, or are you also wanting to experience how it feels to get a bullet in the gut?"

"Do you think about that when you rob banks?"

"That's different. My gun is already drawn. Besides, I'm different."

"Why do you say that?"

Cole released a satanic chuckle. "Because I've faced death so many times that it has become a friend. I flirt and

woo it. Darlin', you have no idea just how mean I can be."
He stepped around her and continued on his way.

Beth stared at Cole's broad back until he disappeared into the night. He had been right. Though she had only wanted a chance to test her speed, drawing on a gunfighter could be filed along with the other stupid things she'd come up with. Like buying an outlaw.

Chapter Sixteen

With no mishaps to delay them, the caravan moved at a steady pace. Everything had long since become routine. They were on the move by dawn and didn't stop until near sunset.

Each night after supper, all but George gathered to hear Cole teach the various aspects of poker. Beth paid particularly close attention.

The nearer they came to Dodge City, the more restless Beth became. She longed to feel the wind blowing through her hair as she sent the gelding galloping across the land. But that wasn't going to happen. She'd promised to stay close to the caravan. She knew what was driving her. Cole would soon be departing. She had tried to prepare herself for the day she would see him ride off, but it wasn't working.

Beth brought her horse alongside Cole's buckskin. Tomorrow they would arrive in Dodge, and Beth had decided the time was right to recoup her losses.

"Apparently your words of prevailing doom were nothing more than air. I can't recall seeing the... What was the name of that supposedly notorious gang?"

"The Turner gang." Cole found it interesting the way Beth's mind worked. Since being unseated by a snake, she rode astride in her buckskin britches and shirt, much to Esther's chagrin.

Beth looked up at the clear blue sky. It was such a perfect day. Antelope were grazing a short distance away, birds were chirping and the wildflowers were in full bloom. It wasn't fair. It should be a cloudy, dreary day to match her disposition. Tomorrow they would be in Dodge City. Shortly after that she would never see Cole again.

"The Turner gang is either in Dodge City, holed up, or out raiding. Even Fort Dodge can't control them. Be glad they aren't after us."

"I don't believe a word of it."

"If you are looking for a fight, you picked the wrong person."

Cole knew her better than she knew him. Of course she was looking for a fight so she could release the tension that was ready to explode. "I want a rematch."

Cole grinned. "What kind of rematch?"

"A poker game. It's only fair that I be allowed to recoup my losses."

"You think you're that good now?"

"Yes, now that I know about keeping a straight face and not doing anything to give away what cards I'm holding. I think I'm every bit as good as you. Well?"

Beth's untamed spirit had always attracted him. "Very well."

"We'll play after supper. In my tent."

"Same rules?"

"Six games. And don't forget to bring your...my money." Beth pulled back on the reins and waited for the others to catch up with her.

By the time Cole entered the tent that night, Beth was already seated at the table, her money piled neatly in front of her. The lady meant business. She hadn't even changed out of her trail clothes. He tossed the cards onto the table and straddled the seat across from her.

"Where is your money?"

Cole pulled it from his pants pocket and placed it on the table. "Would you care to deal, or shall we draw for high card to determine who is first?"

"I don't want you whining afterward. We'll draw for high card."

Cole's jack gave him the first deal.

Beth won the first two hands, and it was all she could do to keep from gloating. "Would you care to double the wagers?" she asked, trying to appear casual.

"It would be my pleasure." Cole dealt.

Beth didn't win a game after that. At the end of the sixth game she sat glaring at him. "You cheated!"

"Prove it."

"Well, I..."

Cole shrugged his shoulders. "I warned you before that calling a man a cheat is shooting words. And you can't even prove it. Like I said, honey, you're nowhere near ready to play with men. But since you have put a considerable amount of money in my pocket, I feel generous. The deck was not only marked, I also dealt from the bottom. There wasn't a time I didn't know what cards you were holding."

Beth's eyes narrowed.

"I didn't do a thing that a crooked gambler wouldn't pull."

Beth threw her cards at him. "You..." She grabbed two pillows and threw them. "No-account..." A vase followed. "Cheating..." She grabbed a small chair and threw it. Cole was already advancing toward her and easily caught the chair in midair.

He circled the table.

Beth opened her mouth to scream, but he cut the sound off by placing his hand firmly over her mouth. She tried to knee him. He easily avoided the attempt by pulling her against him. Cole was enjoying the contest, and being able to contain the fiery woman was an added plus. Then he made the mistake of looking down into her wide brown eyes. The warmth of her body was penetrating his shirt. He moved his hand from her mouth and stared down at her tempting lips. They were parted, waiting for his kiss. She felt good in his arms. His nights had been lonely, and he wanted her. Unfortunately, that would be equivalent to putting a bullet through his head.

Cole leaned down and kissed her nose. "Darling, you're going to have to learn to curb that temper."

Beth's heart was pounding so hard she knew he had to feel it. All her determination never to let him touch her again was quickly slipping away.

Cole backed away and tipped his hat. "Good evening, ma'am."

Dejected, Beth plopped back down on the same chair she had been sitting on. Would she ever learn? Was she so weak and pliable that all he had to do was take her in his arms and she was willing to forgive him for anything? No. Everything would change once he was no longer under her nose. She sighed. No, her feelings would never change. Cole would always be the only man she had ever loved.

The sound of rattling pans told Beth that Magda was already preparing breakfast. Beth set her journal down on the bed beside her. Today they would arrive in Dodge City. Her trip was almost over. In retrospect, she wouldn't have changed a thing, other than Cole's feelings for her. There were so many experiences during the trip that would always be embedded in her mind. Norma and the boys, the sadness of bidding Howard goodbye, the dead cavalrymen, White Horse and the faces of the Indian children were but a few. And of course, there was Cole. There were a thousand and one things about him that she would always remember. She climbed off her bed. She was no longer excited about seeing Dodge City.

Beth spent most of the morning riding off to the side of the caravan, trying to avoid the dust. For some reason she was at peace with herself. She had come to accept Cole's departure and had even managed to acknowledge that he had been right all along. It was for the best. A one-sided love never worked. And, knowing of her jealousy, she would be constantly suspicious of him being with another woman, and always wondering when he would leave her.

The Arkansas River came into view, and on the other side lay Dodge City. They had finally reached their destination.

After crossing the toll bridge Cole led the caravan down a windswept street. It wasn't a big town, but it was almost exactly as Beth had anticipated. Somewhere she had read that a year ago Fort Dodge had banned the use or sale of any alcohol within a five-mile distance. Supposedly some man went exactly five miles and put up a saloon. That was now Dodge City.

"It's only two in the afternoon," Cole explained. "This town doesn't go to bed until five in the morning, so most folks are just stirring from their sleep."

The railroad tracks ran down the center of Front Street. On the side they were traveling, Beth read the signs on the various storefronts. Hover & McDonald's liquor store, Zimmermann's hardware, Dr. McCarty's drugstore, a clothing store, a billiard hall and saloon were but a few of the businesses they rode past. She was delighted when she saw a woman sitting on a beer keg in front of the saloon, smoking a big cigar. When the woman waved, Beth waved back. So did Cole. Was that yet another one of his lady friends?

Beth noticed something hanging from the telegraph pole, but couldn't make it out because of the blinding sun. As they drew nearer, she realized it was three men hanging by their necks. Never having seen such a sight, she stopped her horse and looked up. The morbidness of it momentarily held her transfixed. A queasiness came over her when she saw that the men's lips were blue, their tongues were sticking out and their heads were cocked to one side. It was the buzzing of flies that finally broke the spell and caused her to place her hand on her stomach.

"How lucky you are to see another one of the sights that was on your agenda," Cole bit out.

Beth winced. Without looking at him she kneed her horse forward. She hadn't anticipated the effect a hanging would have on her. But then, she hadn't anticipated anything when she'd decided to take this trip. Looking back, she found it hard to believe that she could have been so naive. Maybe that wasn't the right word. At that time, she hadn't given much thought to anything.

As they continued down the road, Beth's stomach began to settle. Occasionally she heard twangy music or a woman's shrill laughter coming from inside the various businesses. Here cowboys wore their six-guns loosely belted, their pant legs inside their boots and spurs. She had been right. This was exactly what she needed for her research.

As usual, Cole stopped the caravan at the edge of town. Beth sat on a small stool, and while everyone performed their jobs she wrote the day's happenings in her journal, then followed that with sketches.

Beth became lost in thought. She was remembering a conversation she and Cole had had after making love at the Kiowa camp. She had wanted to tell him that other than her husbands he was the only man she had ever let bed her. But she didn't. Instead, she had said, "Have you ever considered marriage?"

"I'm not the marrying kind."

"Everyone is the marrying kind if they find the right person."

"Did all your husbands die in bed?"

She had sat up and looked down at him. "No, but they certainly never made me faint."

"And scream?"

"We'd make a good pair, Cole."

"I'm not the type of man to settle down to one woman. I wouldn't want to make you a widow again. Remember, I'm a wanted man. That alone should tell you to beware."

"I wasn't asking you to wed me. I'm mature enough to realize this is a simple convenience for both of us. I just thought there may have been a woman in your life that you had considered marrying." Oh, how she had lied. It wasn't decent that she should love a man as much as she loved Cole.

"I want you to make sure the men are armed at all times."

Beth looked at Cole, who had come up beside her.

"Why?"

"I was serious about the Turner gang, but besides that, Dodge is made up mostly of bullwhackers, dance girls, saloonists, gamblers and border ruffians. Lewd women and rough men. Any one of them would think nothing of killing someone.''

''But I saw reputable businesses.''

''There are those, too, but they know how to survive under such conditions.''

''Very well.'' Her voice sounded calm, but that wasn't how she felt inside. But then, she always had some sort of reaction when Cole was so near.

Cole went over and struck up a conversation with Tucker, who was sitting beneath a shady tree, reading a book. It also gave Cole a good vantage point to keep an eye on George. It had been a long weeding out process, but Cole was now convinced George was Tex Martin, and at some point, the escaped convict was going to make contact with his old gang.

Cole had no idea how old Tucker was, but he guessed him to be in his late forties or early fifties, as his hair was sprinkled with gray.

With a few well-placed questions he had learned that the doctor and his wife had come on this jaunt for the sole purpose of acquiring money. Tucker said he'd already told Beth that from here they would continue on to Denver, where he felt he could open a lucrative practice.

Cole slowly stood. George had gone behind one of the wagons ten minutes ago, and he still hadn't shown his face again. After a quick excuse to Tucker, Cole hurried to where he'd last seen the blacksmith. He was nowhere in sight.

Cole began making a quick check around camp. ''Have you seen George?'' he asked Decker.

''He took off toward town several minutes ago.'' Decker placed chairs around the long table. ''The man's useless. He never has pitched in and done his share.''

''I'm going to ride to town to see if I can find him.''

232 *The Devil's Kiss*

"Why hasn't anyone told me about this?"

Neither man had heard Beth walk up.

Decker lowered his head. "It wasn't my place, ma'am."

"I will ride to town with you, Cole. I want to see just what Mr. Higgins finds more important than doing what he is being paid for."

"I can take care of it," Cole assured her. "I'll have him back here in no time."

"No, he works for me, and I'm the one who should handle it. We'll go together."

"It's good to have you back, Tex," the thin blond man said, his English accent hardly noticeable. "We expected you nearly a month ago."

"I sent a wire to Jess from Wichita."

"And Jess appreciated it, as did I. As you know, I'm not fond of staying in town for long."

Tex grinned. "When I escaped from prison I headed straight for Independence, like you said. Then something happened that you're gonna like, Turner."

"What's that?"

Tex took a long drink from the bottle sitting on the table, then wiped his mouth with his sleeve. "While I was waitin' around to make sure no one was followin' me, I heard about men being hired to travel west. So I looked into it."

The several men who had arrived with Quin Turner closed in on the table so they could hear what was being said.

"I found out some rich, crazy woman who had a hankerin' to write books about the West was leavin' from Independence and headed here. So I signed up. A perfect cover. By the way, I killed that feller you said in your wire was followin' me."

"And is the woman really wealthy?"

"That she is. I found out from the others that she's even the niece of some senator in Washington. As soon as she's through in Dodge, she'll be paying everyone off. That means she's gotta have a big stash somewhere. She pays real good."

Quin Turner took a long draw on his cheroot, then slowly let the smoke back out. "Then why didn't *you* ride off with the money?"

"There's enough for all of us. Besides, she's travelin' with well-armed men." Tex wasn't about to tell Turner that he'd given it a lot of thought, but there was too much for him to carry alone and someone was bound to have seen him trying to get away with it.

"Is she staying at one of the hotels?"

"No, she's staying with her caravan."

"So, what we have is an eccentric old woman with a small army. Am I right?"

Tex shook his head. "She ain't old and I can't recall seein' anyone prettier. She's got all this red hair.... Well, the widow's a real beauty—but snooty. Thinks she's better than everyone else."

"So, she wouldn't let you in her bed, huh, Tex?" one of the men asked.

The other men laughed.

"Stay out of it, Charley!" Tex threatened. He turned back to Turner. "Mrs. Bethany Alexander—that's her name—is carryin' enough furniture and such for three houses. It's all good stuff. The real expensive kind. But then there's other things I ain't never seen before and I don't even know what they're used for. They gotta be worth plenty because of the jewels on them. No, you don't want just Mrs. Alexander, you want the entire caravan!"

Turner's eyes lit up with interest. "Sounds interesting doesn't it, boys?"

The others grinned and nodded.

"She shouldn't be hard to handle," Turner said.

"Well, that's not right, either. She's a feisty little thing and can shoot and ride as well as a man. And besides the men, she's also hired an outlaw that supposedly has a price on his head. I didn't see the poster, but one of the women in the caravan said she'd seen it."

"Maybe he's planning to get the money, too, boss," the red-bearded man said.

"What's his name?" Quin asked Tex.

"Wagner. Cole Wagner. A big man with hair as black as an Injun's."

"I seen his poster," young Tommy Kidd spoke up. "He's got a five-thousand-dollar reward on his head, dead or alive. Word is that he's a fast gun in these parts. I been itchin' to give him a try."

Tex shook his head. "No, you've got the wrong man. He went to draw on the woman and couldn't even get his steel out of the holster."

"Harry," Quin said, "go get us another bottle."

Harry headed for the bar.

Quin brushed off the ashes that had fallen on his new vest. "Tommy Kidd, are you sure about this Wagner fellow being a fast draw?"

"Positive."

The thin man looked at Tex. Quin was normally a suspicious man, and it was because of that very virtue that he had stayed alive and prospered. "This doesn't quite add up, does it? Why would a man be pretending to be some outlaw? You say you haven't seen the Wanted poster, nor does he have a fast draw. Is there anything about him that would indicate he's an outlaw?"

"Well…" Tex thought a minute. "I don't reckon there is, at least nothing I've seen. But there's something about him… He stays to himself and you get the feeling that he's a man you don't want to mess with." Tex grabbed another drink.

The men had broken out laughing again—all but Turner, who was still staring at him with those ice blue eyes.

"Keeping to yourself is just another way of making people believe you're somebody you aren't. On the other hand, a Pinkerton man or a lawman would probably act the same way."

Everyone became serious and looked at Tex.

Harry brought the new bottle and placed it on the table.

"Tell me you weren't stupid enough to tell anyone anything about the gang, Tex," Turner said as he opened the new bottle.

"I don't know what you're talkin' about."

"Of course you do." Turner poured himself a drink in his shot glass. "Did you by chance brag to anyone in prison about being a member of the gang, or perhaps that you were heading back to join us?"

"I don't like bein' accused—" Tex tried to stand but was shoved back down in his chair.

"Come, come, boys. That's no way to treat Tex," Turner said with deceptive congeniality. He downed his drink. "He's one of us again."

"He wouldn't have been in prison if he hadn't bragged to that Mexican *señorita* about knowing you," Tommy Kidd barked out.

"But he never told them where we were. Now back away and give our friend room."

Tex laughed nervously. "I don't know why everyone's actin' like this. Didn't I bring you a big prize? I didn't have to tell you about the woman and the stuff on the caravan."

"I'm not angry with you," Turner assured Tex, "and we do indeed appreciate your desire to share. And now that we know about the one who claims to be Wagner, we can take care of him. Isn't that right, Tommy Kidd?"

Tommy Kidd grinned. "It will be my pleasure."

"But that leads to another question. Why would this man want to take on someone else's identity? Especially since there is such a high price on the outlaw's head?"

"Maybe so he'd get the job as guide. I told you she pays real well." Tex grabbed the old bottle and guzzled down the contents, some running out the side of his mouth and down the front of his shirt. "I gotta get back to the caravan. Mrs. Alexander ain't gonna be happy when she finds out I left." He wiped his sweaty forehead with his sleeve, anxiously waiting for Turner to say he could go. The words were not forthcoming.

"That's possible, or he could have been trailing you. You know, Tex, I can understand how being a member of the Turner gang would...shall we say...make you a more important man at prison. I'm sure I would do the same thing if I were in jail."

"Well...I mean..."

"I just want to know if you told anyone about coming back to us. That way we'll know and be on the watch," Turner said softly. He leaned forward. "Just between you and me, I got word that someone is on *my* heels."

Tex started feeling good again. Turner had just told him something that he was sure the Boss hadn't told the others. "Well, I did tell my cell mate, but I know he wouldn't tell anyone." He was shocked when Turner reached out and grabbed him by the front of his shirt.

"You stupid bastard!" Turner seethed. "This town is probably surrounded with every cavalryman within a thousand miles."

"I swear, Fly wouldn't tell no one about it. He wants to join us when he gets out." Tex's teeth started chattering. Turner's face was red with anger.

"I should turn you over to Indian Bill and let him cut your tongue out!" The slender man released Tex's shirt and shoved him backward.

"I told you he'd rat on us again!" the red-bearded man declared angrily.

Quin Turner nodded to Tommy Kidd. Though barely twenty, he was the most cold-blooded of the lot. But it was Jess who pulled his gun and shot Tex in the back of the head. No one in the saloon paid attention to the loud shot or the man who now lay dead on the dusty floor.

"Throw him out in the back," Quin Turner ordered.

Red and Jess grabbed Tex under the arms and dragged him away.

"We gonna make a run for it?" one of the men asked.

"No one knows who I am, and Tex can no longer point a finger. I would say we're quite safe for now. I want this man calling himself Wagner killed. He may be innocent, but we can't afford to take a chance that he is indeed following Tex. In the meantime I want to sit and enjoy my bottle and plan how we're going to take over this Mrs. Alexander's caravan." Quin broke out in a coughing fit. Something that seemed to be happening increasingly often. He looked toward the bar to make sure two of his men were there watching the entrance. Tommy Kidd sauntered over to join them.

* * *

Cole had apparently been right. Though it couldn't have been later than four-thirty in the afternoon, Beth found the gambling houses, saloons and dance halls to be much rowdier than when they'd ridden through earlier. Bad music, laughter, gunshots and men staggering about drunk were but a few of the things she saw and heard as they rode by the various establishments. Occasionally she saw painted women standing outside, their brightly colored clothes enough to light up a dark room.

It was Cole who spotted George's horse and pointed it out to Beth.

Inside the saloon, Tommy Kidd hurried to where Quin sat nursing his whiskey. "Boss, two people just rode up outside. They fit that description Tex gave us of the woman and man."

"Well, then, perhaps you should welcome them."

Tommy Kidd walked out the doorway of the saloon just as the pair moved their horses to the hitching rail. "Who you lookin' for, mister?"

The minute Beth saw the stranger she knew he was a gunfighter. He was younger than she and not much taller. His black clothes and brightly embroidered vest gave him the look of a hunter. His stance and the way his gun hung at his side declared his occupation. Beth remembered Cole saying that a gunfighter only pulls his gun to kill.

"What difference does it make?" Cole asked.

Tommy Kidd gave the man a half-cocked grin. "You wouldn't happen to be Cole Wagner, would you?"

Cole sighed. Apparently his luck had run out. There was little doubt in his mind that somehow Tex was behind this. "I'm Wagner."

Beth suddenly realized the danger Cole was in. He couldn't even draw a gun without dropping it. "I'm the one you want to talk to," she called to the man in black.

Cole rolled his eyes and climbed down from his horse. The one thing he didn't want was Beth in the way.

"What's wrong, Wagner? Do you let a woman do all your talking now? It was my understanding you were fast with a gun."

Beth panicked. She couldn't just stand there and let the man she loved be shot down. "No, no," she called. "I'm the one who is fast with a gun. Do you want me to prove it?" The man's steady, steely blue eyes remained on Cole.

"Name's Tommy Kidd. Maybe you've heard of me."

"I've heard of you," Cole replied. His concentration was now totally on the gunslinger.

The sun played on the silver conches circling the crown of Tommy Kidd's hat. Beth nervously watched him step off the board sidewalk and make his way to the center of the dusty street. With the sun behind him, she was practically blinded. Suddenly she realized Cole had also stepped into the street. "No," she cried out.

"I think you would be wise to reconsider," Cole called to the outlaw.

"Oh, no. I don't think you're who you claim to be. Now draw."

"No one can say I didn't warn you."

Kidd went for his gun.

Seeing the movement, Beth reached for her own revolver, ready to protect Cole. Two bullets were fired before she could even clear leather. She looked at Cole, then at the man in black. "Cole?" she whispered. Why didn't he move? Who had been shot? Then Tommy Kidd fell forward, his face buried in the dust.

Beth looked back at Cole. He had been so fast—she hadn't even seen him holster his gun.

To Beth's astonishment, a wagon came around the corner. As if it had been planned, the man driving it climbed down, picked up the gunslinger's body, tossed it in the back and a minute later drove off. It was such a cold, feelingless act. Beth was suddenly engulfed with a horrid reality. Had she followed her original plan, that would have been her lying dead instead of Tommy Kidd! She gasped. Her so-called quick draw didn't exist.

Beth turned toward Cole. His eyes were colder than ice, and his face was molded in steel. She had never suspected . . . had never dreamed he was that fast. Why had he dropped his gun when she'd challenged him before? To humor her?

Her nerves still raw, Beth hurried after Cole, who was already marching into the saloon. Coming in from the bright sunlight, it took a minute for her to adjust her eyes to the dark, musty room.

As she followed closely behind Cole, Beth saw men scattered about, and even dance hall girls. There were "nice" men with white neckties and good clothes, and dealers sitting at tables. Cole referred to them as well-turned fingers and smooth tongues.

Everyone moved aside, giving Cole a wide berth as he maneuvered about, looking for George. Beth had to practically run to keep up with him. When he didn't find the blacksmith, he went upstairs and started banging doors open. Some of the prostitutes screamed, and more than one man cursed loud enough for the whole place to hear, but George was not to be found.

When they were back outside, Cole stood staring at George's horse, still tethered to the hitching rail.

"We really don't need him any longer," Beth said breathlessly. Cole looked up and down the street. Apparently he hadn't heard her. "He'll come riding back later," she tried again.

Cole nodded. "Very well."

He headed for his horse and Beth hurried toward hers. The ride back to the caravan would allow her time to reconcile her thoughts. Cole had once told her she had no idea just how mean he could be. She hadn't believed him. She did now.

Turner stood just inside the doorway and watched the pair ride off. He nodded for one of his men to follow. It might take a little convincing, but he could use a man like Wagner in his gang. Especially now that Kidd was dead. But the only things Tommy had been interested in were money, women and his reputation with a gun. Quin had heard that Wagner was not only fast, he was clever.

Quin returned to his table. "Please note, gentlemen, Tommy made an unwise judgment and paid for it. Jess!"

A thin, scruffy man scurried to the table.

"Tonight I want you to sneak into Mrs. Alexander's camp and tell Wagner I want to meet with him. Make it tomorrow at noon."

"Sure thing, boss."

"And make sure no one sees you."

"Anything else?"

"No, that will suffice."

Chapter Seventeen

As Beth sat in the middle of the floor with pencil and journal in hand, her gaze traveled from the colorful pillows scattered about the tent floor to one precious object after another. Gifts from across the world. She had cared for the men—in her own way—but none had compared to Cole Wagner.

She resumed her writing.

Cole is full of contradictions and complexities. Every time I think I understand who he is, a different person seems to emerge. At some point I had foolishly thought of him as being gentle and pliable. There was nothing gentle or pliable about him when he stood in the middle of Front Street. He had nerves of steel, and, though he warned the gunslinger, I never saw a drop of compassion for the other man. And when he marched through the saloon looking for George, there wasn't a man in the place that dared to get in his way. So far my tour has proven my stupidity at every turn. How could I have been so addled as to think I had a fast draw? I will, however, give myself credit for having the tenacity to try to save Cole's life.

Beth held her handkerchief to her nose and inhaled the pleasing odor of lavender perfume. She had to admit that it was that manly, dangerous side of Cole that fascinated her the most. He represented everything she had ever dreamed of in a man. Gentle with a sense of humor, yet very dangerous. Her hand moved over her breast. And when it came to making love, he had released a woman of such fervor that it shocked even her. Just thinking about him ignited desire. The nights were the worst. Remembering but not feeling his hands and mouth caressing every inch of her body, not having him turn her into a wanton woman, not experiencing the delirious ecstasy when he entered her—making her forget everything except what the two of them were sharing—had taken its toll.

Beth sat up, unsettled at how the remembering could have such an effect on her. Her love for Cole made her extremely vulnerable. Looking back, she wasn't even sure when or how it had happened. She did know how it hurt to acknowledge that what they had shared had been nothing more to him than a means of satisfying his lust. She preferred to think that they had shared something very special.

Beth stood, refusing to let her thoughts of Cole continue to eat away at her. However, the thoughts didn't subside, and by noon she had become a mass of nerves. He had once said that if she wanted to know anything, she should just ask. That was exactly what she intended to do. She wanted Cole to tell her if he had any feelings for her. She needed to know so she could stop deluding herself and try to get on with her life. She took off in search of him.

Seeing that Cole's horse was gone didn't help Beth's declining spirits. After talking to Esther and the cook, Magda, Beth knew Cole had left a short time ago. No, he hadn't told either of them where he was going, but there was nowhere to go except town. Why had he done that? She was, after all, the one who had declared she wanted to see Dodge City.

A thought occurred to Beth. Perhaps going into town would lighten her mood.

"Is something wrong, Bethany?" Esther asked as she entered the tent.

"Why should there be anything wrong?" Beth went to the chifforobe and swung open the doors.

"You left in such a hurry when I told you Cole was gone. Surely you're not wanting to change dresses already?"

"Yes, I am. I want the white ruffled blouse, the blue bolero jacket and matching skirt. The small black hat will go quite well with the black braiding."

Beth began pulling out drawers as Esther took down the clothes.

"Where is my reticule?"

"It's on the top shelf. Are you planning to go to town? Cole warned us to stay close to camp. Here, move away," Esther said in an exasperated tone of voice. "I'll get everything." She began pulling out the clothes. "I don't think you should go anywhere, and certainly not alone."

"Hogwash. All types of people live in town, Esther. I saw perfectly respectable women walking down the street yesterday."

"Why not wait and let Cole go with you?"

"Cole! How strange that I have always been quite capable of taking care of myself until Cole came into our lives!" Beth sat on a stool and was about to pull off her boots, but changed her mind.

"I'll tell Jeff and Evan to saddle their horses so they can go with you."

"You'll do no such thing. Instead, go have a horse saddled for me. And hurry."

"I'll help you dress first."

"No, I'll do it myself."

"But you never put a decent amount of petticoats on, and I've noticed that as of late you don't wear your corset."

"If I don't worry about it, neither should you. Now go."

Esther shook her head. There was nothing more she could do to keep the stubborn woman in camp.

As Beth rode past A. J. Peacock's saloon, she saw Cole's buckskin tied to the hitching post in front. The same place George's horse had been. It wasn't there now. Though she was tempted to ride on, her curiosity overruled common sense.

Beth dismounted and tethered her gelding next to Cole's. Reticule in hand, she squared her shoulders and moved forward.

The moment Beth stepped inside the smoke-filled room she was met with broad grins and leering eyes. She had started to scan the long room for Cole when she spotted a mountain of a man headed toward her. His jacket was made of s variety of pelts, leaving Beth to believe he had to be a trapper. A saloon girl grabbed the big man's arm and whispered something in his ear. The bear of a man quickly glanced across the room, then returned to the bar.

"Slumming, honey?" one of the girls decorated like a peacock called.

Beth ignored her. By looking in the same direction the trapper had, she'd discovered Cole seated at the back with another man. Four others stood nearby. A brazen-faced blonde hovered over Cole, sending a shard through Beth's heart. The woman had the audacity to drape her arm around Cole's neck, shoving her bosom directly in his face!

Bitter and feeling used, Beth turned away, ready to leave—until she saw a man sitting at a table playing a game of cards by himself. Maybe she couldn't do anything about Cole's lack of feelings for her, but she could certainly show the outlaw that she could indeed play poker. She'd prove it by winning the biggest pot he had ever seen! Not much of a victory, but a victory nevertheless.

Beth went to where the gentleman with slicked-back hair and an artistically twisted mustache sat. "Is it too early for a game?" she asked sweetly.

Duke looked behind him to make sure the lady was talking to him. "It's never too early, sweetheart, but aren't you in the wrong place?"

"Not at all."

"Well, then, what is your fancy?" Duke rolled three dice on the table. "Chuck-a-luck or poker?"

"Poker." Beth tried to pull a chair out with the toe of her boot, the way she'd seen men do. Instead of moving backward, it started to tip over and she had to move fast to catch it before it hit the grungy floor. She cleared her throat to hide her embarrassment, then sat with the stranger.

"The name is Duke, ma'am." The gambler smiled, exposing a gold tooth. "Anyone else care to play with the lady?" he called out. The other three seats were quickly filled.

Quin had watched Cole closely to see if he showed any signs of compassion for the charming lady who had entered the saloon minutes ago. No one could help but notice Mrs. Alexander. Besides being beautiful, she looked completely out of place. "I assume that is Bethany Alexander."

Cole nodded.

"An amazingly beautiful woman, wouldn't you say, Mr. Wagner?"

"I would indeed." Cole looked toward Beth.

"Don't pay her any attention, sweetie," the blonde whined. "I can give you more than she ever dreamed of."

Cole said nothing. It infuriated him that Beth had sat with the gambler. Would the woman ever learn to stay out of trouble? Well, she was on her own this time.

"Get out of here, Sally," Quin ordered the trollop. "We have business to discuss."

"But I—"

A slight nod of Quin's head and Sally was yanked away from the table.

Cole turned his back on the girl. He couldn't afford to get involved. Besides, he was having enough trouble with Beth's antics. He was still furious at her for even being here, let alone looking as if she was ready to hold a tea. Sure as hell, there was going to be trouble. He could feel it in his bones. Dear Bethany was going to be the cause of it and he would have to finish it.

Determined to take his mind off Beth, Cole concentrated on Quin Turner. The man looked nothing like Cole had envisioned. To begin with, Turner was much younger than he had expected. He had one of those faces that never seemed to age. Cole guessed him to be in his early forties. He was a frail sort of man who wore wire-rimmed glasses and looked as if he had never had to shave in his life. Had Turner not introduced himself, Cole would never have suspected him to be the notorious outlaw who was behind the murders of countless people.

"Now we can talk." Quin leaned forward. "I had my man contact you in camp because I have a deal I think you might be interested in. There is no doubt that you have plans for the widow, whether it be to bed her, take her money, or both."

"You seem to be well-informed."

"Yes. Tex was good at telling everything he knew. That is how he ended up in prison."

"I'm not interested in anything you have to offer. I'm doing nicely on my own."

"Tex was certain the lady is carrying a considerable amount of money."

"By the way, where is Tex?" Cole asked casually.

"I believe someone discovered him lying in the alley, quite dead."

"It couldn't have happened to a nicer man."

"My proposal is quite simple. We share the money she's carrying and the ransom I can get for her."

Cole chuckled. "Now, why would I want to do that?"

"Because I have contacts, and you will end up with more money by doing it my way. We could get a handsome sum for a senator's niece."

Cole pretended to be surprised. "Senator's niece?"

"That's right. Apparently Tex learned more than you did about the fetching lady."

Even in the dim light, Cole could see the twinkle of amusement in Turner's eyes. "Since you have this all figured out, why do you need me?"

"The cavalry."

"The cavalry? What about the cavalry?"

"They are keeping a close watch on the widow's camp. Jess had a hell of a time getting past them to give you my message." Quin took two cheroots from his vest pocket and offered one to Cole. He still wasn't sure he trusted the man, but time would tell. If he proved trustworthy then he'd be useful.

Cole gratefully accepted. It took solid determination for him not to look at Beth. He rolled the cheroot in his mouth before biting off the end. One of Turner's men held out a lit match for him. After several puffs to get it going, Cole held the cigar in front of him and watched the smoke curl toward the ceiling. "Is the cavalry your doing?" he asked Turner.

"I had wondered the same about you," Turner replied. "However, it doesn't make much sense that a wanted man would make himself available to the military, unless you're actually a spy."

"A spy?" Cole chuckled.

"I was giving it some serious consideration until you shot down my best man. He told me Cole Wagner was suppose to be a fast gun, and you certainly proved it. But that doesn't mean I trust you. I'm curious. How would you explain those pony soldiers suddenly sitting in wait, and waiting for what?"

Cole leaned back in his chair, seemingly giving the situation thought. "I'd say that considering Mrs. Alexander's uncle is a senator, she is probably the one we should be suspicious of. Perhaps her caravan was outfitted so as to attract me, but more likely you."

Cole raised the bottle of whiskey sitting on the table and looked at Quin. "Do you mind?" he asked.

"Not at all. Help yourself."

Cole poured the amber liquid into one of the used shot glasses, then downed it.

"Your analogy has merit. I've already stayed in town longer than usual, so I need to head out before the fort discovers I'm here."

"I'll go with you. I have no desire to be arrested either." Cole started to rise but stopped when Turner held up his hand.

"If she wanted you arrested, it would have already happened. You'll stay here. I want you to lead the wagons due north. There is a mountain of rock with a trail going right through it. The cavalry will be hard put to follow. We'll be waiting on the other side."

Cole leaned back in his chair and stared at Turner. "And how do I know you won't take care of me, as well?"

"You don't really have a choice. If you refuse to cooperate, one of my local friends would be more than happy to report you to the army. He could use the reward money." Quin stood. "Don't worry, Wagner, I need a fast gun, especially now that I've lost Tommy Kidd."

Cole watched Turner until he and his men left the saloon. The man was much shorter than he appeared while sitting. His gaze shifted to Beth, just in time to see her tip a shot of whiskey. The laughter that followed indicated the woman was well on her way to getting drunk. He knew he should just get the hell out of there and leave the woman on her own. Maybe she'd even follow him out. On the other hand, maybe she wouldn't. A saloon girl walked up behind the auburn-haired minx. No question about it, Beth was being set up.

No matter what reasoning Cole used for leaving, he knew he couldn't abandon Beth. Accepting his fate, he positioned his chair so he could keep an eye on her, then reached for the bottle still sitting on the table. From where he was sitting, he could see she was winning—so far.

Cole stuck the cheroot back in the side of his mouth. Should he go to Beth's aid, or should he let the gambler and his partner take Beth's money? She deserved to lose, though it wasn't likely she'd learn anything from it. Five minutes later he sidled over to the poker table.

Beth became excited when she saw Cole headed in her direction. Now he could see the money she'd already won. He needed to know that she was as good at poker as he, especially when marked cards weren't being used.

Cole stopped to the left of the dealer, but Beth avoided eye contact by looking down at the cards she was holding. A pair of twos. Was it her imagination or were the cards a bit blurry? She drew three cards and called the bet. Her pair won, and she greedily raked in the pot.

"Ma'am," Cole said, "if I were you, I think I would quit."

"You're not in this game," the gambler protested, "so keep your comments to yourself, mister."

Beth was about to heed Cole's advice when the hussy returned who had been hanging over Cole earlier. She even wrapped her arm around his neck as if she owned him. Beth chose not to react.

One man dropped out of the game, and Beth was certain Cole would take his place. She was disappointed when he didn't. He apparently had no desire to participate in an honest game.

After five hands Beth was again digging in her reticule for a seemingly endless amount of money. Cole knew the card shark was wondering just how much she had with her. Cole was wondering the same thing. If she didn't lose everything, there was sure as hell going to be someone waiting outside to take what she had left. And it wouldn't be difficult, because Beth continued to down her liquor.

Cole had no problem seeing how the saloon girl behind Beth signaled Beth's cards to the gambler. Still Cole chose to keep quiet. However, when Beth looked up at him, he motioned to her with his eyes. One of Beth's many attributes was her quickness. She turned in her chair and looked at the woman dressed in a gaudy purple gown.

"I don't like anyone to stand behind me. Either move or I leave."

Unsure what to do, the brunette looked at the gambler.

"Go find some customer to entertain, Bell." Duke touched the garter circling his arm. "I'll talk to you later."

Bell walked away.

"Thank you, sir." Beth picked up the cards she'd been dealt. She gave Duke her brightest smile. "I'm sure you wouldn't be foolish enough to try something underhanded, would you?"

Duke nervously glanced at the other two players. Neither the trapper nor the storekeeper was looking particularly friendly, especially when they noticed saloon girls standing near them, as well. "I hope you're not suggesting I'd cheat."

Beth shook her head. "Of course not. You don't strike me as a man who would be that foolish." She hiccuped.

Waiting for the trader to place a bet, Beth glanced at Cole for his approval. Instead all she could see was the blond hussy whose hands had become entirely too friendly with Cole's body. "You'd best keep your hands to yourself," Beth called out to her. "That man is real particular whom he beds and when!"

Sally laughed. "It sounds to me like the lady is jealous," she said to Cole, making sure Beth heard.

"Don't be ridiculous," Beth snapped. "I wouldn't have him even if he was wrapped up in ribbons."

Cole suppressed a smile. He had to agree with Sally. He looked at that black hat Beth wore and shook his head. Why in the hell had she chosen to wear such attire? The hat was the final touch to the ridiculousness of it all.

Beth's winnings started to rebuild. She even praised the other players when they won, pouring on the charm. Each hand began to take longer and longer as the men showed more interest in her than the card game. By the looks on their faces, Cole could tell the saloon girls weren't taking kindly to the attention Beth was receiving. To Cole's surprise, he wasn't taking kindly to it, either. Especially when other men started collecting around the table.

Still angry at having been caught, Bell had the piano player strike up rollicking strains of music. It took little encouragement for the ladies of the night to begin dancing in wild abandonment. In an effort to get even more attention, Bell and another girl stood by the piano loudly singing the words to "Camptown Races." Instead of accomplishing what they wanted, the tactic caused Beth to begin clapping her hands. Thoroughly enjoying herself, she quit the game and stuffed her money in her reticule. Cole saw her momentarily sway when she stood.

Convinced the dizziness was due to having sat so long, Beth was soon dancing with the men. In no time a line had formed, each man awaiting his turn. Beth laughed and completely enjoyed herself, oblivious to the girl's angry taunts and Cole's glare.

Cole heard something rip as Beth sashayed past him. It had to have been her skirt. He'd had enough. He snatched up Beth's reticule before someone else did. From the moment she had walked in, he had known there was going to be trouble. Looking for a quick way to get the prima donna out of there, he scanned the room, then shifted his glance back to Beth.

Lord almighty! She had walked over and joined the others in song. Cole began maneuvering his way toward his feisty boss, but he didn't reach her in time to prevent Bell from delivering a hard slap to Beth's cheek. Beth slapped the brunette back, and then all hell broke loose. Others of the profession were about to converge on Beth, some breaking bottles on the edges of tables on their way. They were ready to cut the unwanted uppity woman to pieces. The men started grabbing women to prevent anything from happening to Beth, and fights quickly broke out everywhere.

Cole finally managed to get a hand on Beth's wrist and jerk her to him just as an unconscious trapper hit the floor where she'd been standing. Cole slung Beth over his shoulder, strapping the arm holding the reticule across her legs. Still full of fight and determination, she reared straight up, pounding her fists on his head and shoulders and calling him names he hadn't thought she even knew. The thought of what she had been like when he first met her caused him to break out in laughter. Talk about misjudging someone.

As Cole wove his way toward the swinging front doors, he had to dodge and plant a fist on more than one man's face. The sock he landed on Duke's jaw was strictly for pleasure. Cole stepped over the gambler's prone body and continued on his way. He briefly wondered why Beth had ceased her struggling, but he was too busy trying to get them out of the saloon to find out.

As soon as Cole made it out the doors, he inhaled the welcome fresh air. He had been right about trouble brewing. Unfortunately he'd also been right about men waiting outside for Beth. The look on their faces was proof enough that they sure as hell hadn't expected to see someone carrying her.

"You can put her down," the biggest of the men stated. He put his hand on the revolver shoved under his belt. "We'll take care of her from here."

"I don't think so. I'd as soon leave peacefully, but on the other hand I'm in just the right mood to kill the three of you." Cole whipped his revolver out, taking the men by surprise. "Now, you tell me which it's going to be, gentlemen. A killing or a peaceful retreat."

"Well," the big man said as he backed away, "we didn't mean no harm. You know times are hard and a man's gotta do what he can to make it from day to day." He stopped. "You gonna shoot us in the back?"

"Get the hell out of my sight."

The men hurried away and disappeared into an alleyway.

Until he saw the confounded sidesaddle, Cole had thought to sling Beth over the saddle of her horse. Left with no choice, he placed her limp body across his saddle. The liquor had finally taken its toll. She had passed out.

After winding the roan's reins around the pommel of Beth's saddle, he looped the reticule over it. Knowing the gelding would follow, he hurriedly untied his own horse. He didn't have time to waste. Men were already being knocked out the door. Some had resumed their fight outside, and windows were being broken.

Cole swung up behind Beth, and as soon as she was cradled in his arm, he had his horse racing out of town—the roan trailing right behind them. After determining that they hadn't been followed, Cole slowed the buckskin and looked down at his sleeping beauty's peaceful face. Thick lashes brushed an eye that was already turning black, and there were smudges all over her face and her dress. The "doves" had been ready to tear her to shreds, but even as small as she was, she'd held her own. He studied her perfectly shaped lips that now had a small cut close to the side. Ah, yes, her lips. He couldn't resist raising her and kissing them.

"Mmm," Beth muttered, "now that's what I need."

Cole grinned and moved his horse on down the road. Beth would never remember her trip back to camp.

Cole's good mood didn't last long. Turner's threat was looming over him.

Chapter Eighteen

Though the others had left the long table, Cole continued to nurse his coffee. Turner had put him in a bad position and there was nothing he could do about it. For certain, he couldn't afford to be turned over to the cavalry. For appearance's sake they would have to arrest him and he would have no way of locating the gang's hideout. As long as Turner wanted Beth for ransom, she would be safe. It was the rest of the caravan he was mostly concerned about. They could easily end up dead.

Cole watched Beth leave her tent. He didn't know how she managed to look so sprightly after yesterday's spree. The spring in her step indicated she was feeling cheerful. And, other than the black eye she sported, there didn't even appear to be any aftereffects from the soiree. He chuckled at his use of the word. The next man she chose to marry would have one hell of a job on his hands keeping her out of trouble. For some reason, the thought of her marrying didn't sit well with him.

"Good morning," Beth greeted in a blithe manner. She refused to let Cole see how miserable she felt. The night's sickness had been bad enough, but having to walk out into the bright sunlight verged on the unbearable. Not only did it make her head pound, but her swollen eyes felt as if they could burst out of their sockets. She ran her hand over the top of her head. "I know I must look awful. Esther told me you brought me home. I wanted to thank you."

"You look beautiful. Truly a sight any man would be pleased to see in the morning," Cole replied.

Beth forced a smile over her clenched teeth. "Is that something you tell all your women?"

Cole chuckled. "Darlin', when it comes to beauty, I don't know a woman who could compare to you."

Beth cocked a smooth eyebrow. "And I'd wager you told that hussy at the saloon the same thing yesterday. You certainly didn't mind the way her hands were all over you."

"Do I detect a note of jealousy?"

"No, of course not."

"If you're talking about Sally at the saloon, it wasn't what it seemed. There was nothing to be concerned about. How could I even be interested in such a woman? It was business. I was talking to Quin Turner—"

"You mean the notorious leader of that gang you told me about?"

"One and the same." Cole finished his coffee.

"What did he want?"

"He wanted me to join his gang. Seems he'd heard of my reputation."

"And what did you say?"

"I told him I wasn't interested."

"Magda," Beth called, "bring Cole and me some coffee." She looked back at Cole, trying to appear uninterested. "How did he get in touch with you? Did he know you were guiding the caravan?"

"No, but apparently George did. Turner told me George's real name is Tex Martin," he lied. "Apparently George escaped from prison and joined your caravan to avoid the law and come here. Oh, by the way, George is dead. One of the band took care of that."

Magda set a kettle of coffee and a cup on the table in front of Beth, then walked away.

"George not only told Turner about me, he also told him all about you."

Beth refilled his cup before pouring her own coffee. "Do you think he will try to get in touch with you again?"

"I'm sure of it. He wants to ransom you."

Beth's intake of breath was audible. "He's after me?"

"He knows your uncle is a senator. There are also the money and precious items you're carrying about. We need to get out of here, Beth. I gave it a lot of thought last night, and decided we should head north. There are a group of rocks with a trail through the middle of them. They won't be able to come after us."

"I'll think about it."

"There isn't time. Beth, you have to realize what danger you're in. We have to leave as soon as possible."

Beth ran a tapered finger around the rim of her cup. She couldn't tell Cole that the most important thing in her life was gone. "I haven't seen enough of Dodge City."

"Beth, we have to leave."

"I said I'd think about it," she snapped at him.

Cole stood. "Let me know when you've made up your mind."

Beth watched him walk away. His tense shoulders told her he was angry, but she didn't care. She didn't care about anything. The only feelings she had were feelings of bitterness. Of course, it was all her fault. All along Cole had warned her. But instead of listening, she had let her love blind her.

Beth remained in her tent the rest of the day. Even as she ate her mutton supper she still couldn't decide on an excuse for not heeding Cole's warning and moving the caravan away from Dodge City.

Cole sat on the bedroll cleaning his revolver. The small campfire he'd built allowed just enough light to see by. He reassembled his gun. Beth left her tent just as he shoved the gun into his holster. He was surprised when she turned in his direction. He'd expected her to avoid him. He'd told her of danger, yet she had chosen to ignore him. "Have you changed your mind about leaving?" he asked when she came to a stop in front of him.

"Something suddenly occurred to me."

"Oh?"

"You were lying about meeting with Turner, weren't you?"

Cole was at a loss as to where she'd come up with that idea. "Why would you even think such a thing?"

"When I stopped playing cards at the saloon, Bell told me all about you and Sally making so much noise upstairs that everyone downstairs could hear you."

Cole smiled. "Tell me, when was this romp with Sally supposed to have happened?"

"You needn't try to act so innocent. It was that morning."

"Now, darlin', you know I prefer to take my time, and you entered the saloon not very long after I did. I simply can't figure out how I managed to do what I'm being accused of."

Beth remembered being told he had just left camp when she had inquired. She had changed clothes quickly and she had galloped her horse all the way to town. If he'd walked his buckskin... He was right. There wasn't enough time.

"When are you going to start believing me over others?" Though he'd fought against it, Cole knew what he was going to have to do to get the caravan moving. He had used the tactic many times to get what he wanted, but for the first time it left a bitter taste in his mouth. Beth deserved better.

"I just didn't want you to think you had to keep your word about not bedding others. That was all said in the throes of passion. One's liable to say anything under such circumstances."

Cole sat there listening to Beth and watching her twist her hands.

"I just didn't want you to be under the illusion that because we made love you have to find excuses to be with other women. Why, I've had men all over the world and most of them were a lot better at making love than—"

Cole reached up and roughly yanked Beth to the ground beside him. He rolled on top of her, pinning her beneath him. The firelight danced in her thick auburn mane, which had spilled like a fan onto the dirt. "Who you've taken to your bed is your business," he growled, "but I don't want to hear about it."

Beth's struggling ceased when she looked into a pair of steely eyes. The same eyes she'd seen when Cole had shot down Tommy Kidd.

"And don't try telling me other men were better, sweetheart, because during the height of your passion—when you were out of your mind for the want of me—you declared no man had ever made you feel that way."

"Oh, well..." Lies suddenly were not coming easily. "I... I was pretending. Let's talk about this Turner—"

"Pretending, hell!"

Cole's kiss was hard, punishing, but just the feel of his lips on hers had blood rushing through her veins. He sucked at her bottom lip, and Beth's passion soared at the feel of his hand on her breast.

"Tell me to stop, Beth," Cole whispered in her ear. "Tell me to stop and I will."

Just the thought of Cole carrying her to the tent had her quivering with anticipation, but she couldn't allow it. There were other considerations. She couldn't allow him to have so much control over her emotions. "Stop," she blurted out, already regretting the words. She dropped her hands to her sides, determined not to let him see the effect he had on her. "If you can so easily pull away from me, why should I be any different with you?"

Cole rose up on his elbows and studied her face. Her brows were pulled together and her mouth was pinched. She was lying all the way. "Have I told you that I love you?"

Beth tensed. "I've had enough lies."

"Why do you think I went so long without touching you?"

"I've asked myself the same question."

"I was attracted to you from the start, and that worried me." He smiled. "You see, I never thought I would find a woman I would want by my side for the rest of my life." He leaned down and kissed her chin. "I know that isn't possible." He kissed her nose. "You could never be happy with a no-account outlaw." He kissed each eye closed. "Nor would I be any kind of a man to ask it of you. It wouldn't—" he outlined her lips with his tongue "—be fair to expect you to keep running from the law."

"Anything is possible if you truly love me."

Cole rolled onto his back. Dammit, Beth, he silently cried, get up. Run like hell! Can't you see this is all a ploy? But then she was leaning over him, excitement already shining in her eyes. He pulled her down on top of him. "After we first met, it seemed as if I saw your face everywhere I looked. In the clouds, the grass and even across the prairie. At night when I lie alone on my bedroll I think of you. I see you in my dreams.''

''Oh, my dearest, I didn't realize. I was so afraid you didn't love me, and it kept eating at me.''

''I shouldn't have said anything. I have nothing to offer you.''

''Your love is all I ever wanted.'' She leaned down and kissed him. ''Make love to me, Cole.'' She began working at the buttons on his shirt.

''Are you sure you want to give an exhibition for the others in the caravan?''

Beth's fingers stilled, then she broke out laughing. ''I had forgotten all about them. See what you do to me?''

Cole attempted to kick dirt onto the waning campfire before rolling Beth into the shadows. ''You present too tempting an argument,'' he said softly. ''I want you too much to wait.''

Knowing they could no longer be seen, Cole slowly undressed the beauty, the full moon bathing Beth's ripe body in gold. His hands moved to the firm breasts. His fingers played with the pert nipples while his tongue danced a minuet with hers. He nipped at her chin before trailing his tongue down her neck—between her enticing breasts. He nibbled at her flat stomach, causing her to squirm with delight. He continued down until he found what he wanted. As he tasted her sweetness, Beth writhed from the pleasure he was giving her.

Beth continued to tug at his shirt, wanting to feel his nakedness, until he finally rose to his knees and undressed. Devoured by the throes of passion he had ignited, Beth lay with her eyes open, watching his every move. ''You're beautiful,'' she whispered.

''So are you.'' His clothes discarded, he lay on top of her, gently running his finger up the inside of her arm.

"Did you know your skin is softer than a lily petal, or that a rose pales when compared to the beauty of your lips?"

Beth had never had such words of loveliness spoken to her. "Cole, I'm sorry I questioned you about Sally." She ran her hand down his muscled back. "I had to know the truth. I had to know what your true feelings were. I didn't want to be lied to."

Cole thrust himself deep within her, causing her buttocks to rise from the ground. "I love you," he said simply. He smiled when she moved her hips against him, wanting more. "Don't you know by now that I could never enjoy another woman after having you?" He moved slowly in and out of her, giving them both what they wanted. "That's why I was so concerned about you remaining here where Turner can get to you." He leaned down and sucked on her tongue, which was tracing her lips. Her eyes were closed and she was already near her climax, but he knew she could hear him.

"We'll start packing tomorrow," she whispered. She opened her eyes. "Please, Cole," she pleaded. Her arms curled around his neck and she raised herself high enough to kiss his shoulder.

Her tightness and quivering body were rapidly pulling Cole into her web of eroticism. "Oh, sweetheart," he whispered in her ear, "you're so beautiful." He wrapped his powerful arms around her. Holding her tight against him, he carried them both into a world of fiery passion, where nothing mattered but their love for one another.

Esther was smiling as she packed what was left in the tent. She had never seen Bethany so happy. The woman was practically dancing from one place to another, helping where she could to get the caravan on the move. Esther hadn't failed to notice how Beth's face radiated love every time she looked at Cole. She had known from the beginning that Cole was the one man who could tame Beth's wild spirit. He had not only accomplished the task, he'd even gone on to show her what it meant to be a woman.

She folded the sheets and placed them in the trunk. Now the question was, what came next? Would Cole and Bethany marry after they were safely away from that nasty gang?

Lizzy came hurrying in. "I came to help and inform you we have a problem." She began stuffing pillows into a different trunk.

"What kind of problem?"

"Decker has broken his arm."

"Oh, bless his heart." Esther looked at the doctor's wife. "How did that happen?" she asked worriedly.

"He was pulling a bad wheel when the jack collapsed, and the wagon fell on his arm. Tucker has set it, but says it won't be possible for him to drive the wagon. It's going to hurt mightily when he's riding. He was lucky that he didn't get his body pinned under that wagon."

Esther shook her head. "Our first accident. Who will drive the wagon?"

"Apparently Cole is going to do it. He'll put it in lead. My, my, that is one fine man. You should have seen his muscles ripple when he lifted that bed so Wilber could pull Decker from beneath it." She closed and locked the second trunk. Seeing there was nothing else to do, she walked out of the tent with Esther. "I think Beth will have her hands full with that one. What do you think?"

Esther grinned. "I think you're absolutely right."

"Do you know where we're headed next?"

Esther shook her head. "Some rock formation. Cole told her we would be safe once we got there."

"What's to keep the gang from seeing us leave, or attacking?"

"According to Beth, they are off raiding farms. That was why they wanted him to keep us here for another week."

"Now I can understand what the big hurry is."

"As it is, it is going to take three days to reach those rocks."

The two women went off to help Magda prepare the noon meal.

It was shortly after noon that Cole cracked the whip over the oxen's broad backs and set the caravan on the move. It was a beautiful day for traveling. Pleasantly warm and not too hot. He had been surprised at how quickly Beth had had everyone up and on the move this morning. It was almost as if she knew what he was about. But that couldn't be possible.

Cole knew he should be pleased the way everything had turned out, but his mood was black. He was fighting his own devils about delivering the caravan right into Quin's jaws. It wasn't going to be easy keeping everyone safe, but he was going to give it one hell of a try. Would Beth still love him once she discovered he had lied and used her? Not likely. He'd known all along that the fates had never been on their side. There had never been any choices. He hadn't meant to hurt her. He'd done what he had to do. Suddenly he was racked with sadness. It was never in the cards that they would end up together, but what a hell of a couple they would have made.

Chapter Nineteen

Perched on the wagon seat next to Jake, the young man who had taken Doolan's place, Beth continued to watch the wagons move along the crevasse in the mountainous rocks. Her beloved Cole was delivering them to safety.

Beth's heart was so full of pride and joy it was a wonder it didn't burst. There couldn't possibly be a more wonderful, experienced leader in the entire territory than Cole. Spending the past few nights wrapped in his arms had been equivalent to being in heaven. She felt warm, loved and protected. She had to smother a giggle. She was so madly in love she was becoming silly.

Beth could see the opening at the other end, and her excitement grew. Once they were safe she would ask Cole to marry her. If he said no, that was all right. But he wasn't going to ever leave her side, not if she could help it. She'd follow him anywhere.

When Jake drove the wagon into the open, Beth felt like a woman reborn. They were free.

"We'll stay here tonight," Cole announced.

Beth jumped off the wagon as they lined up to make camp. Though Wilber hadn't yet driven the last wagon through the opening, Magda was already starting to prepare supper and Beth's tent was being erected. Setting up camp had been done so often that now the operation was like a fine tuned violin. Everyone worked in complete unison.

Once her tent was in order, Beth hurried in to bathe. She wanted to be perfect when Cole joined her.

It was a scream that brought Beth straight up in her bed. Then bullets were being discharged. She turned to Cole. He had already left the tent. Another scream. Beth jumped off the bed and ran to the chest. It seemed to take forever to pull on the buckskin britches and tunic, though it could have been only minutes.

When Beth ran outside, it was complete mayhem. Wilber and Tucker were running for their shotguns, but mounted men on horses were in pursuit. A bullet rang out, catching Wilber in the leg. Beth groaned when the kindly doctor was struck on the back of the head with a six-shooter. He slumped to the ground unconscious. Lizzy tried running to her husband, but she was cut off by one of the mounted men.

Beth spun around, ready to retrieve her gun. Her effort had come too late. She was one of the last to be herded into a circle.

"What is this all about?" Beth demanded. No answer was forthcoming. Where was Cole?

While three men kept their guns pointed at the collected men and women, others knocked down the tents and tossed everything back into the wagons. Beth had never seen a meaner or more degenerate bunch of men. Everything about them bespoke filth.

Beth suddenly recognized one of the men. He was as thin as an ice sliver, and his hair was absolutely white. He had been standing near the table when Cole had had that blond whore hanging on him. She remembered Cole saying he had been with Quin Turner that afternoon.

Again Beth looked for Cole. Where could he have gone? Was he hiding until he could help? Beth didn't want to believe what this was all adding up to. She tried to shut off her mind. She tried telling herself she had to have faith in the man she loved. She tried reminding herself that she had been wrong before. Or had she? Had Cole misled her with one lie following another? Had he delivered them to the Turner gang?

As soon as the camp area had been thoroughly cleaned, two of the villains tied everyone's hands behind them. They were then ordered to climb on top of the farm wagons. Beth was too small to accomplish such a feat. Some man grabbed her around the waist and tossed her onto one of her crumpled tents.

The animals were quickly collected and hooked up to the wagons. Again the caravan was on the move, and Beth had a gnawing feeling that she would soon be seeing an outlaw gang's encampment.

Not knowing how long they would be traveling, Beth wiggled about until she was fairly comfortable. She was hurting badly. She couldn't convince herself that Cole wasn't somehow involved in all this.

Waking later, Beth had no idea when she had dozed off, but the sun told her it was still morning. Having sunk down in the tent, she had to rise up to see. Not until she had looked to the front, back and sides did she allow her excitement to build. She wasn't being guarded. To make her position even sweeter, the wagon she was on was now bringing up the rear of the caravan. Being the only one aboard, she could only surmise the villains had forgotten where they had put her. Or possibly the man who had tossed her in the wagon hadn't known who she was.

Beth tested her wrist bindings. They were secure. She thought a minute. Why couldn't she slip the rope under her hips? Then she could... By lowering her shoulders she managed it, the feat not as difficult as it seemed. Then it was a simple matter of bending her knees to her chest and slipping the bindings past them. With her arms where they should be, she quickly scooted to the back of the wagon. She didn't stop to think about the danger. She simply pushed with her feet and jumped.

The ground Beth landed on was hard and ungiving, but she hadn't sustained any serious injuries. She rolled behind a bush and held her breath. Had the driver seen her jump? She peeked around the bush. The wagon was still continuing on its way. Now she had to get far enough away that she couldn't be found. But before she could do anything she had to rid herself of the bindings around her wrists. She raised her hands and worked at the knot with her teeth.

Quin Turner glared at the prisoners lined up before him. "Where is Bethany Alexander?" His voice was soft and deadly.

Jess paled. "I don't know, boss. We must have had her when we left."

"Are you saying she simply disappeared?"

"Yes . . . ah, no! She must have escaped somehow."

"She's a wily one," Cole commented as he joined Turner.

"You traitorous son of a bitch," Decker accused. He lunged forward.

One of the raiders rammed his fist into Decker's broken arm, dropping him to his knees.

"See what happens when you misbehave?" Cole's cold smile sent shivers through each one of the prisoners. He grabbed Decker by the shirt and lifted the man to his feet, disregarding the man's pain. "Where is Beth?"

"I don't know, and if I did, I wouldn't tell you."

"Such brave words. I'm impressed." Cole released the shirt, then looked each of the others in the eye. "They don't know where she is," he finally told Quin.

"I tend to agree, but how do we know for sure?"

Cole chuckled. "These people aren't like us. I've traveled with them long enough to know lying doesn't come easy."

Quin looked to his own men. "Which one of you saw the redhead last?"

"It was too dark to see who was who. I tossed a woman in one of the wagons," a huge bear of a man answered.

"Which wagon?"

Bull looked at the wagons and scratched his head. "It was one of them—" he pointed to a farm wagon "—but they all look alike."

"I brought up the back with one of them wagons," another man stated.

"There are also two men missing," Cole said. "Where are they?"

"We left them behind, *señor,*" a young *bandido* said. "I laid the colored one's head open with the butt of my *pistola*. Cowboy shot the other one."

Lizzy broke out in sobs. Esther gathered her friend in her arms, trying to comfort the woman.

"Somehow, Beth managed to escape. I'm going after her."

"First I'll take your gun."

"Even after I delivered the caravan to you?"

"Just a precaution."

Cole pulled out his six-shooter, handed it to Quin, then headed for his horse.

''Two of my men will go with you.''

Cole mounted and moved his horse close to Quin. ''Don't you trust me?''

''Not yet.''

Laughing, Cole sank his heels in the buckskin's sides. The two men Quin motioned to follow had to do some fast moving to get to their horses and catch up with Cole.

Cole kept his horse in a canter, easily following the wagon tracks. His mind was racing. The territory was wild and Beth was vulnerable. A big cat or even an Indian could put an end to her life. Had she stayed put, she would have been safe.

He clenched his jaw. During their travels he'd made a point of staying off to himself. In his profession it was dangerous to become attached to others. It distorted his vision. He could no longer think only of himself. Beth hadn't allowed him that privilege. Over the weeks he'd come to care what happened to her as well as the others, and he was suffering the consequences. Even now he was worried about Beth and wondering if Tucker and Wilber were dead. He should be able to say to hell with all of them. He was on an assignment for President Grant, and that was all that he should be thinking about.

Cole tried to cleanse his mind. He needed to come up with some strategy. Turner's den of thieves was much larger than anyone had realized. The place was a veritable town. In the short time he'd been there he'd discovered that it was actually an association for the lawless. The president was going to be surprised to find out such a thing existed. Just the men on Wanted posters would have brought in a fortune. Tearing it down was going to have far-reaching effects. More so than anyone had anticipated. The question now was how he was going to accomplish that feat.

Cole looked out over the land, continuously searching for the woman he'd come to love. The realization had hit him between the eyes when he'd found out Beth was missing. A thought occurred to him. Beth was the answer to everything. If she could reach the fort or cavalry, she could give them the directions. The scouts would pick up the same tracks he was following. Their invasion certainly wouldn't catch everyone, but it would sure as hell destroy the association once and for all.

Cole pulled back on the reins. He'd caught sight of Beth ducking behind a bush. Her buckskin clothing blended in with the terrain, making it almost impossible to see. Even her hair wasn't noticeable. Probably because it was full of dust. They weren't far from the rock formation. Last night he'd instructed the cavalry commander, Captain Scott, to hold his troops there until he received word to move. Now it was all up to Beth.

"Whatcha stoppin' for?"

"We should have already caught up with her. Why, she's only a mile from where the cavalry has probably positioned itself." He had spoken loudly enough so Beth would be sure to hear. "They have to be near the rocks."

"Turner ain't gonna be pleased about this. If she makes it that far she's bound to send them after us."

"A lady like that could never make it this far," Cole assured them. "We'll have to backtrack and see if we can pick up her footprints." Cole laughed. "If we don't find her some hungry cougar sure as hell will."

Cole turned his horse and headed back the way he'd come. Now it was all up to Beth. He knew her well enough to know she would stop at nothing to see her people safely out of danger.

The three men were well out of hearing distance before Beth removed her hand from her mouth. Her dirty face was already stained with wet tears and they were still flowing. She sat on the ground, her heart torn into a million shards. Never had she known such complete devastation. How big a fool could a woman be? Cole had laughed at the possibility that she could be dead. To think that only this morning she had thought of herself as the luckiest woman in the world.

Time became a blur. Nothing mattered. Beth wanted to die.

It was concern for Esther and the others that finally penetrated Beth's consciousness. They were her responsibility. The thought of them suffering caused her to look at the sun for direction. She had to get help. The outlaws had said she was close to the rocks. She looked southward. They were tall enough to be seen from miles away, but apparently she had been too fatigued to notice.

Beth forced herself to her feet, then staggered forward. The fall off the wagon had had a worse effect than she had thought. She was sore all over.

Her mouth dry and needing water, Beth picked up a small stone and stuck it under her tongue the way she had observed the Kiowa doing it. It had been a three-day trip from Dodge City to the rocks. She could only pray that the vermin had been right about the cavalry patrol finding her. It was doubtful she could make it all the way back to Dodge.

Quin sat in the parlor of his two-room abode, holding a sheath studded with rubies and emeralds. The handle of the blade nestled inside was equally adorned. It was worth a king's ransom. But he could never sell so priceless an item. He had given all of Mrs. Alexander's money and other possessions to the association, just so he could keep this one piece.

Quin rose and walked to the open doorway. The eight empty wagons still hadn't been removed. It was amazing how fast rabble could go through so much. He looked toward the stockade where the prisoners had been placed. The council had decided to keep them as slaves rather than hang them. His loins were already aching to claim the redhead. But he liked to think about how it was going to feel and what he would do with her. Then, when he was consumed with lust, he'd have her brought to him. She would do just fine until the ransom was delivered. Then he'd take off with both—the money and the woman.

He thought about how he had planned to leave next week. The association had no idea how much money he had gained from the grain. He was now rich enough to live nicely in Europe for the rest of his life. Of course, there would have been a stop at the fort to report he had seen where Turner's gang was holed up. He had formed the association and he would end it. But seeing the Alexander woman had delayed his intentions. He wanted the money she could bring and he wanted her.

He was about to go back inside when he saw the three riders returning. The woman wasn't with them. His hands balled into fists as he waited for the men to bring their horses to a halt.

"Where is the woman?" Quin demanded.

Bear scratched under his hat. "We couldn't find her," he reported.

Quin looked at Cowboy.

"He's tellin' it like it is. We searched all over the land. Couldn't find any tracks and couldn't find her."

Quin shoved his wire-rimmed glasses up the bridge of his nose. "Then you two get your asses back out there and don't come back until you find her. Wagner, you go talk to the prisoners."

"They know I double-crossed them."

"Then they should believe you when you inform them that if they don't come forth with some answers they'll be hanged . . . one at a time! I want to know what happened to Mrs. Alexander."

Cole nodded, then headed his horse toward the stockade. He had seen it this morning when he was checking out "Turner Villa," as it was called.

The town was nestled against rocks, and because it was an adobe, it was impossible to see from any distance. Because of the way the adobe rooms were laid out, and the underground well, he was convinced it had to have once been an Indian dwelling. The disadvantage for him was that the residents had a panoramic view of anyone approaching. He had to figure out a way to see the cavalry advancing before the gang did.

Cole swung out of the saddle and handed his reins to the stockade guard. "I'm going in. Lock it behind me."

"What you wantin' with them?"

"To see if I can talk some sense into the lot of them. Turner needs information."

"Don't harm the older woman. I done bought that one for a servant."

"Servant?"

"And other things." The fat man spit a wad of tobacco juice, some of it running down the sides of his mouth.

"I figured they'd probably be hung."

"Too many women wantin' servants. Now that they're getting money under their belts, they've begun thinking of themselves as fancy ladies. Anyway, the council went along with them, at least for now."

He untied the rawhide and pulled back the pole, allowing the tall, wooden-spiked gate to open. Cole entered. He didn't turn when the gate was closed behind him. He was looking at the eight angry faces staring back at him from the other side. He moved forward.

"I don't know why you're here," Decker called. "You can just turn your yellow ass around and go back out!"

Cole could see the pain on Decker's face as he stood. Apparently Lizzy and the others had reset his broken arm.

"I'm not going anywhere until we have a talk."

Young Jake charged forward, ready to defend the others.

"Stop," Esther called, stepping in front of the boy. "Did you find Bethany? Is she all right?"

"I didn't find her."

"Then what else could you possibly want from us?" she asked bitterly.

"I want you to tell me which wagon Beth was riding in."

"The last one," Magda replied. "Now you can leave us."

"Decker, I want you to listen to me," Cole said softly.

"To hell with you," Decker spat out.

"And while I'm talking to Decker, I want each of you to talk loudly, as if you were making angry replies to my questions."

"That won't be difficult." Lizzy spoke up.

Cole moved closer. "Are you listening, Decker?"

"I'm listening."

Amy, the girl who had replaced Molly Dee, began giving Cole a loud tongue-lashing.

"Now, you listen real close, Decker, because I haven't much time and I'm not going to be able to repeat it. I'm going to save your hide."

"Surely you don't expect me to believe that?"

"And don't interrupt. I want someone sitting on that fence rail at all times. I'm hoping Beth has made it to the cavalry."

"She's in on this?"

"Of course she is. When whoever is on the fence sees what could be the cavalry, I want to hear a loud, blood-curdling scream. Then I want you all to yell, pound the fence, whatever it takes to get attention. I don't want these cutthroats to see the cavalry coming. I'll take care of the rest."

"How do I know you're telling the truth?"

"You don't, but what other chance do you have of getting out of this with your lives? Everyone I've talked to can't talk of anything but the coming hangings."

Cole backed away and motioned that the women could quiet down now. He nodded, tipped his hat and left.

Cole went directly to Quin. He was quick to inform the leader that Beth had indeed been in the last wagon. He added that it was his men he could blame for allowing her to escape. When he left Quin, Cole headed for the small cantina. There was nothing more he could do but wait. There were too many keeping an eye on him.

An hour passed. More than one woman had sauntered by wearing one of Beth's dresses. Another hour passed. Sunset was quickly approaching. *Come on, Beth, I know you can make it.*

The shrill scream startled even Cole. But within seconds he had slipped the bowie knife from the scabbard inside his boot and was headed toward Quin's place. As he had hoped, Decker and others were making one hell of a noise and drawing everyone's attention.

Cole was standing beside the door when Quin stepped out to see what all the commotion was about. In one swift motion Cole moved behind him and had the sharp blade on the outlaw's throat.

"One move and you're a dead man." It wasn't a threat, it was a statement.

"You'll never get out of here alive."

"Then neither will you. Now start backing into the house." Cole could feel Quin shaking. Like most killers and thieves, he was a coward.

"Now what?" Quin asked.

"Now we wait."

"Why are you doing this? Think about it. I can see that you make all the money you ever wanted."

"It won't work, Turner. I'm an agent for the president, and he wants to see you real bad. However, after what I've learned about you, I wouldn't be averse to ending your miserable life here and now."

When the cavalry rode in, there was fighting, but the melee didn't last long. Cole removed his knife from Quin's throat and shoved him back outside. A corporal came forward and placed him under arrest.

"Sir!" Captain Scott dismounted and saluted. "We have everything under control. May I say thanks to you, from all the farmers and even myself, for cleaning out this gang once and for all. I'm certain you know it is something we have been trying to accomplish for five years."

Cole nodded his acknowledgment of the captain's compliment, but his eyes were on Beth. She was standing no more than ten feet away, with Esther and the others behind her. Her face was smeared. He could see streaks where she had been crying. She looked so small and helpless. Even her clothes were torn in places. He wanted to grab her in his arms and again feel her soft body pressed against his, but the cold hate in her eyes prevented it. He smiled briefly at the captain then moved toward Beth.

"Tucker and Wilber?" he asked.

"They are going to be all right."

"I knew you could make it to the cavalry."

"You saw me?"

"Yes. That was why I turned the men around and headed back the way I came. Would you care to take a walk? I'm sure there are a hundred questions you want to ask."

"Not quite that many. Captain Scott has been kind enough to fill me in on some of it."

Cole took her arm and led her away from the others. They strolled for some time, neither knowing where to start. They stopped near some rocks and stared at the yellow sun as it began its descent.

"You lied to me, Cole. From the beginning you lied to me."

Cole turned and faced her. "I love you, Beth."

"Do you honestly expect me to believe that?"

Cole felt his gut twist with pain, but he refused to apologize or turn away. "I did what I had to do, Beth. I'm first and foremost the president's man. I do whatever he sends me out to handle."

Beth brushed the tears from her eyes. "When did it start?"

"The moment you sent a wire to John Smyth, informing him you wanted to buy an outlaw and tour the West."

Beth gasped. "You mean from the very beginning?"

"The arrangements had to be made quickly. I knew one of Turner's gang had gotten out of prison and would be traveling with your caravan. However, I wasn't able to get his description before I had to leave. It became a weeding-out process as to who was the man I was searching for."

Suddenly everything was becoming so clear to Beth. "Is Norma also a government agent?"

"Norma was my dead brother's wife."

"And you knew about Howard wanting to return to farming?"

"I knew."

"You used your own sister-in-law?" Beth backed away. "My Lord! Is there nothing you won't sully?"

"I warned you more than once that I was dangerous, but you refused to back off."

Beth brought her hand forward. The slap to his face surprised even her. She sat on one of the rocks, her strength suddenly gone. "By all means, don't stop now. I deserve to hear the rest. It will be great material for my book. It must have really been a chore to keep me in line and headed the right direction." She thought about the clippings of Dodge City that she'd found in her hotel room. She didn't have to ask if they had been planted. She had thought she was so smart, and the entire time she was being manipulated. "I'm surprised you helped me with the train robbery."

"The first train robbery was set up, including the lawmen inside. It was to convince you that I was indeed an outlaw. I arranged it by telegram when Doolan and I went to town for supplies. I didn't expect you to make another try."

"Why did you get rid of Molly Dee?"

"You were getting upset at the way she was attracted to me."

It made Beth sick to think how shy he had appeared when they'd first met. All an act. "The Kiowa incident?"

"That wasn't planned."

"Are you really Cole Wagner?"

Cole raised a foot and placed it on the rock beside where Beth was sitting. "Yes."

"And the outlaw posters?"

"It has been my cover for nearly four years."

"I'm not going to ask about the words of love, or what I thought we shared. I know now that there is no level you wouldn't stoop to if it means getting what you want."

"That's not fair. What I do is far more important than you or I. But then, I guess you just can't see it that way. Don't do this, Beth. I meant it when I said I love you."

"You're right. I don't see it that way. I don't understand how any man could put the woman he supposedly loves in jeopardy. I could have been killed!"

"Put your life in jeopardy? Aren't you the one who continually professed she wanted to see the real West and that she could certainly take care of herself? All that blood and gore so you could write a damn dime novel!"

"That's not the point." Beth held her head proudly. "I've changed my mind. Instead I am going to write a book on my experiences while traveling across the West with the lowest, most miserable man I have ever had the misfortune to meet...." She looked up at the tall, bronzed man. "You lied to me, Cole. You used me in every way possible. Who knows, maybe I even deserved it, but I will never forgive you for what you've done."

"I do love you."

A tear left the corner of Beth's eye and trailed down her cheek. "No. Had you loved me, you would have trusted me enough to tell me the truth." She saw his jaw muscles twitch. "Don't look so angry. In time you'll think of me as just another woman in your many adventures."

"You're making a mistake, Beth. We're good for each other."

Beth stood. "I'll make this easy for both of us. I never want to see your face again."

"Do you mean that?"

Beth walked to where several cavalrymen stood. "Lieutenant, if I am no longer needed, I would like to collect my people and head for the fort. An escort would be most appreciated."

The lieutenant glanced at Cole. Receiving a nod, he said, "I'll attend to it right away, ma'am."

Cole went in search of his horse. Five minutes later he was riding away.

Beth stood on the rim of the low mesa and watched Cole leave. Even when she could hardly make him out, she could see the puffs of dirt being kicked up by his horse. She had loved her outlaw more than she had thought humanly possible. Now she would pay for it.

"We're ready, Mrs. Alexander."

Beth brushed away the tears and turned to the sergeant. "So am I."

Chapter Twenty

Boston, One Year Later

Alice brushed the pesky fly away from her face. "I've said it before and I'll say it again. You were very fortunate that you didn't have your money tied up in the stock market. The crash was horrible. I've been told men committed suicide over their losses. Thomas came home nightly with horrible tales."

Beth and her cousin strolled to the small table beneath the arbor. The silver tea set, a plate of delicacies and finger sandwiches had already been set for their convenience. Alice was a cousin, but they had never really been close.

"Are you and Thomas financially stable?" Beth asked.

"Thomas says we suffered losses, but thanks to the money you've given us, we will be fine."

The women sat on the wicker chairs, and Alice proceeded to pour.

"So, are you all packed and ready to leave Boston?"

"Nearly packed. I depart in two days."

"I still can't believe you're selling your home and I'll never see you again."

"I'll come back for visits."

"You were born here, and you only returned a short time ago."

"Time passes quickly. Try to remember that my book has already been published. Have you read it?"

Alice placed her hand on her breast and gazed sadly at her cousin. "I'm afraid not. You know I'm not much for reading. I understand it's going to make you another fortune." She handed Beth her cup of tea. She had never seen her cousin looking more beautiful. It was as if something within her had come alive. But at the same time there was sadness in her eyes. "Bethany, I know we have never been as close as I would have liked, but I do care deeply about you."

Beth nodded. "I know."

"You've been unhappy ever since your return. Won't you tell me what is bothering you? It helps to confide your problems to another. I promise not to be judgmental."

Beth looked toward the open French doors leading into the house. "It's quite simple. I fell in love with a man who didn't love me."

"My poor Bethany. Why didn't you tell me about this sooner?"

After a year of keeping her feelings a secret, Beth suddenly felt the need to confide in someone other than Esther. "I guess I thought you wouldn't understand." She cleared her throat. "It was the only time I have ever experienced complete love, Alice." She fought back the tears that threatened to explode. She had done enough crying over the past year.

"And you still love him."

"He is the only man I will ever love."

Alice reached out and patted her cousin's hand. "It hurts now, but I promise a day will come when you will love again. It will never be the same as the first time, but it will be more comfortable. Many years ago I was also madly in love. His name was Marco. He was handsome, wild and the gardener's son. I was positive I would die without him."

Mindless of her satin town suit, Beth scooted her chair forward. "I never dreamed—"

"Few people knew about it."

"What happened?"

"Father put an end to it. He wasn't about to allow his daughter to marry a gardener's son, and he was convinced Marco was only after Daddy's wealth. Daddy was right, of course. He gave Marco an unknown sum of money and the rogue disappeared." Alice laughed softly. "I wanted to die from the humiliation and the love I still carried in my bosom. I would have gladly run away with him. Instead, I rode to the lake, determined to drown myself. You'll never guess who pulled me out and saved my life."

"Thomas?"

"Yes, Thomas. I ended up telling him my story, including the part about being a tarnished woman. I was certain no man would ever want me for a wife. He looked at me, smiled and said, 'I would.' We were married six months later. He made me whole again. I don't love him in the same way I loved Marco, but I care very deeply."

Beth was in awe. She had never thought of Thomas as being capable of such depth. "Did you ever see Marco again?"

Alice held her napkin over her mouth to smother her laugh. "Yes. He didn't age well. He was fat and bald."

"I think you made that up." Beth took one of the sandwiches. "Cole didn't leave me. I left him. He used me. From the very beginning he lied and used me. And as if that wasn't enough, after risking my life, he expected me to believe he loved me! I told him I never wanted to see him again."

"If he was that despicable, you were right to turn away."

"Then why am I so miserable?"

Alice smiled sadly. "We seem to have a knack for picking the wrong men to fall in love with."

The two women continued their afternoon visit. Their moment of closeness had passed.

Washington, D.C.

The three impressive gentlemen were standing in the center of the room when the senator slammed his fist down on the president's desk. "I have been waiting for you to show your face, Cole Wagner. A month ago I finally found out you were the culprit who placed my niece in danger. I have also received information that states you sullied her reputation. She is not the sort of woman who would willingly bed a man she is not married to!"

Cole's eyes turned pitch-black. "Are you accusing me of forcing myself on her, Senator?"

"Now, now gentlemen, let's try to hold our tempers."

"This man may work for you, Mr. President, but I think he should be hung! Everyone has heard of his infamous way with women."

President Grant clasped his hands behind his back. "As you said, sir, he is *my* man. He will not be hung. He caught Quin Turner and his gang at considerable risk to himself. Something that for the past five years no lawman or soldier has been able to accomplish. Besides that, for nearly four years Mr. Wagner paraded about as a wanted man, which certainly brought with it its own dangers. During that period he also put various other attempts at corruption to a successful halt. This last year he has been instrumental in helping gather men guilty of fraud against the United States of America.''

''And he nearly cost my niece her life! The man is every bit as ruthless as Quin Turner.''

''Nevertheless, your niece came out of this completely unscathed.'' President Grant turned his back on the senator. ''I don't want to hear any more about it.''

Realizing he was being dismissed, the senator scurried out of the room. He pulled a silk handkerchief from his pocket and mopped his damp forehead. He should have demanded a duel of honor, even though it was illegal. However, he knew of Wagner's reputation with a gun. Such a duel would be tantamount to suicide.

''Well,'' Ulysses said to Cole, ''what are you going to do now that this has all come to an end? As I remember, prior to sending you off to clean up this Turner mess, you were expressing a desire to resign.''

''We've been together a long time.''

Ulysses laughed. ''And look where we ended up. Tell me about this Alexander woman. Is the senator right? Did you keep your hands off her as I ordered?''

''Actually—''

''Never mind. I don't think I want to know. Would you care for a drink?''

Cole nodded.

''Port or whiskey?''

''Whiskey.''

Ulysses poured the drinks then handed Cole his. ''Earlier the senator was telling me his niece has booked passage from Boston to Europe...or someplace like that. So the matter is no longer something that has to be dealt with. As for being a wanted man, all the bounty posters have been removed, but you might still need to lie low for a spell."

"I could use the rest, anyway." He walked to the window and silently downed his drink. Hearing Beth being discussed brought back strong memories. Staying away from her hadn't been easy. On more than one occasion he had come damn close to telling the president he was leaving. He'd had a stupid notion of stealing Beth during the night and taking her to some mountains where no one would ever find them. Too late he'd come to realize just how deeply he loved Bethany Alexander. He smiled. Obviously he had been one of those men who had to be knocked over the head before he came to his senses.

The president sipped his port. "Perhaps you should go to California, or... possibly Europe?"

Cole turned. There was a definite twinkle in the older man's eyes. "Are you implying what I think you're implying?"

"We've known each other for over ten years, Cole. Hell, you were in your early twenties when we first hooked up together. I have met the lovely widow and can easily understand how you might have feelings for her."

"We didn't part under the best of circumstances, and that was a year ago. Maybe there is already another man in her life."

Ulysses Grant let out a hoot of laughter. "Who am I talking to?" he finally asked. "The Cole Wagner I know would never let a minor thing like that stand in his way."

Cole grinned. "People change."

"Not you, Cole."

Cole set his glass on the desk and picked up the fine felt top hat beside it. "If you will excuse me, I'll be on my way."

The two men shook hands. They both knew they would probably never see each other again. In some ways it was a sad parting, but for Cole it carried the hope of a new beginning. When it came to Beth, fate had played with a crooked deck. He had ended up losing her, but now it was time to get on with his life.

He opened the door and was about to leave when the president called, "Cole?"

President Grant picked up a book from his desk and walked to where Cole waited. "I almost forgot to give you this. My wife read the story and said it was excellent. It's a going-away present."

Cole took the book Grant held out to him. "Please express my appreciation." A cocky smile spread across Cole's lips. He knew Grant worshiped his wife. "Take good care of the lady, or I may come back for her."

Grant laughed. "See? You haven't changed."

Cole tipped his hat and left.

He was a wealthy man and now he had nothing to do except decide what he wanted to do and where he wanted to go. It would be interesting to see if he could lead a gentleman's life. He'd once told Beth that flirting with death had become a sweet addiction. He'd told the truth.

Cole opened the door and entered his hotel suite. It was the same suite he'd always stayed in while in Washington. Getting rid of it made everything seem so final.

He entered the bedroom and tossed the book on the gilded lounge chair. He'd left word at the restaurant to send his supper up. He hoped it would arrive soon, because he was feeling hungry.

He removed his coat and ascot and laid them on the bed. He'd always dressed in the highest fashion when in Washington and had an extensive array of clothes in the three armoires lining one wall. Remembering the outlandish suit he'd worn when he first met Beth made him chuckle. At the time he hadn't known what he needed to wear or say to get on the lady's good side. Having nothing to go by, he'd had to play it all by ear. He had certainly guessed wrong when he'd purchased that itchy suit.

He released the top buttons of his shirt. Feeling more comfortable, he glanced around the room. Suddenly he was at a loss. What was he supposed to do with himself now? Not since he was a young boy had he had so much time on his hands. The book Mrs. Grant had given him caught his eye. What could have possessed her to give it to him? He left the bedroom and sat in a salon chair. As soon as he turned the book over, he had the answer to his question. The cover read, *The American Legend,* by B. F. Alexander.

He opened it to the first page.

He was a tall, uncompromising outlaw with a bounty on his head. Not a bit trustworthy and wearing the most ridiculous plaid suit she had ever laid eyes on. Amelia Harding should have been leery, but wasn't. Who better to show her the West? Not the one described in novels, but the real West. So the infamous Lance Webber became her guide.

Cole kicked off his shoes and made himself comfortable. An hour later his supper was delivered, but he was no longer hungry. He was too absorbed in the tale being woven before his eyes. The memories were flooding back, but this time he was seeing everything through the eyes of another. Beth had made good use of the journals she'd kept so meticulously while they were together.

Other than elaborating on things of no importance and changing their names, Beth told everything as it had happened. Including his hesitation to make love to her. She did of course leave out the actual lovemaking, but she alluded to it. The reader would have no doubts as to what happened.

Cole wasn't just reading the book, he had started reading between the lines. Beth painted a clear picture of how he had brought out the best and the worst in her, but he hadn't realized that she perceived him as looking down on her. The fact that she had felt the need to prove she was as good as he came as a complete surprise. So she had tried things that she would never have thought herself capable of. In the long run she felt it had made her a better person. At first he was portrayed as a hard, ungiving bastard who upon rare occasions showed a softer side. Cole found it interesting the way she had him evolve into a man of tenderness, but a man who had a job to do.

Daylight was shining through the window when Cole snapped the book closed. He stood, raked his fingers through his tousled hair and headed for the bedroom. He was tired, but when he flopped down on the bed, his eyes remained wide open. He stared at the ceiling, thinking of the nights they had spent together. Since she'd left, keeping busy had helped somewhat, but there were still the lonesome nights when he did nothing but think about the woman he'd loved and lost. She had done the right thing when she'd sent him away. He was every bad thing Beth had put in her book. That was why he had never gone after her.

Cole suddenly jumped off the bed and snatched up the book again. He quickly turned to the last five pages and reread them. In Beth's story, Amelia looked past her hurt at having been used and came to realize that Lance truly had had no choice in what he had done. And after the tears and blaming, she loved him all the more for it. In Amelia's heart she knew Lance loved her, making his job as an agent all the harder. She loved him all the more for that, too. On the last page Amelia was headed for San Francisco. Lance had said he planned to retire there after he had finished showing her the real West. She was going to find him.

Cole read the pages again. Beth would never have been allowed to know where he was after they had parted. More than once he had said he was going to San Francisco and buy land.

He could feel his pulse racing. Had Beth been trying to tell him of her love and that all was forgiven? Did he dare hope that out of all the lies they could still have a life together? He couldn't afford to be let down again, it took too much out of him. Besides, it was more likely to be nothing more than hopeful fantasizing. Still, what if she was waiting for him. Like it or not, he had to find out the truth. He would go to San Francisco, but he was going to be damn cautious.

Chapter Twenty-One

Esther followed closely behind Beth as they entered the Cosmopolitan Hotel. Her ward had spent yet another trying day shopping, and Esther could hardly wait to get to the room, where she could soak her sore feet. It was time Bethany realized that her companion wasn't as young and spry as she used to be.

They had been here for three weeks. There had to be a purpose for all this, but so far Esther had no idea what the purpose was. However, if Beth persisted in keeping secrets, then so be it. Beth came to an abrupt stop and Esther ran right into her back.

"He's here," Beth whispered excitedly. She glanced around the spacious lobby.

Esther straightened her hat. "Who is here?"

"Cole."

"That's foolish talk. I don't see him."

Neither did Beth. "But I felt him. He was so near."

Esther placed her arm around Beth's slender shoulders. Only she knew the suffering Beth had gone through. "It's only your imagination."

Beth took one last look around the comfortable lobby. "Perhaps you're right." She started walking toward the stairs, then stopped again. "I have to find out if anyone has inquired about me."

"Don't do this to yourself, Beth."

Beth wasn't listening. She was already headed for the registration counter, her satin petticoats rustling as she walked.

"Ah, Miss Alexander," the bespectacled clerk greeted her. "What can I do for you?"

"I . . . I was wondering if anyone had inquired as to my whereabouts. I've been shopping."

"Not from me."

Beth's excitement faded.

"Let me ask the other clerk."

Beth wanted to disappear into the ground. The man probably thought she was crazy asking such a question. No one had visited her since her arrival. She watched the clerk return.

"Yes, Miss Alexander, a man did inquire about you."

"I knew it. I knew it! I could feel it."

"I beg your pardon?"

Beth blushed. "Pay no attention."

The clerk grinned. "The gentleman left a note." He handed it to Beth.

Beth's fingers shook as she took the piece of paper. She was almost afraid to open it. She decided to wait and read the message upstairs.

As soon as Beth entered the large suite she went straight to her bedroom and closed the door behind her. She hadn't told Esther about the caller. She wanted to be sure. Slowly, carefully, she unfolded the piece of paper and read.

My beloved Beth,
After reading your book, I have come to hope you

might still have feelings for me. I have been invited
to a ball and would be honoured if you would ac-
company me. I will arrive this evening at eight. If you
are not waiting in the lobby, I will understand that the
error was mine. It has been a long, cold year, my
love.

Beth held the paper to her breast. Cole had come for
her. She had tried every way she knew to locate him, but
even her uncle hadn't been able to tell her where to find
him. The book had been the only way she'd known to
reach him.

She ran to the door and swung it open. "Esther! Esther! I need my very best ball gown! I only have three
hours to get ready!"

Cole hesitated leaving the carriage. Would Beth be
waiting for him, or would he go to the ball alone? He was
afraid of the truth. Not knowing if she would be in the
lobby almost seemed better than knowing he had foolishly built up false hopes. He took a deep breath and
stepped out. Waiting would accomplish nothing.

Beth had her back turned when Cole entered the lobby,
but he would have recognized her anywhere. Then she
turned and looked straight at him as if she knew he was
there. A smile was playing at the corners of her lips. Ah,
those lips. From the first they had been his downfall. She
was beautiful. Absolutely beautiful. He moved toward
her, still unable to believe fate had smiled on him. Had
any man ever loved a woman the way he loved her?

Beth's feet were glued to the floor and her heart was
pounding. She couldn't move. Coming toward her was the
most magnificent man she had ever seen. His evening
clothes were absolutely perfect. Top hat, cane and all. She

had never seen him dressed in such a fashionable manner. Across his arm was a beautiful bouquet of white roses.

Cole stopped, handed Beth the flowers and offered his arm. She gladly took it.

He grinned. He felt as if the weight of the world had been lifted from his shoulders. "Would I be out of line, madam, if I said I loved you?"

"I know you do." She smiled, her love shining in her eyes. "It just took me a terribly long time to realize it."

Cole led Beth out of the hotel and helped her into the carriage. "Am I to believe I am forgiven?"

"Only if you marry me." Beth ran her hand along his cheek when he sat beside her. "Am I moving too fast again?"

"Never." Cole gently pulled her to him, unable to go a moment longer without touching her. "It seems a lifetime since we made love."

"Must we go to the ball? All I want is to be in your arms again."

Cole released a hearty laugh, the first one in many months. "Beth my darling, how have we managed to be so blessed?" He knocked on the top of the carriage with his cane.

"Where to, sir?" the driver asked.

Cole gave him the address of where he was staying.

"Do you intend to marry me or not? I will not tag after you without a ring on my finger."

"It would be my pleasure, my love. But I must tell you that had you waited, I would have asked you."

Beth and Cole lay naked on the bed, their desire for one another temporarily satiated.

"Cole?" Beth ran her fingernail across the flat of his stomach.

"What, love?"

"Did you really quit working for President Grant?"

"I did. Why?"

"I was just thinking what a great pair we would make at undercover work."

Cole rolled on top of her. "No. I've already put you through too much danger." He kissed her. "We're going to live properly as husband and wife." His hand slid down her thigh.

Beth returned his kiss with fervor. She had been right. She could never love any man the way she loved Cole. However, he had not heard the last about them working as a team.

* * * * *

HARLEQUIN®

Scandals

A passionate story of romance, where bold, daring characters set out to defy their world of propriety and strict social codes.

"*Scandals*—a story that will make your heart race and your pulse pound. Spectacular!"
—Suzanne Forster

"Devon is daring, dangerous and altogether delicious."
—Amanda Quick

Don't miss this wonderful full-length novel from Regency favorite Georgina Devon.

Available in December, wherever Harlequin books are sold.

Look us up on-line at: http://www.romance.net

The collection of the year!
NEW YORK TIMES BESTSELLING AUTHORS

Linda Lael Miller
Wild About Harry

Janet Dailey
Sweet Promise

Elizabeth Lowell
Reckless Love

Penny Jordan
Love's Choices

and featuring
Nora Roberts
The Calhoun Women

Weddings by DeWilde

Since the turn of the century the elegant and fashionable
DeWilde stores have helped brides around the world
turn the fantasy of their "Special Day" into reality. But now the
store and three generations of family are torn apart by the
separation of Grace and Jeffrey DeWilde. Family members
face new challenges and loves in this fast-paced, glamorous,
internationally set series. For weddings and romance, glamour
and fun-filled entertainment, enter the world of DeWildes....

**Watch for *WILDE MAN*,
by Daphne Clair
Coming to you in January, 1997**

The sophisticated image and spotless reputation of DeWilde's
Sydney store was being destroyed by tacky T-shirts and
unmentionable souvenirs! And Maxine Sterling was not going
to let swaggering DeWilde Cutter get away with it! He'd have
to take his gorgeous looks and puzzling name and find
another business. And she was certainly *not* going to fall in
love with a man whose life-style symbolized everything
she'd fought so hard to escape!

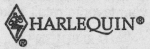

HARLEQUIN®

1997
Reader's Engagement Book
A calendar of important dates
and anniversaries for readers to use!

Informative and entertaining—with notable
dates and trivia highlighted throughout the year.

Handy, convenient, pocketbook size to help you
keep track of your own personal important dates.

Added bonus—contains $5.00 worth of coupons
for upcoming Harlequin and Silhouette books.
This calendar more than pays for itself!

 Available beginning in November at
your favorite retail outlet.

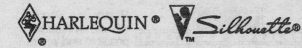

HARLEQUIN ® Silhouette®

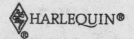

Not The Same Old Story!

HARLEQUIN PRESENTS®
Exciting, emotionally intense romance stories that take readers around the world.

Harlequin Romance®
Vibrant stories of captivating women and irresistible men experiencing the magic of falling in love!

HARLEQUIN Temptation.
Bold and adventurous—Temptation is strong women, bad boys, great sex!

HARLEQUIN SUPERROMANCE®
Provocative, passionate, contemporary stories that celebrate life and love.

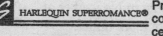
AMERICAN ROMANCE®
Romantic adventure where anything is possible and where dreams come true.

HARLEQUIN® INTRIGUE®
Heart-stopping, suspenseful adventures that combine the best of romance and mystery.

LOVE & LAUGHTER™
Entertaining and fun, humorous and romantic—stories that capture the lighter side of love.